JOANNA BLALOCK WAS A DOCTOR WHO WOULDN'T TAKE NO FOR AN ORDER

Forensic pathologist Joanna Blalock was told by her superior at Los Angeles Memorial Hospital not to probe too deeply in her autopsy of the lovely young nurse who had plunged to her death from the hospital roof.

Instead Joanna ripped through the smoke-screen of suicide to expose the horrifying truth—it was murder, the work of a serial killer with medical expertise.

From that shock point there was no turning back on a path that took her into battle against the peril that hid behind the prestige of the mighty medical center where doctors played God, where science had become the perverted plaything of those in power, and where women were the targets and the victims of a twisted branch of medicine gone mad. . . .

"*Deadly Medicine* makes a shuddery venture, worthy of Robin Cook or Michael Chrichton, into the cold grey corridors of a hospital that confirms our very worst fears."
—Donald Stanwood,
author of *The Memory of Eve Ryker*

Watch for the next Joanna Blalock medical thriller from Signet.

Leonard S. G⋯⋯⋯⋯⋯⋯⋯⋯ting physician in L⋯⋯⋯⋯⋯⋯ with the UCLA Me⋯⋯⋯⋯⋯⋯ical professor. He ⋯⋯⋯⋯⋯⋯ina.

Deadly Medicine

BY

LEONARD S. GOLDBERG

A SIGNET BOOK

SIGNET
Published by the Penguin Group
Penguin Books USA Inc., 375 Hudson Street,
New York, New York 10014, U.S.A.
Penguin Books Ltd, 27 Wrights Lane,
London W8 5TZ, England
Penguin Books Australia Ltd, Ringwood,
Victoria, Australia
Penguin Books Canada Ltd, 10 Alcorn Avenue,
Toronto, Ontario, Canada, M4V 3B2
Penguin Books (N.Z.) Ltd, 182–190 Wairau Road,
Auckland 10, New Zealand

Penguin Books Ltd, Registered Offices:
Harmondsworth, Middlesex, England

First published by Signet, an imprint of New American Library,
a division of Penguin Books USA Inc.

First Printing, November 1992
10 9 8 7 6 5 4 3 2 1

Copyright © Leonard S. Goldberg, 1992
All rights reserved

 REGISTERED TRADEMARK—MARCA REGISTRADA

Printed in the United States of America

PUBLISHER'S NOTE
This is a work of fiction. Names, characters, places, and incidents either
are the product of the author's imagination or are used fictitiously, and
any resemblance to actual persons, living or dead, events, or locales is
entirely coincidental.

BOOKS ARE AVAILABLE AT QUANTITY DISCOUNTS WHEN USED TO PROMOTE
PRODUCTS OR SERVICES. FOR INFORMATION PLEASE WRITE TO PREMIUM MAR-
KETING DIVISION, PENGUIN BOOKS USA INC., 375 HUDSON STREET, NEW YORK,
NEW YORK 10014.

For Paige and Julie

For I have in me something dangerous . . .

—Shakespeare, *Hamlet*

1

The helicopter hovered above the ground, its floodlights streaking the misty night air. It slowly descended the final forty feet to the heliport at Los Angeles Memorial Hospital. Medical personnel stood off to one side, waiting for the rotary blade to stop turning. Security police were in attendance to discourage the curious.

From the rooftop of the Psychiatric Institute, Karen Rhodes stared down at the aircraft, her forehead pressed against a protective wire-link fence. The door of the helicopter opened and a patient was lifted out and placed on a gurney. Karen couldn't see the patient's face, but she knew his identity. He was a famous movie star critically ill with AIDS, who had just returned from France, where he had received an experimental drug. He had lived a wonderful life, Karen thought, and now his name would be forever tainted by a horrible disease. Even in death the scandal would not die. They would never leave him alone.

Karen turned away, sadly shaking her head, remembering the words of her father. Public scrutiny, he had told her, was the price one paid for fame or wealth or power. He had advised her over and over again always to think twice, never act impulsively, never bring embarrassment to herself or the family name. And she had followed his advice carefully, exactingly. Up until six months ago. That was when the nightmare began.

How could I allow it to happen? she asked herself for the hundredth time. *How? I'm a highly trained nurse and I should have known the dangers. I should have realized the risks, but I didn't—or didn't want to. And now I'm caught, trapped in a prison I helped to construct.*

But there was a way out. She had been promised that. What was done could be undone. The memories might haunt her, but those too would fade.

And if there were no way out, she would make certain those responsible paid heavily. Either she would be freed tonight or they would be disgraced tomorrow. Maybe even imprisoned. Her family would see to that.

Karen glanced at her watch. It was 11:30 P.M. She walked across the rooftop to a weathered lounge chair and looked down on it, filled with disgust and shame. Here was where it started, here was where it would end. She lay on the chair and closed her eyes, waiting for the promise to be delivered.

In the distance, the helicopter engine whirred to life. The noise turned into a deafening roar as the helicopter began its ascent. Karen could not hear the footsteps approaching from behind. With sudden quickness, a man was on top of her, powerful hands on her neck, knees pinning her shoulders to the mattress. She twisted and squirmed, legs kicking wildly in the air. Her cry of terror was muted by thumbs of steel that crushed her throat. She jerked spasmodically, sucking for air that could not pass the bone and cartilage blocking her windpipe.

He loosened his grip and stared down at her. So inviting. So irresistible. He leaned over and gently nibbled at her neck, careful not to break the skin. She tasted so fresh and sweet. He wished he could spend more time with her.

He lifted her and carried her to the edge of the roof, then hesitated, waiting for the helicopter to gain altitude and disappear into the night.

Karen Rhodes offered no resistance as she was heaved over the railing and fell ten stories to the pavement below.

2

Simon Murdock paced back and forth across his office, a tightly rolled up newspaper in his hand. He was a slender man in his early sixties, with neatly groomed white hair and narrow brown eyes. His face was heavily lined and dotted with early age spots. Murdock had been dean of the medical school for fourteen years and was known for his even-handed, controlled temperament. Only those closest to him knew how explosive his temper could be.

He jabbed angrily at the intercom button on his desk and spoke to his secretary. "Where the hell is Blalock?"

"On the way, sir."

Murdock mumbled to himself, then placed the wrinkled newspaper on his desk and smoothed it out. Karen Rhodes's suicide at Memorial had made the front page of the *Los Angeles Times*. Murdock clenched his teeth, hating the adverse publicity. He had spent every day of the past fourteen years transforming Memorial into a world-renowned medical center. Institutes had been built, endowments tripled, honors bestowed. One faculty member had won a Nobel Prize, another was thought to be steps away. Murdock considered any blemish on the Center's reputation a personal affront, something to be quickly scraped off and smoothed over.

His eyes went back to the newspaper, his mind trying to envision the grief and shock of the girl's family. She was so young, he thought, and had so much to live for. A tragic suicide. A needless waste. He wondered if the girl had any idea of the repercussions her death would set off. The Rhodeses were a prominent California family, rich from oil and land, powerful in politics. Her father, Senator Alexander Rhodes, was a shining light in Washington, a man being groomed for the presidency. A brother would almost surely be the next attorney general of California, a steppingstone to the governorship. The family was accustomed to power and praise, not shame and embarrassment. The news media would have a field day, and the Rhodes family would cringe every time they picked up a newspaper or turned on the television.

Murdock began to pace the floor again, reminding himself of things yet to be done. A memorial service should be scheduled for Karen Rhodes, to take place in a week or so. A nursing scholarship would be established in her name. Murdock would fund it from one of the discretionary accounts he controlled. And he needed to speak with the coroner's office again. After he had spoken to Blalock.

The intercom on his desk buzzed. "Dean Murdock, Mr. Mortimer Rhodes is here to see you."

"I'll be with him in just a moment."

God damn it! Murdock growled to himself. Mortimer Rhodes was the last person he wanted to see at this moment. He had already spoken to the old man a half-dozen times about his granddaughter's death. The same phone conversation over and over again. But Mortimer Rhodes had to be coddled. He sat on the board of directors at Memorial and was the hospital's largest benefactor.

Murdock straightened his posture and adjusted his tie. The newspaper was swept off his desk and into the wastebasket. He pushed the button on his intercom. "Please have Mr. Rhodes come in."

Mortimer Rhodes strode into the office, bundled up in a topcoat and scarf. The old man, slightly bent at the waist, sat down heavily in the wingback chair, his eyes riveted on Murdock. "Anything new since we last talked?"

"I'm afraid not. May I offer you coffee or tea?" Murdock asked, struck by how much Rhodes had aged over the past few months. His hair was now snow white and the lines in his face had deepened into crevices.

The old man flicked his wrist impatiently. "Have the police been called in?"

"We can't do that unless there's evidence of foul play."

"My granddaughter did not jump off that damned roof. You know it and I know it."

"We must wait for the result of the postmortem examination, Mortimer. We have no choice."

"Who will perform this examination?"

"Dr. Joanna Blalock, a forensic pathologist."

"A woman?"

"I can assure you that she is highly qualified."

"Blalock . . . Blalock," the old man muttered, trying to place a name he recognized from the distant past. "Do you know anything about her family background?"

"Her family was in banking."

"In San Francisco." The old man nodded to himself. "They're the ones who went bankrupt."

Murdock nodded back. "Apparently Joanna's father was the driving force behind all of the Blalock enterprises. When he died in a plane crash, everything came apart. The family lost all of their holdings. Joanna was a sophomore in college at the time."

"Who put her through school?"

"No one. She got scholarships and had to work part time, even in medical school. She had a rough road, but she made it."

"You seem to know a great deal about this woman's personal life," Rhodes said suspiciously.

"That's because I headed the search committee that recommended her appointment to our staff two years ago."

"She's only been on the staff two years?"

"That's correct."

Rhodes took a deep breath, exhaling loudly. "I prefer someone else do the postmortem examination. Not this Blalock woman."

"I think you're making a mistake, Mortimer. If your granddaughter met with foul play, a forensic pathologist has the best chance of spotting it. Unlike other pathologists, they're trained to uncover criminal acts."

"And she's the best you've got, eh?"

"Her qualifications are impeccable. Let me show you her curriculum vitae." Murdock went to a nearby file cabinet and extracted a thick folder. He flipped through it, pleased with himself for having reviewed the folder an hour earlier. Murdock was very good at anticipating people, particularly demanding ones like Mortimer Rhodes. He handed the folder to the old man.

Rhodes put on his reading glasses and turned in his chair to maximize the light. He thumbed through reprints of scientific articles Joanna Blalock had published. Most dealt with unusual bullet wounds and fragmentation of high-velocity missiles. Her curriculum vitae showed that she had graduated from Stanford, then Johns Hopkins Medical School with honors. After completing her internship, she went to El Salvador with Operation Hope for three months. "What is this 'Operation Hope'?"

"It's a nonprofit organization that provides medical care to impoverished areas, particularly in Latin America."

"Is the usual tour of duty three months?"

Murdock shook his head. "Usually a full year. But the village where the medical group was stationed came under a rebel attack and a number of the group were badly wounded. Joanna's injuries were so serious she had to be airlifted back to America, where she was hospitalized for several months."

"What kind of wounds?"

"The nature of her injuries was not disclosed."

Mortimer Rhodes went back to the folder. His eyes narrowed noticeably as he turned a page. "She was resident in psychiatry here at Memorial?"

"Correct. After her injuries healed, she applied for and was accepted into the residency program at the Psychiatric Institute."

"And she stayed only six months?"

Murdock nodded. "After six months she resigned and accepted a residency position in forensic pathology at Johns Hopkins. Apparently her interests had changed.''

"Was that the real reason or just the reason she gave?''

Murdock knew what Mortimer Rhodes was thinking. The old man was aware that resignations from residencies were rare and when they did occur it was almost always due to illness or some breach of morals. ''The real reason. I checked her old file. There was no mention of illness or misconduct.''

The old man closed the folder and handed it across the desk. ''I'll trust your judgment on this, Simon.''

"Good. We'll bring everything to a conclusion as quickly as possible.''

"So young,'' Rhodes muttered, now staring out into space. ''So young to pass on.'' His lower lip began to quiver and then his stoic face came apart. But only for a moment. He quickly reached for a handkerchief and blew his nose loudly. When the handkerchief came down, the face was firm again. ''I want the examination done as soon as possible, and I want to know the results the moment they're available.''

"Of course, of course.'' Murdock glanced over at the intercom unit. A light blinked silently. Someone was waiting in the reception area, probably Blalock. Murdock got to his feet and walked over to help Mortimer Rhodes up. ''You might wish to depart via my private door. I'm afraid the news media people are lurking everywhere.''

"Thank you, Simon.''

Murdock waited for the old man to leave, then pushed the intercom switch. ''Is Blalock here?''

"Yes, sir.''

"Show her in."

The door opened and Joanna Blalock entered. She was a slender, attractive woman wearing a beige tweed suit and a silk blouse. Her skirt was tight—not too tight, but enough to show the outline of a marvelous pair of legs. She had soft, patrician features with dark, very brown eyes. Her sandy blond hair was drawn back and held in place with a simple barrette. She was thirty-four years old but looked five years younger.

"Thank you for coming so promptly," Murdock said.

"Your secretary said it was urgent."

Murdock gestured toward a wingback leather-upholstered chair. "Have a seat, Joanna."

As she sat down, Joanna glanced around the room and noticed the changes that had taken place since her last visit to the office two years ago. The floor had a new deep brown carpet and the plastered walls were now covered with pale yellow grasscloth. Rich, lime-colored drapes had replaced the venetian blinds. Behind the huge teak desk—which was also new—were built-in shelves lined with medical textbooks and journals. She wondered which of the school's philanthropists had footed the cost of the renovations.

The two physicians glanced briefly at each other, then looked away. There was no warmth between them, yet no dislike either. Their personalities simply did not mesh, and both knew it and accepted it.

"You've heard about the nurse's suicide?" Murdock asked.

"I heard she fell to her death."

"And you're aware of her family background?"

"Of course."

Murdock looked over at the buttons on his telephone, all still lighted. "Since this tragedy occurred, my phone has not stopped ringing. I've spoken with the senator twice. He's now flying back from Spain, where he's been on a congressional junket. Her grandfather calls me hourly. During my last phone conversation with the old man, I had the mayor and the chief of police on hold. And the calls keep coming. Everyone is demanding a complete investigation."

"She should be a coroner's case."

"She should, but she won't." Murdock rocked gently in his swivel chair. "The coroner's office is now in a state of transition," he added delicately.

Joanna nodded. The former coroner had not run a tight ship and the end result was a tremendous backload of cases, sloppy work and disgruntled workers. The old coroner had not tended to business, preferring to spend his time writing books and giving interviews on sensational cases. He was now looking for employment elsewhere.

"We can't afford any mistakes here," Murdock went on. "Like it or not, we're in the public eye. This story is front-page news and will continue to be until all matters pertaining to the girl are sealed once and for all. Everyone agrees that the postmortem examination should be done here at Memorial by a forensic pathologist. Someone with impeccable qualifications. Namely, you." He paused and stared into Joanna's eyes. "Any objections?"

"None."

"Good. I want this matter settled very quietly and very quickly. Understood?"

"Speed is not one of my talents, Simon. Thoroughness is."

Murdock's face reddened. "Of course. I—ah—I meant—"

The intercom on Murdock's desk buzzed loudly. He angrily pushed a button. "No interruptions, damn it!"

"It's Mortimer Rhodes again, sir. He's calling from his car."

Murdock sighed wearily. He picked up the phone and listened as the dead girl's grandfather again insisted on a complete investigation, leaving no stone unturned.

"Of course," Murdock said sympathetically into the phone. Mortimer Rhodes was demanding absolute confidentiality. "We'll be very careful."

Murdock tuned him out. He wished that the autopsy were being done somewhere else, but if it had to be performed at Memorial, then Blalock was the person to do it. No one would push or intimidate her, not even the Rhodes family. And most importantly, she would know how to handle any delicate matters that arose. There would be no sensationalism, regardless of the findings. *What findings?* Murdock thought miserably. He hoped it was a simple suicide.

At that moment, Mortimer Rhodes informed him that he did not want the girl's brain examined at autopsy. There would be no further disfigurement of the head.

"But Mortimer," Murdock protested mildly, "that might be very important."

"I don't give a damn," Rhodes roared over the phone. "You make certain my instructions are carried out."

"All right. There will be no examination of her brain." Murdock looked over at Joanna Blalock.

"The hell there won't be!" Joanna said sternly.

"Hold on a moment, Mortimer, hold on," Murdock said quickly, covering the phone with a palm. "Is it that important?" he asked Joanna, almost whispering.

"Absolutely. Either we do this correctly or we don't do it."

Murdock went back to the phone, listening intently, nodding, all the while trying to find a way out of the dilemma. His eyebrows suddenly arched. "You say you've talked with the chairman of Pathology and he agrees that examination of the brain is unnecessary?"

Joanna resisted the urge to storm out, knowing that she was the only forensic pathologist at Memorial and that if she didn't do the autopsy the chair of Pathology would. And screw it up. And then find a way to blame her for his inadequacies.

"Of course, of course," Murdock was saying, nodding, his head bobbing up and down like a yo-yo.

Joanna took a deep breath and calmed herself. She knew the kind of pressure that people like Mortimer Rhodes could bring to bear. They were the rich and powerful, giving generously to a number of causes but always holding a marker and expecting favors when needed.

"By all means," Murdock said to Mortimer Rhodes. "Everything will be done just as we discussed."

"Keep me informed," Rhodes commanded and hung up.

Murdock placed the phone down. "That man is impossible." He waved a hand in disgust and waited for his anger to pass.

Joanna got to her feet and walked over to the partially opened drapes. She looked out on a fine spring day. Blue sky, a few clouds, no smog. "Tell me everything you know about Karen Rhodes."

"She was a very fine nurse who got along well with patients and staff. Last night she worked three to eleven, which was her usual shift. She seemed in good spirits. Nobody noticed anything unusual."

"She left the ward alone?"

"As far as we know."

"Did she have any serious illnesses?"

"No." Murdock quickly flipped through a folder on his desk. "According to her medical record, she was quite healthy. She had surgery three years ago for a ruptured ovarian cyst. No complications. This morning I spoke with her family doctor, who assured me her health was excellent."

"Who was her doctor?"

"Eric Van Horn."

Joanna groaned inwardly. Van Horn was physician to the socially prominent of Los Angeles. He was smooth and charming and medically mediocre. He believed that tranquilizers were the greatest drug ever invented and prescribed them so often that the house staff at Memorial referred to him as Valium Van Horn. "Was she taking any drugs?"

Murdock hesitated. "Are you referring to prescription drugs or others?"

"Both."

"Van Horn told me that she took small amounts of Valium on occasion. There was no mention of illicit drugs."

"Did you ask?"

"No."

"Was she seeing a psychiatrist?"

Murdock shrugged. He suddenly grimaced as a sharp pain stabbed at his temple, followed by a flash of light. The onset of a migraine caused his face to lose color. He quickly opened his desk drawer and took out a propanolol tablet, swallowing it down without water.

"Are you all right, Simon?" Joanna asked, concerned.

"Goddamn migraine," Murdock grumbled, now massaging his temples, waiting for the pain to ease. "Joanna, we have to be very careful so that we don't create a circus atmosphere around this poor girl. I know that Memorial is a teaching hospital and that autopsies are usually attended by throngs of interns and students. And in this case, the turnout will be even larger. If any of them talk to the press, God only knows how grotesque the stories might be. Is there any way that the autopsy could be performed in a restricted area with only essential personnel present?"

"We have a special room that's used for contaminated cases."

"Good," Murdock said approvingly. "And the staff needed?"

"Myself and the chief resident."

"We should also include one representative from the coroner's office, if you don't object."

"Who?"

"The acting coroner, Robert Nagura. Do you know him?"

"Only by reputation. He's supposedly quite competent." Unlike the jackass he replaced, Joanna thought.

"I've already talked with him and he's freed up his schedule. He's waiting for my call now. What time will you begin?"

"In one hour," Joanna said and started for the door.

"Joanna, if you discover anything that would cause embarrassment to the girl's family . . ." His voice trailed off as he reached for another propanolol tablet. "Remember how much they've suffered already. We don't want to add to their burden."

Joanna nodded. "Her brain should be examined, you know."

Murdock shrugged.

"And if I find the slightest reason to open her head, I will."

Murdock's migraine came back with a vengeance.

David Rodman, the chief resident in Pathology, looked down at the corpse of Karen Rhodes and shivered to himself. He had known the woman socially—not well, but still he had known her. She used to date a good friend of his, a surgical resident, and six months ago they had shared a table at a house staff dinner-dance. She was so damn pretty, he thought sadly, and now she's a mangled mess. He studied her face once more, then turned away.

Rodman walked over to a wall mirror and gazed at his reflection. He was a tall, lanky man in his late twenties, with fair skin and auburn-colored hair. His slender face was unmarked except for early crow's-feet at the corners of his eyes. Rodman wondered how he would age, how he would look with gray hair and lines in his face. *What the hell difference does it make?* he asked himself. *Everybody grows old unless they die young, like Karen.* He cursed softly, annoyed by the thoughts of his own mortality.

The room he was standing in looked more like an operating room than a place where autopsies were performed. Everything was tiled in white, glistening and aseptic. In the center of the room was a large stainless-steel table, with the corpse on top and a microphone hanging overhead. X-ray viewboxes were mounted on the wall, lights on, films up. Rodman walked over and turned an x-ray right side up. It showed Karen Rhodes's pelvic bones, crushed beyond repair with multiple fractures.

He sat on a steel stool and folded his gloved hands atop the black plastic apron he was wearing. Sweat began soaking through his green scrub suit. He closed his eyes and started reviewing the pathological findings that were found in people who had jumped from great heights.

Rodman sprang to his feet as the door opened. It was Harry Crowe, the diener, the keeper of the corpses.

"Good, good," Harry chuckled. "You should always come to attention when I walk in."

"Fuck off, Harry!" Rodman sat back down and glared at the short, heavyset man who had bee-bees for eyes and a wide mouth that seemed to grin perpetually. He was sixty years old and had spent over half of his life working at Memorial.

"Shame on you. A distinguished doctor, and you use such bad language." Harry walked over to the stainless-steel table and patted the corpse's forehead. "No brain examination for you. Your family says no."

"What the hell do you want?"

"I got a Japanese doctor from the coroner's office and he says he's supposed to be in on the autopsy.''

''So?''

''You know anything about it?''

''No, but that doesn't—''

''Yes or no?'' Harry snapped. ''You're the chief resident. Make a decision.''

''Ask Blalock.''

''I'm asking you. You always try to be like Blalock. So do it now. Yes or no.''

''Well, I—um—I—''

''Your answer is yes. I'll give him a scrub suit. If you change your mind, let me know and I'll throw his ass out.''

Rodman watched him leave, disliking him even more than usual. Harry was a fixture at Memorial, a pain-in-the-ass know-it-all whose abrasiveness was tolerated by the house staff because he could make life miserable for them if he wished. And he was right about Rodman trying to imitate Joanna Blalock. Rodman's dream was to become a mirror image of Blalock, to be an authority in forensic pathology, to charge her reputed fee of a thousand dollars a day to testify. *Sweet Jesus*, he thought as his mind drifted. *At that rate, I could work for fifty days and pay off my medical school loan. Make that a hundred days*, he recalculated, remembering taxes.

The swinging doors opened and Joanna Blalock walked in. She put on a black apron over her scrub suit, then worked her hands into latex gloves. ''Did the fellow from the coroner's office show up?''

''He's changing now,'' Rodman said, walking over.

''Good.'' Joanna looked down at Karen's body,

then turned away as her face lost color. "I—ah—I forgot something in my office."

She hurried out into the hall and took several long, deep breaths, trying to regain her composure. Joanna had thought she could be totally objective with Karen's corpse, but she couldn't. Karen had been a close friend over the past year, someone Joanna really liked and enjoyed being with. They had met at the Music Center during the first intermission of *La Traviata*. The women had so many things in common they hit it off right away. They became quite close, sometimes sharing their deepest secrets; they were solid friends who knew they could always count on each other. They had last talked a day ago and Karen had given no indication of being suicidal. Karen had said she wanted to talk with Joanna about something at the Psychiatric Institute that was bothering her. Something about a research program. It was important, but she said it could wait.

Joanna steeled herself to go back into the autopsy room. She knew that there were some pathologists who would advise that she withdraw from the case because of her friendship with the deceased. But Joanna felt otherwise. She was convinced she could be objective and push her feelings aside. More importantly, Joanna was the only forensic pathologist at Memorial. If Karen had committed suicide, Joanna might be able to determine why. If there had been foul play, Joanna would be the most likely one to uncover it. She felt she owed that to her friend.

Joanna took a deep breath and reentered the autopsy room. She reached for a magnifying glass and went to the end of the table. Motioning to

Rodman to come closer, she leaned over and began examining the soles of Karen's feet.

Rodman watched the ritual, knowing that Blalock always started with the soles. Blalock believed that the bottoms of the feet were the most frequently overlooked part of the anatomy. She had told Rodman about a case where the heels provided a critical clue. A woman had been strangled, presumably in the parking lot where her body was discovered. Blalock had found rug burns on her heels and had managed to extract fibers from the abraded skin. The fibers matched those taken from the living-room carpet of the prime suspect. He was now serving a life sentence at San Quentin.

"Nothing," Joanna reported.

Rodman moved to the side of the table and stared down at the girl's battered body. "She's really been mashed."

"That's what happens when a body falls ten stories traveling thirty-two feet per second per second."

"You'd think she could have come up with a better way to do it."

"Like how?"

Rodman shrugged. "She could have injected herself with a massive dose of insulin or started an I.V. on herself with ten-percent potassium chloride."

"You're thinking like a doctor now. Remember, she was a nurse."

"She worked on a ward. That stuff was readily available."

"Not in a psychiatric hospital."

"Then she could have OD'd on drugs."

Joanna shook her head. "Too risky. Most overdoses fail, and there's always the possibility of ending up a vegetable.''

Rodman stared at the girl again, now nibbling on his lower lip. "What a waste!"

"Did you know her?"

Rodman nodded. "She used to date Bob Hannah, a surgical resident. I sat across from them at the house staff dance last year."

"What was she like?" Joanna asked, wanting to get a male's view.

"Pretty, reserved, very nice. She looked like real money."

"Oh?"

"Everyone was commenting on her watch. It was one of those ten-grand Piagets."

"Did she use drugs?"

Rodman hesitated. "I don't know."

"Then guess."

"I'd say not. I was at a beach party once and she and Bobby were there. Someone lit up a joint and passed it around. I remember Karen refusing. She didn't make a big thing out of it. Just said, 'No thanks.' "

Joanna nodded to herself. That was the image that Karen wanted to project—or had been trained to project. But she could loosen up around good friends. She and Joanna had often talked about men, but they had never discussed Bobby Hannah. "You mentioned that she *used* to date this resident?"

"They were together for six months. Then they split apart."

"When?"

"Three or four months ago."

"Was she broken up over the split?"

"You'll have to ask Bob Hannah."

Robert Nagura entered through the swinging doors. He was a slender, middle-aged man with healthy groomed black hair; a high, unlined forehead; and almond-shaped, very Oriental eyes.

"I'm Bob Nagura from the coroner's office. Sorry to be late. The freeway traffic was a bitch."

"No problem. I'm Joanna Blalock. This is our chief resident, David Rodman."

Everyone nodded, preferring not to shake with gloved hands.

"Do you know the background in this case?" Joanna asked.

"Only what I've read in the newspaper," Nagura said.

"Then you know as much as we do." Joanna blew a piece of lint off her magnifying glass and headed for the stainless-steel table. "Feel free to ask any questions or make any suggestions."

"I'm here only as an observer."

Joanna started again with the soles of the feet and worked her way up. There was a fracture-dislocation of the left ankle and a compound fracture of the left tibia. The jagged end of bone sticking through the skin was encrusted with dirt and grime. Her right thigh was swollen, loaded with blood, and her pelvis tilted peculiarly. A small, well-healed scar was present in the right lower quadrant of the abdomen. The anterior chest wall was intact.

Joanna took a deep breath, preparing herself for the most gruesome part of the examination. From the neck down, Karen was a corpse. But from the neck up, she became recognizable. A friend.

Joanna stared down at the corpse's neck and with the use of her magnifying glass studied the black-and-blue area over the larynx. It was an inch wide, covering the Adam's apple and surrounding tissue. Carefully she palpated the area and felt the fragments of bone just beneath the skin. At the base of the neck, Joanna spotted some teeth marks. She examined the marks closely with the magnifying glass. It looked like a love bite. She reminded herself to do a vaginal smear for sperm.

Joanna lifted Karen's head. Brain and blood clots stuck to her gloves. There was a blowout fracture of the posterior skull with tissue oozing out. At the nape of her neck there were discrete red marks, less than an inch in width, running horizontally. Her back was abraded and badly bruised.

Joanna stepped over to the x-ray viewboxes and studied the films of the patient's neck. Three of the upper cervical vertebrae were fractured, two of them subluxed, but only to a modest degree.

Joanna came back to the table. "Dr. Nagura, would you care to examine the body?"

"Oh, no," Nagura declined politely. "I am here only as an observer."

"Your turn, David."

Rodman picked up a magnifying glass and began at the feet, imitating Blalock's style and manner. He saw the same things Blalock had seen. The fractured bones, the tilted pelvis, the bruised area over the larynx, the posterior skull fracture dripping blood and brain tissue. He even checked the x-rays, duly noting the cervical fractures and subluxations.

"Well?" Joanna asked.

Rodman cleared his throat, quickly organizing his thoughts. "The injuries are consistent with those caused by falls from great heights. The evidence indicates that she landed on her back with the greatest force being transmitted through her skull and left lower extremity. Death was probably instantaneous as a result of her massive head injury.''

''Good,'' Joanna said approvingly.

Rodman breathed a sigh of relief and stepped back.

''Now tell me what happened to her before she fell,'' Joanna added.

Rodman blinked rapidly, not certain he'd heard the question correctly. ''*Before* she fell?''

''That's right.''

''I—I don't know.''

''But you will,'' Joanna told him. ''Now, reexamine her neck carefully. Very carefully.''

Rodman spent a full two minutes examining and reexamining the neck—with and without the magnifying glass. He finally gave up. ''I don't see anything.''

''What about the bruise over the laryngeal area?''

''That could be from a trauma.''

''What trauma?'' Joanna demanded.

''The fall.''

''But you told me she landed on her back.''

''Maybe she hit something on the way down.'' Rodman was groping, his brain racing for an answer.

''Like what?''

''A railing.''

''There are no railings or balconies at the Psychiatric Institute.''

Rodman thought for a moment. ''Maybe it was self-induced. You know, she hits the ground and a hand flies up and slams into her throat.''

Joanna rolled her eyes upward in disbelief.

"Not too likely," Rodman admitted.

"Which leads to the conclusion that if it wasn't caused by the fall, it must have happened before she fell."

Rodman's eyes widened. "You mean somebody hit her with a karate chop?"

Blalock shook her head. "Put your thumbs on her larynx, one on each side."

"Like this?" Rodman bent over, touching her neck ever so lightly.

"Exactly. Could you crush her larynx with just your thumbs?"

"No. But I probably could if I put my fingers around her neck."

"Yes, you probably could," Joanna said softly.

Rodman quickly lifted the head and inspected the back of the neck. Red finger marks stared at him. "Holy shit!"

Robert Nagura watched with an impassive face, but inwardly he was thanking his lucky stars he had chosen not to examine the body. He too had seen the bruise marks, but like Rodman he wouldn't have made much out of them.

"So," Joanna concluded, "her larynx was crushed prior to the fall. Since people with crushed larynxes tend not to move as they gasp for air, we can safely assume that she didn't jump from that rooftop."

"She was pushed off," Rodman said in a barely audible voice. "Somebody crushed her throat and pushed her off."

"So it seems."

Joanna walked over to the wall phone and dialed Simon Murdock's number.

3

Detective Lieutenant Jake Sinclair hurried into Memorial Hospital and went directly to the men's room. He quickly wetted a paper towel and dabbed away at the mustard stain on his tie—his favorite tie, the only one he owned that really went with his brown houndstooth sportscoat. The yellow came off, replaced with a huge water spot. Jake cursed and resigned himself to the loss of his pale-green tie. He buttoned his jacket to hide the spot, then glanced in the mirror. Behind him a cubicle door opened and an emaciated man in his early twenties stepped out.

Jake studied him in the mirror and saw the telltale signs of drug addiction. Twenty pounds underweight; hollow cheeks with acne; and wide, spacey eyes. His long-sleeved shirt probably hid needle tracks, Jake guessed.

The man went to the basin next to Jake and ran water over his trembling hands. There were letters tattooed on the knuckles: *HATE* on the right, *LOVE* on the left. The "L" was a coiled snake with its tongue sticking out.

"What are you looking at?" he hissed.

"Your tattoo," Jake said and turned to face the young man.

He backed off a step, eyes even wider now. He

knew he was looking up at a cop. Jake Sinclair was just over six feet tall and weighed two hundred pounds, most of it in his shoulders and trunk. He had a fair complexion, high-set cheekbones, and piercing blue-gray eyes. His thick brown hair was swept back with no trace of gray despite his forty-four years. Jake's good looks were marred by a straight, well-healed scar that ran along his chin—compliments of a dope pusher's wife protecting her husband with a metal stoker.

"I'm here for the drug program," the man said nervously.

"Then move your ass along."

Jake shook his head in disgust as the addict dashed out. A piece of shit, he thought, with no redeeming features except one. His tattoo. Jake loved tattoos. And the fancier the better. They were excellent marks of identification. Witnesses tended to remember them in detail. He thought again about how the addict looked and filed it in his memory bank—along with the tattoo.

Even in the john, Jake Sinclair was all cop. Police work was his whole life and he liked it that way. His few friends were cops or ex-cops. He drank in cop bars, ate in cop restaurants. He had no family except for an aunt back east with whom he never communicated. He lived alone in a one-bedroom apartment and shared his patio with a black cat that walked in a few years ago and decided to stay. The cat, like Jake, spent most of his time on the streets, coming back to the apartment only to sleep.

For the past sixteen years Jake had been a homicide detective. Early in his career he had solved a tough case—a retired dentist who was raping and killing old women. There was a lot of publicity and he got the reputation of being a super-sleuth, which he felt he didn't deserve. So he began working twenty-four-hour days and seven-day weeks, trying to live up to his press clippings. He still put in long hours, but he didn't have to. Six months ago word came down that Jake was being considered for promotion to captain. He quickly let it be known that he was not interested. Jake knew what his strengths were, and shuffling papers was not one of them.

He had one flaw. Neatness. Compulsive neatness. It was like an anchor around his neck, but he had long ago accepted it and learned to live with it.

He glanced in the mirror again, eyes focusing in on the stained tie. He wondered if there was a men's shop close by.

Jake left the rest room and after a stop at the information desk found the Department of Pathology. Dr. Blalock was not in. The secretary escorted Jake into an empty office and asked him to wait.

Jake sat down carefully, sidesaddle, into a soft, cushioned chair. His hemorrhoids were flaring badly, and he thought again about the doctor who had suggested he be treated with lasers. Jake had no idea what lasers were, but he envisioned strobe lights, sparks, and plenty of electricity. He declined the suggested therapy. Not that his hemorrhoids weren't bothering the hell out of him. It was just that the thought of someone sticking high voltage up his ass bothered him more. He decided to continue medicating himself with over-the-counter ointments.

He glanced around the office, trying to get a feel

for the man he was about to question. The desk was rich mahogany with everything on top neatly and carefully arranged. The carpet was a soft gold, the drapes deep brown with faint yellow streaks. The walls were painted a cream color. There were no hanging diplomas or plaques. Jake liked that. No advertising. It told him that Blalock was a man who knew who he was and expected others to know as well.

He shifted around in his chair, wondering if Blalock was really any good. Blalock might be a university professor, but that didn't mean much to Jake. A few years back, Jake had worked with a forensic pathologist who had been flown in from some college in Philadelphia. The man was supposed to be a wizard. He turned out to be a turkey. Jake could have done better picking a medical examiner at random from the Los Angeles Coroner's office.

"Sorry to keep you waiting," Blalock said, walking into the office. "I'm Joanna Blalock."

Jake's jaw dropped noticeably. *Christ*, he groaned to himself, *a woman*. The detective quickly regained his composure and stood, displaying his ID and shield. "Lieutenant Jake Sinclair from Homicide."

"Sit, sit," Joanna said genially. She plopped into a swivel chair behind the desk, her eyes fixed on the detective. His response had been typical. Women were expected to be nurses and secretaries, not forensic pathologists. It was something Joanna had had to put up with all of her professional life. By now she should have been used to it. But she wasn't and probably never would be. At length she asked, "You usually work alone?"

"My partner is out with bronchitis." Jake eased

himself into the cushioned chair. The doc looked so damn young, he thought. She couldn't be much over thirty. And she was too good looking to have brains. He wondered how much help she was going to be. "How long have you been on the staff at Memorial?"

Joanna kept her expression even, hiding her irritation. Now the detective was trying to find out how experienced she was. "Two years here and before that I was on staff at Johns Hopkins for two years, and before that I was a resident in Forensic Pathology for three years. My final tally is seven years. How long have you been a cop?"

"Too long."

"Then you must be very wise."

Jake gestured noncommittally with his head and smiled thinly. He took out a ballpoint pen and a small writing pad. "You want to fill me in?"

Joanna leaned forward, elbows on the desk. "Last night—sometime between 11:10 and 11:40— a twenty-five-year-old nurse fell from the roof of the Psychiatric Institute. She was brought to the emergency room and pronounced DOA. Twelve hours later a postmortem examination was performed. She had the usual injuries one would expect from a ten-story fall. In addition, there were bruises over her throat in the area of the Adam's apple, and fingermarks on the back of her neck. The larynx was crushed, badly fractured. She was strangled before she fell."

Jake jotted down a note, then looked across at Joanna, expecting more.

Joanna stared back.

"Was she dead before she hit the ground?" Jake asked.

"I don't think so. There were too many bruises

over her body, too much blood in the subcutaneous tissue. Dead people don't bruise or bleed."

"She put up a fight?"

"Not that I could see. Her nails were long and manicured—no breaks, no chips. There was no blood or skin or fibers under her nails."

Jake tapped his pen against the writing pad. That bothered him. People being strangled fight like hell. "Did you say the fingermarks were on the back of the neck?"

"Right."

"So the assailant came at her from the front?"

"Correct."

"And she didn't put up a fight?"

Joanna shrugged her shoulders. "Maybe he surprised her."

"Or maybe she knew the murderer." Jake put his hands out and wrapped them around an imaginary neck, squeezing. "So the thumbs did the heavy work, huh?"

"And some."

"Oh?"

"This was not a simple strangulation. The bone and cartilage in her larynx were crushed by a very powerful pair of hands."

"And that's not a common finding in people who've been strangled?"

Joanna shook her head. "It's rare. You don't need that kind of force to shut off someone's airway. Moreover, in young people those tissues have a fair amount of elasticity. They're a bitch to crack."

"But fractures do occur in people who've been throttled?"

"Yes, but they're small and difficult to find. In her, the bones were crushed."

Jake stood and started pacing. He thought better on the move. "Are we sure she fell from the roof?"

"The campus police found her purse up there."

"You said she was a nurse. Did she work at this Institute?"

"Yes. She had just finished working the three-to-eleven shift. None of her coworkers noted anything unusual. She left the ward alone."

"This Institute, is it a research place or a hospital?"

"Both. But mainly a hospital."

Jake groaned inwardly. Shit! A nuthouse filled with wackos, every one a possible suspect. "Are any of them violent?"

"Probably."

"I take it that there are no witnesses to her fall?"

"None that have come forward." Joanna rocked back in her chair, watching Jake pace. He was a big man with large hands and feet, but he walked with soft, effortless steps, like a cat. She wondered if he was as powerful as he looked.

"How did she get from the Institute to the emergency room?"

"On a stretcher, I would guess."

Jake looked over at her, his lips almost smiling. "I meant, who brought her in?"

"I don't know. We can check it out in the ER."

Jake started pacing again. "Was she sexually assaulted?"

"No." Joanna knew that the majority of strangled women showed signs of rape or sexual abuse. "But I did a vaginal smear looking for sperm."

"Was there evidence that she had been fooling around?"

"Maybe. She had a love bite at the base of her neck."

Jake spun around on his heels. "A what?"

"A love bite. Teeth marks."

"I want to see it."

Joanna looked at Jake strangely, now sensing a change in his demeanor. Before, he was a cop going through the motions. But not now. Something had set him off. "Am I missing anything?"

"I'll tell you after I've looked at that bite."

Joanna pushed her chair back. "The autopsy room is across the hall."

Moments later they were looking down at the corpse of Karen Rhodes. Her body was covered with a sheet, with only her head showing. As promised to her family, the skull had not been opened, the brain not examined. Joanna pulled the sheet back to expose Karen's neck and upper chest. She handed Jake a magnifying glass and pointed to the teeth marks.

Jake leaned over, studying the marks with his naked eye, then using the magnifying glass. "It's a love bite, all right."

"I've already established that."

"Uh-huh."

Joanna looked at him, exasperated. "Would it be too much for me to ask what the significance of that love bite is?"

"He didn't break the skin this time," Jake observed.

"Who is *he*?"

"I can't be positive, but I think he's a wacko who's running around Los Angeles killing women. He also likes to nibble on them."

Joanna shivered. "How many has he killed?"

"This is the third we know about."

Joanna looked down at Karen's face. Several strands of hair had fallen over her forehead. Joanna gently lifted them and patted the strands back into place. *My God.* Joanna shivered again, sensing the terror Karen must have felt.

Jake watched intently. "She was a friend of yours, huh?"

"Yes." Joanna pulled the sheet up over Karen's face.

"Close?"

"We were good friends."

Jake hesitated for a moment, trying to find the right words. "You know, when a cop is killed, it's a rule that nobody who was close to him is allowed to be part of the investigation. No family, no close friends, even if they're the world's greatest cops. It's a good rule, too, because feelings can interfere with your thinking. They've got the same kind of rules in medicine, don't they?"

"If it's a member of your family, yes."

"But not if it's a close friend?"

Joanna looked at him sharply. "I can handle it."

"That's what they all say."

"Why don't you mind your end of the business and I'll take care of my end, okay?"

"Fine. Except when your side of the business begins to affect mine."

"Have I done something you don't approve of?"

"It's something you haven't done."

Joanna stared at the detective, disliking him more by the minute. "Like what?"

Jake stared back, trying to keep his calm. "Like you fixing the dead girl's hair, when you should have stayed focused on the love bite. The killer left his teeth marks. You can make a dental mold from that, can't you? And then we can see if it matches up with the others. And maybe—just maybe—if we can find a suspect, his teeth marks will match.''

Joanna felt her cheeks blush. ''I was going to get to that.''

''I'm certain you were,'' Jake said, stepping back from the table. ''Now, where are her personal effects?''

''In my office.''

They walked back in silence. Joanna started to say something but decided against it. She was still fuming, still upset by the way the detective had lectured her. She didn't have to take that from anyone, much less a cop. But she was upset because she knew that Sinclair was partly right. She should have stayed focused on that bite. And she should have immediately connected it to the murder. Concentrate, she reminded herself. Concentrate on every positive finding. Milk it for all it was worth. That's what her old professor at Johns Hopkins told her a hundred times. But he also told her that there was no substitute for experience. And that any forensic pathologist with less than twenty years of experience was still a babe in the woods. Joanna had sixteen years to go.

She led the way into the office. She reached down behind her chair and picked up a large plastic bag, then placed it on the desk.

Jake broke the seal and took out a Chanel leather purse. He emptied it carefully. Kleenex, lipstick, brush, keys. Her wallet contained forty dollars, credit cards (American Express Gold Card, Visa, Nieman Marcus, Chevron), and a photograph of a handsome young man. Her driver's license had been recently renewed.

Joanna studied Karen's picture on the license. Beautiful, she thought, even in a driver's license photo.

Jake was now studying a Cartier watch, stopped at 11:32. Jake doubted that even a Timex would still be ticking after a ten-story fall. "Well, Doc, what do you think?"

"It wasn't robbery."

Jake nodded. "And it wasn't rape."

"After money and sex, there's not much left, is there?"

Jake grinned sourly and wondered if Blalock really knew how right she was. He swept the contents back into the purse and pocketed the victim's driver's license and the photograph of the young man.

His hand went into the bag and came out with a pair of bloodstained pantyhose. They had been cut open, toe to top. He turned the hose around and around until he found the crotch. Then he held it up to the light and looked for stains. "Why are these hose cut open this way?"

"When trauma cases are brought to the ER, they cut the clothes off," Joanna explained.

Jake grumbled under his breath, still examining the crotch.

Smart, Joanna told herself, *very smart and very compulsive*. Most cops would have taken her word that no sexual attack had taken place. But sometimes it had, and there was no evidence at autopsy to back it up, particularly if the rapist was quick and small and withdrew just prior to ejaculation.

"Nothing," Jake reported, discarding the hose. He took out a bloodied nurse's uniform, also cut open. "Her blood?"

"Probably, but we'll check it out."

Jake extracted a bra, a pale-blue cashmere sweater, and a right shoe—white, loafer, size 7. He looked down into the empty plastic bag. "Where the hell is the other shoe?"

Joanna shrugged her shoulders. "Any number of places. It could have been thrown off at the moment of impact or it could be down in the ER."

Jake swept all the items back into the plastic bag. "Do you have time to go down to the emergency room with me?"

"Sure." Joanna took off her tweed jacket and put on a long white coat with her name embroidered above the upper pocket.

"Why the white coat?"

"It's like your badge. It'll open doors quicker."

They walked down a long corridor, past offices and laboratories, then up a flight of stairs and through the Radiology department. They came to a set of swinging doors. Posted on both of them were large signs that read: ABSOLUTELY NO ADMITTANCE. They entered, Joanna leading the way.

The back area of the emergency room was quiet. They went past a small lounge where two nurses were drinking coffee and smoking cigarettes. An old man on a stretcher was talking loudly in a language that neither Joanna nor Jake recognized. The young intern standing over the patient had a blank look on his face.

Up ahead they saw a middle-aged nurse swinging her arms back and forth, stretching her muscles. She was a thin, attractive woman, big-busted, with curly brown hair. She turned as they approached.

"We're looking for the head nurse," Joanna said.

"That's me. What can I do for you?" She had a nice smile, but her face looked very tired, the bags under her eyes dark and obvious. Her name tag stated that she was Nancy Evans.

"I'm Dr. Blalock and this is Lieutenant Sinclair from the Los Angeles Police Department. We need some information on Karen Rhodes. She was the nurse who fell from the Psychiatric Institute last night."

"Christ, what a mess!" Nancy winced.

"Were you on duty then?"

"Uh-huh."

Joanna glanced at the wall clock. It was 2:30 P.M. "Are you working a double shift?"

"Naw. We're trying a new schedule." Nancy yawned widely, quickly bringing a hand to her mouth. "Twelve hours on, twelve off. For three consecutive days. It's a bitch."

"She was DOA, huh?"

"Oh, yeah. I knew it the second they wheeled her in, but I went through the motions anyway. We cut her clothes off. An intern tried to get a line started. But there were no vital signs. Zilch."

"Who wheeled her in?" Jake asked.

"I don't know. It was a zoo down here last night. We had a big freeway crash with bad head injuries. All the rooms were going full blast."

Jake scratched the top of his head. "Lot of confusion, huh?"

"A circus! When they told me they were bringing in a jumper, I had no rooms available. We had to double up."

"Who told you she was coming in?"

She gave Sinclair a blank look. "Somebody barked it over the intercom."

"Do you keep a record of incoming calls?"

"Not for that kind of thing," Nancy said, stifling another yawn. "Are you her private doc?"

Joanna shook her head. "Who handles triage down here when there's a crowd of patients?"

Nancy shrugged. "Doctors, nurses. It varies."

"Who decides which patients go into which rooms?"

"It depends. Last night all the doctors and nurses were tied up, so Luther did it."

"Who's Luther?"

"One of our medical assistants."

"Can we talk to him?"

"Sure." The nurse walked over to an intercom, spoke briefly into it, then returned. "He's on his way."

Jake asked, "Did the girl who jumped have shoes on when she was brought in?"

"I didn't notice," Nancy said. "I remember her uniform was bloody and she had pantyhose on. Jesus, what a mess!"

"Did she have a sweater on?"

"I'm not sure."

"Think about it."

She stared into space, her eyes blinking. "I remember a sweater, but I'm not certain it was hers."

"What color?"

"Blue."

Jake nodded. The nurse's memory was accurate, despite her fatigue.

Nancy turned as a huge black man dressed in a scrub suit approached. He was six feet four, weighed at least two-fifty, and had hands the size of hams. His face had a very pleasant quality about it—big, expressive eyes; a droopy mustache; white, even teeth.

"What's up, Nancy?" Luther asked in a soft, almost lyrical voice.

"This is Dr. Blalock and Lieutenant Sinclair from the police department. They want some information on the jumper we had last night."

"Sure," Luther said genially, obviously not intimidated by the doctor or the cop.

Jake quickly sized up the big man. He could easily envision Luther calming down a frightened kid with a broken arm, particularly with that voice of his. On the other hand, Luther could just as easily scare the shit out of some punk who tried to act tough in the ER. "You remember the jumper?"

"Hard to forget that."

"How'd you know she was coming into the ER?"

"A medical student came running in from the parking lot, screaming at the top of his lungs. He was walking to his car when he found the body."

"But he didn't see her jump?"

"No."

"So what did you do?"

"Sent two orderlies with a gurney."

"No doctors?"

"They were all tied up."

"Did you see her when they brought her back?"

"Yup," Luther said tonelessly. "She was gone. One of the doctors came in and pronounced her, and that was it."

"And everybody returned to business as usual," Jake said, more to himself than to the others.

"Not quite."

"How do you mean?"

Luther hesitated for a moment. "It's kind of different when one of the medical staff dies, you know. It's like it was one of your own. Same thing must happen when one of your fellow officers is killed. You just feel something different.''

Jake nodded. He had experienced that feeling. Too many times. ''Did she have shoes on when she was brought in?''

Luther smoothed his mustache down, gazing at the ceiling. ''Can't remember. We put all her things in a bag, cleaned the room, and got ready for the next one.''

''Could we look in the room now?''

The nurse nodded and led the way. The room was spotless, empty. No white shoe.

''What's so important about her shoe?'' the nurse asked.

''It's missing,'' Jake said evenly.

''I mean, so what?''

Jake ignored the question. ''Which door was she brought in through?''

They walked out into the corridor and the nurse pointed to the automatic sliding doors.

''Thanks for your time,'' Jake said, nodding to the nurse and Luther.

''She did jump, didn't she?'' the nurse asked, suddenly interested.

Jake headed for the door, Joanna a step behind. They walked out into a huge parking lot filled with cars. There were no sidewalks or ramps.

Jake shielded his eyes from the bright glare. ''Where is the Psychiatric Institute?''

''Straight across the lot.''

Jake gazed out at the mammoth brick building. ''Would there have been this many cars here last night?''

Joanna shook her head. ''It would have been virtually deserted.''

"Then we'll walk straight across. That's the route the orderlies with the gurney would have taken."

They weren't able to walk straight across the lot. Instead, they zigzagged around cars. Jake had his head down and his eyes glued to the ground, like a bloodhound trying to pick up a scent. Several times he dropped to his knees and peered beneath vehicles.

"Is the shoe that important?" Joanna asked.

"I don't know," Jake muttered, head moving back and forth, eyes constantly searching. He really didn't know if the shoe had any importance. He only knew that it was missing and shouldn't have been. A long time ago Jake had learned never to overlook the small things. There were no perfect crimes and no perfect criminals. Even the best of them fucked up—usually in small ways.

They came to the side of the building. Joanna led the way to the spot where the victim had landed. Jake walked over and examined the pavement. There were two dried pools of blood, equal in size, separated by three feet of pavement. They were both equidistant from the side of the building. Jake studied them for a moment. "She landed parallel to the building, right?"

"Correct."

Jake tilted his head way back and looked up at the roof, trying to envision the girl's flight. His gaze came back to the ground. "How'd she land?"

"On her back," Joanna told him. "Most of the force went through her skull and left lower extremity."

Jake again studied the pools of dried blood. "Where was her head?"

"Probably here." Joanna pointed to the spot closer to him. "When I examined these pools earlier, I found a piece of tissue that looked like brain in this one."

Jake carefully placed the heel of his right foot at the inner edge of the pool, then paced off the distance to the building. It measured out just over ten feet. "She wasn't pushed. She was thrown off."

Joanna tried to figure it out, but couldn't. "What do you base that on?"

"People who jump drop like deadweight. They land maybe three, four feet from the building. Her body hit ten feet away." Jake looked back up toward the roof again, wondering what sort of nut or sadistic bastard he was dealing with. "You said the killer's hands were powerful?"

"Very."

"So were the bastard's arms." Jake jotted down a note in his pocket pad, closing it with a slam. "Let's look at the roof."

They entered the building through a side door that a guard opened for them.

Jake checked the knob. It opened only from the inside. But that didn't mean a damned thing, he thought grimly. The killer could have waited for someone to exit and just before the door shuts, the killer grabs it and walks in—nice and easy.

They took the elevator, sharing it with a patient and her medical attendant. The patient was a thin, frail middle-aged woman with unkempt gray hair and a glassy stare in her eyes. She looked straight ahead, like a blind person seeing nothing. A peculiar sour odor emanated from her. Jake studied her arms. They were poles, skin covering bone with no muscle.

The elevator stopped at the sixth floor and the woman and her attendant left the car.

Jake turned to Joanna. "What was that smell?"

"It might be related to her mental illness. There are some psychiatrists who believe that schizophrenics emit an unusual odor."

"Can they make a diagnosis based on the smell?"

"Hardly."

They got off at the tenth floor and walked down a long, deserted corridor. It was very quiet. The only sounds they heard were the clicks of their shoes on the tiled linoleum. Every door they passed was closed.

"What is this place?" Jake asked in a low voice.

"The BRI. Brain Research Institute."

"It's eerie as hell."

"No," Joanna grinned, "it's all in your mind. If I had told you that this floor was used for storage, it wouldn't have bothered you one bit."

"Maybe." And maybe not, Jake thought. He still had the odor of that woman in his nostrils. He wondered if the whole place smelled that way. "Do you have to go through this floor to get to the roof?"

"Yes."

"Who works up here?"

"A very distinguished group of physicians, some technicians, a few secretaries."

"Have you spent time up here?"

Joanna nodded. "A long time ago. Would you like me to show you around?"

"Later. Let's do the roof first."

They went through a fire exit and climbed the metal steps to the roof. Jake checked the doorknob. It opened from outside and inside.

The roof was virtually bare. It was composed of a gritty rocklike material and ringed by a five-foot-high chain-link fence. A rusty folding chair was off to one side, an old weathered lounge chair behind it.

Jake moved toward the wire enclosure, his eyes darting back and forth across the flat surface of the roof. He saw a shining object and reached down for it. A broken button. He picked it up by its edges, wrapped it in a handkerchief, and pocketed it. Head down, he walked on until he reached the fence. He held his arms up, holding an imaginary body. The killer had to stand back a couple of feet from the fence, Jake thought. And that meant the woman was really thrown twelve feet, not ten. The killer must have had unbelievable strength. But why bother to throw her off the roof? Her throat was already crushed. A wacko? Or somebody very smart, trying to cover up murder?

He examined a closed gate in the fence, held shut by a rusty lock. Beyond the gate a metal ladder went from the edge of the roof to the floor below. It probably connected to a utility room, Jake guessed.

"Lieutenant!" Joanna waved him over.

Jake walked across the roof, his eyes still searching, looking for the small things.

Joanna was standing next to the lounge chair, pointing down at a white loafer. It was made out of a suede material, the type that wouldn't hold a fingerprint. But Jake picked it up with his ballpoint pen. It was a size 7, the same size and style as the shoe in the plastic bag.

"Where did they find her purse?" Jake asked.

"According to the campus police report, on the lounge chair."

"Then she was sitting here just before she was attacked."

"Why'd she take one shoe off?"

"Maybe she kicked it off, fighting for her life."

"You mean the murderer caught her lying down?"

"Or pushed her down."

Joanna looked down at the weather-beaten cushion atop the chair. She leaned over and studied an old stain.

Jake peered over her shoulder. "What's that?"

"A stain."

"Yeah, but *what*?"

"I'm not sure," Joanna said cautiously. "But if someone were lying prone on this chair, the spot would be at the level of the pubis."

"Maybe you can find some sperm."

"I doubt it, but we can try."

Jake rubbed his chin. "She wouldn't have been banging somebody up here. Not with her pantyhose on."

"Just a wild shot," Joanna said.

"Keep taking them. You might get lucky." Jake frowned, trying to envision the brutal murder. He curled his arms and picked up the imaginary body, then headed for the fence. "So the killer crushes her throat and carries her across the rooftop. Like so."

"She's already anoxic at this point, gasping for air." Joanna was just behind Jake.

"No fight left in her."

"He could have taken his time. There was no rush."

Jake stopped. "He? How do you know it was a he?"

"Three reasons," Joanna told him. "First, women don't usually strangle their victims. They use poison, knives, occasionally a gun. But not strangulation. Secondly, there were no nail marks on the victim's neck. Women usually have nails long enough to at least make indentations. And thirdly, the incredible strength of the killer."

"Good points. But not proof."

"True. But I'll give you ten-to-one odds it was a man."

Jake began walking again with slow, deliberate steps. At the fence he raised his arms up over his head. "And then the bastard throws the girl over the railing."

They stood in silence, staring out at the sky. Both were thinking the same thought. Was the girl aware when she was thrown over? Did she realize what was happening?

The noise of a helicopter engine drew their attention. It made a wide turn, then slowly descended, finally resting down gently on the landing pad.

"Do they fly in here often?" Jake asked.

"All the time. Memorial is the biggest trauma center on the Westside."

"Did any of them land last night?"

Joanna smiled to herself. This cop wasn't going to overlook anything. "Probably. I can check it out with the people in ER."

"We're interested in landings and takeoffs between 11:00 P.M. and 11:45 P.M." Jake stretched his back, then rotated his neck as vertebrae cracked pleasurably. "You know, Doc, in almost every case I've ever worked, there's always been one question—one big question—that has to be answered. And as soon as you get the answer, you can find out who did it and why they did it. Of course, in this case that doesn't necessarily hold because here we are probably dealing with a serial killer, a wacko. Even so, there's still one question that needs answering. One thing that keeps gnawing at me.''

''What's that?''

Jake stared out at the overcast sky. ''What the hell was she doing up on this roof at eleven-thirty at night?''

4

Dr. Richard Wong, the chief of Clinical Pathology at Memorial, adjusted the focus of the microscope and carefully studied the vaginal smear. Joanna Blalock watched him impatiently. The clinical pathologist—thin and in his early forties, with a sparse, stringy mustache—moved the slide back and forth slowly.

Joanna glanced at her watch. "Well, what do you think?"

"It's overstained."

"Can you read it?"

Wong nodded slightly. "If you stop bugging me, I can."

They were sitting across from each other in a small, windowless room. There was just enough space for a tiny desk, two metal chairs, and a filing cabinet. On the wall behind Richard Wong there was an overhanging shelf that was crowded with books and papers. Joanna ran a hand through her hair, her eyes now on the wall clock. It was almost eight in the evening and she still had things to do.

"Ah, here's a good area!" Wong said at last, refocusing the microscope. "Take a look."

Joanna squeezed her way around the desk. Wong pushed his chair back, giving her room. The vaginal smear was overstained, but Joanna could still see a cell with a long, threadlike tail.

"It looks like a sperm," she said.

"That's because it is a sperm," Wong said pleasantly.

Joanna pulled away from the microscope, hitting her head on an overhanging shelf. "How many did you see?"

"Two for sure, maybe a third."

"Which means she probably had intercourse on the day of her death."

Wong scratched an ear. "Twenty-four hours at the outside—assuming she received a full load."

"Is this the only smear that shows sperm?"

Wong nodded, watching Joanna clean the slide and pocket it. "Was the girl raped?"

"No."

"Well, then, all we can say is that she got laid sometime during the last day of her life." Wong rocked back in his chair, stifling a yawn. "And according to Simon Murdock, I'm not supposed to say anything to anybody about this. Right?"

"For now."

Wong sighed. "Are we being so secretive just because she was the daughter of Senator Rhodes?"

"No," Joanna lied easily, "we're doing it because she was murdered."

Her mind went back to the meeting she'd attended earlier with Simon Murdock and Mortimer Rhodes. All the facts had been brought out, including the gruesome details. The old man had been livid, torn between grief and anger. Over and over he had demanded absolute confidentiality. He also demanded that the son of a bitch who did it be caught and hanged.

"Tell me about the blood studies," she said to Wong.

"All the specimens were B-positive."

"Did you type them out all the way?" Joanna asked, remembering a case in which both the victim and the assailant were type A-positive. When they checked for the lesser-known antigens on the red blood cells, it became clear that the bloods were from two different people.

"Of course I did," Wong said, exasperated. "What the hell kind of show do you think I run down here?"

Joanna held out a hand and flipped it back and forth, grinning down at the man who had been a friend for years.

"All of those blood samples came from her body," Wong went on. "But the stuff on that piece of canvas didn't."

Joanna's eyes widened. "Did you find sperm?"

"No-o-o," Wong said slowly, making her wait. "But it had a sky-high level of acid phosphatase."

"So it had to be semen?"

"Almost surely," Wong said, now smoothing the edges of his mustache. "Where did the canvas come from?"

"A lounge chair."

"Somebody was fooling around on it," Wong said.

Somebody was strangled on it, too, Joanna thought. She glanced at her watch. "Well, I've got to run. Thanks for your help."

"Joanna," Wong said in a soft voice, "Lois asks about you all the time. She'd be thrilled if you'd stop over and visit us."

Joanna nodded. Lois Wong was a pediatrician Joanna met eight years earlier while working with

Operation Hope in El Salvador. She too had been wounded by the mortar attack on the village, but not as badly as Joanna. Every time they saw each other socially the conversation always drifted back to El Salvador and the village and the attack. And Joanna would relive the nightmare. The awful nightmare. "Soon," she said at last. "I promise."

An hour later Joanna was driving westward on Sunset Boulevard. Traffic was light, with most cars going in the opposite direction. She took the curves at a careful thirty miles per hour, staying in the inside lane just in case her car decided to die on her again. The eight-year-old Toyota was on its last legs and had required extensive repairs over the past year. Joanna needed a new car badly, but there was no way she could afford it. Not on her income of $90,000 a year. It sounded ludicrous, but it was true. She went over the numbers in her mind again and they came out the same again. Her gross income was $7,500 per month—$5,000 after taxes. She had to pay $1,500 per month on the large loan she had taken to cover the cost of her medical school education. And $2,000 per month went to a nursing home outside San Francisco where her mother, who had Alzheimer's disease, was a patient. That left $1,500 a month to live on. In Los Angeles, that was barely enough to get by.

Joanna reflexively took her foot off the accelerator as her car's engine began to make a grinding sound. The noise gradually subsided and she drove on, now at twenty miles per hour. Maybe the car will last another year. Two years would be great, she thought. That was when her medical school loan would finally be paid up. Her mind drifted back to her college days when her wonderful father was still alive, the family wealth still intact. She could have gotten a new car simply by phoning home. But that was another world, a dream. Gone forever.

Joanna turned off Sunset and drove into an underground garage. It was situated beneath an apartment complex she had moved into shortly after her return to Los Angeles. The building itself was a large, rectangular structure, two stories high with chimneys dotting the roof. Rents started at $800 per month.

Up ahead Joanna saw Lieutenant Sinclair standing in her parking space, waiting. She sighed wearily. The last thing she wanted to do at this moment was to discuss Karen's gruesome murder.

"Anything wrong, Lieutenant?" Joanna asked, getting out of her car.

"Naw," Jake said. "Just something we have to talk about."

Joanna wondered what it was and why it couldn't wait until tomorrow. "How long will it take?"

"A while."

They walked up a short flight of steps and stopped at the mailboxes. Joanna checked her mail, groaning at the stack of bills. One letter was from the nursing home where her mother was a patient. Joanna remembered that she had paid that bill last week. Probably another rate increase, she thought dismally.

They went through a passageway and into a large garden area filled with sweet-smelling plants and shrubbery.

Jake gazed around the quadrangle, impressed.

"I didn't know there were any apartments like this left in Los Angeles."

"I'm told this is one of the last. It's owned by a nice old man who doesn't want anything changed. He apparently designed the building himself."

"And what happens when the old man dies?"

"His family will tear it down and put up a huge condominium complex. At least, that's what I'm told."

"Too bad."

"Nothing lasts forever, Lieutenant."

They came to Joanna's apartment, located on the ground level at the easternmost end of the building. A folded note was taped to the door. She quickly read it.

"A sometimes roommate," Joanna said, pocketing the paper.

Jake noted the warm grin on the doctor's face. A man, he decided.

They entered a spacious living room, tastefully decorated and very feminine. The chairs and couches were French antique and upholstered in deep-blue silk. The walls were covered with oils, lithographs, and watercolors. Jake studied them briefly, thinking about his own apartment. The only thing on the wall was a faded print of a Japanese geisha. It had been there when he moved in.

"Let me just say hello to my roommate," Joanna said, excusing herself.

Jake wandered around the living room, figuring it to be twice as large as his entire apartment. Everything was neat and in place, yet it had a comfortable lived-in feel to it. Jake stopped and looked down at two battered suitcases, adorned with stickers from foreign countries. Next to them was a soiled knapsack and a pith helmet. He nudged them with his foot and saw the ID tags. Kate something-or-other. The last name was smudged. Son of a bitch, Jake muttered to himself, the doc's roommate was a woman. He figured that Blalock was in her early thirties with plenty of money—and women like that didn't have roommates unless they were lesbians. He moved quickly to the door that led off the living room, concentrating on what he heard. All he heard was a running shower and a woman's laugh. Then footsteps. He darted back to the center of the room.

"Sorry about that," Joanna apologized.

Sinclair noted the water spots on Joanna's shirt and coat. He envisioned two women kissing passionately and felt a wave of nausea.

"Care for a drink?"

"A beer, if you got it."

"Heineken's all right?" Joanna headed for a small wet bar that was tucked away in a corner and connected to the kitchen.

"Perfect." Jake's eyes went back to the suitcases. "Your roommate travels a lot, huh?"

"Only nine months a year."

"Why so much?"

"She's an archaeologist."

"And she still pays half the rent?" Sinclair asked, then realized how stupid his question was. People like Blalock didn't take in roommates to split the rent.

Joanna laughed softly. "Lieutenant, my sister has no permanent address. When she returns from her travels, she simply moves in with the nearest relative or friend."

Sinclair grinned, relieved and feeling a little foolish.

Joanna came back with two bottles of Heineken's and frosted mugs. They sat on couches across from each other, a coffee table with leather inlays between them.

Jake took a giant gulp of beer, so cold it felt like ice going down. Delicious. "You've got to be wondering why I'm here."

"I assumed it has to do with Karen Rhodes."

Jake drank more beer, hesitating, hating to ask a favor from a civilian. "The manure has hit the fan. There's flak coming from everywhere."

"Are you talking about the girl's family?"

"Yeah."

"It doesn't surprise me." Joanna poured her Heineken, then waited for the foam to settle. "I was just at a meeting with Mortimer Rhodes. He's probably out forming a vigilante posse right now."

"He's doing worse than that," Jake said sourly. "He wants the army and navy called out, with the marines as a backup. And he keeps reminding everybody that he's got one son who's a senator and another who's going to be the next attorney general of California."

"Your future boss."

Jake nodded. "Every cop's future boss."

Joanna leaned back, wondering if the detective was going to ask her to intercede and try to cool Mortimer Rhodes down. If that was the purpose of his visit, he was wasting his time.

"And it's only going to get worse," Jake said. "If we don't catch this killer in a real big hurry, I can tell you what they'll do next. They'll form a task force."

"That's not such a bad idea."

"It's a crummy idea," Jake said tonelessly. "And even the brass knows it. We'll end up with fifty dicks stumbling over one another. In the end all we'll have is a mountain of paperwork and no murderer. He'll be walking around laughing his buns off."

"If it's such a bad move, why do it?"

"Public relations," Jake said. "It makes it look like we're doing something. It's also a matter of covering your ass. If you spread the blame out thin enough, nobody gets hurt too much."

Your tax dollars at work, Joanna thought. "Well, it seems as if you have your work cut out for you."

"Which brings me to the purpose of my visit." Jake placed his mug down on a silver platter. "Let me begin by telling you that I think the murderer may have made his first mistake by killing that girl at the Psychiatric Institute."

"What mistake?"

"It's only a hunch, but I'll tell you the way I figure it. His first two victims were kind of non-descript. A teenaged hooker who no one knew or cared about. She could have talked to a hundred guys the night she got whacked and nobody would remember one of them. And if anybody did remember, they weren't going to talk about it. The second victim was a young divorcee who walked down a dark, deserted alley at the wrong time. Again, no witnesses. But his last hit was different, wasn't it?" Jake sipped his beer, waiting for Joanna to make the connection. His gaze dropped to the graceful outline of Joanna's thighs and he had to force himself to look away.

Joanna slowly nodded. "He killed Karen on the

roof of a very large building. He had to walk into that building and he had to climb ten flights just to get to the BRI. Then he had to walk through the BRI to get to the roof. Somebody may have seen him.''

"Without even knowing it."

"Someone might have seen an unfamiliar face."

"Or one they'd seen before."

Joanna's eyes widened. "You think the killer works at the Psychiatric Institute?"

"No. But he's probably been there before."

"Maybe," Joanna said dubiously, "but it still could have been someone who walked in from the outside for the first time."

"Oh?" Jake smiled thinly. "You figure this guy just happened to stroll into the Institute at midnight?"

"It's possible."

"And then by chance he goes to the tenth floor and finds the only door with steps leading up. Then he decides—what the hell, I may as well take a look at the roof."

"That's unlikely," Joanna conceded.

"So," Jake went on, "whoever went to that rooftop was probably familiar with it."

"That doesn't narrow it down much," Joanna said. "There are a lot of people always coming and going in the Institute, even at night."

"How many?"

"Hundreds."

Jake's brows shot up. He had expected fewer, far fewer. "Why so many?"

"It's like a regular hospital. There are doctors, patients, visitors, nurses, technicians, aides, house staff, and on and on."

"Shit," Jake muttered under his breath.

"You're going to need some help," Joanna said, thinking that a task force might not be such a bad idea after all.

Jake suddenly brightened, seeing his chance. "What I need is someone who knows the inside of a hospital, how it works, what the people do, who should be there and who shouldn't." He paused again, waiting for her to make the connection. "I need someone like you."

Joanna's jaw dropped. "You want me to assist you?"

"Right." Jake sat back, his eyes still on her face. "Only for a day or two. I'm just going to be looking for someone who may have seen the killer."

"I—I'm not sure how much help I would be."

"A lot," Jake said and meant it. He had given the idea a lot of thought, at first resisting it, asking himself over and over, "Who the hell needs to work with a civilian?" But the more he thought about it, the better it sounded. He had worked plenty of homicides in unfamiliar settings—a museum, an art gallery, even one at the Music Center. Those places were foreign to him. He had no grasp, no feel for what usually went on there. But he always had other cops he could rely on for the expertise he needed. He didn't know any cops who were experts on hospitals.

"Do you want me to serve as a guide?"

"A guide!" Jake spat the word out. "If I wanted a guide I'd find one of those candy-stripers. I don't need a roadmap. I need someone who will see things I don't see, hear things I don't hear."

"Give me an example."

"Remember when we were in the emergency room questioning that nurse?"

Joanna nodded.

''She told us she was on duty at midnight when the girl was brought in. I accepted that, you didn't. You looked at the wall clock and asked her if she'd worked a double shift. Now, why did you ask her that?''

Joanna thought for a moment. ''Because most nurses work eight-hour shifts beginning at 7:00 A.M. If she was on duty at midnight, she had to be working the 11:00 P.M. to 7:00 A.M. shift. She should have been off when we got to the ER.''

''Yet there she was, on duty at 2:30 P.M.'' Jake drained the last of his beer. ''You knew something was off, so you questioned her about it. She could have been lying through her teeth and I would have bought every word.''

''Why would she lie?''

''Everybody lies,'' Jake said flatly. ''Presidents, mothers, friends. Everybody.'' He looked at Joanna, not certain he'd made his point. ''You know things I need to know and don't have time to learn.''

Joanna gestured with her hands. ''Of course, I'll help. But it'll have to be cleared through the dean's office.''

''It's already been done. He thought it was a good idea, particularly after he got a phone call from Mortimer Rhodes.'' Jake lied easily. But what the hell, he figured. He'd call the captain and the captain would call the chief and the chief would call old man Rhodes. It'd work out all right.

Joanna gave him a long look. ''Then why did you go through all the preliminaries? You could have asked me on the phone.''

''Because I wanted to get a feel for you. Before I work with someone—particularly a civilian—I'm going to damn well know about them.'' Jake lied so convincingly that he was even impressed himself. He had come to her apartment because he wanted to see her again, away from the hospital. Joanna Blalock was good looking as hell, with the best pair of legs he'd seen in a long, long time. Even better than his ex-wife's, which was really saying something.

"And what did you find out about me?"

"That you're a good listener and don't ask stupid questions. Also, you're not a pain in the butt."

High praise, indeed, Joanna thought. "Where do we start?"

"At the Institute, ten o'clock tomorrow morning."

"On the roof again?"

"Nope," Jake said, eyes on his empty mug. "The crime unit went over it late this afternoon."

Joanna pushed her half-full Heineken's bottle over. "Did they find anything?"

"Some smudged fingerprints on the lounge chair." Sinclair poured and drank deeply. A rim of foam was left on his upper lip. He swiped it away with a finger. "The boys weren't too happy about the swatch you cut out of the cushion."

"Somebody had intercourse on that cushion," Joanna said.

"You sure?"

"Positive. That swatch contained a sky-high level of acid phosphatase."

Sinclair rubbed his bristled chin. "Is there any way to tell whether it came from the girl?"

Joanna shook her head. "Acid phosphatase is found only in semen. Women don't have that enzyme."

"And you're certain she wasn't raped?"

''No way. But she did have intercourse some time during the day she died.''

''How do you know that?''

''We found a few sperm in her vagina.''

''Well, well,'' Jake mused, trying to fit the new pieces into the puzzle. ''Can you give me the approximate time she was laid?''

''It's impossible to tell,'' Joanna said. ''There are too many variables.''

''Like what?''

''The man's sperm count. If it was low to begin with, we'd find only a few sperm in her, even if she'd had intercourse an hour before her death.''

''What if her boyfriend was a healthy stud?''

''Then I'd guess she had intercourse eighteen to twenty-four hours before her death. Maybe longer.''

''But not a lot longer.''

''Right.'' Joanna watched as the detective's eyes narrowed, his brain concentrating, weighing the possibilities; his head moved ever so slightly, discarding one thought, replacing it with another. ''Any ideas?''

''A million of them,'' Jake said hoarsely. ''And none of them worth a damn.''

''Do you have any clues at all on this killer?''

''Not really. I met with a shrink last week and he tells me this guy falls into the category of a sadistic killer. He gets real pleasure from it.''

''Does he pick his victims randomly?''

''Probably not. He's either attracted to them or something drives him to them. There is no way to be certain, but the love bites convinced the psychiatrist he was right. They signify that the killer feels very close to his victims. He gets attached to them, and that takes time. The bite is an act of intimacy, the grand finale."

The phone in the bedroom rang and Joanna excused herself. Passing the closed bathroom door, she heard the shower running full blast, Kate singing loudly.

Joanna sat on the edge of the bed and picked up the phone. It was a television reporter who had learned that Joanna had performed the autopsy on Karen Rhodes. She wanted to ask some questions. Joanna hung up abruptly. The circus was beginning and poor Karen's life and death would become public property.

She glanced over at the telephone answering machine, now remembering that she hadn't listened to her messages last night. Joanna had given a lecture at a hospital in Santa Barbara and hadn't returned to her apartment until after one in the morning. She had practically fallen asleep with her clothes on.

Joanna pushed the rewind button and lay back on her pillow. The first message was from her hairdresser, canceling her appointment. There had been a small fire in his shop and they would be closed for a week. The next sound was a click: Someone had called and hung up without leaving a message. The next voice on the machine was Karen Rhodes.

Joanna bolted to a sitting position and turned the volume up.

"Hi, Joanna, this is Karen. I tried to reach you at your office, but you'd already left for Santa Barbara. I've got to talk with you. It's very important. Please call me as soon as you get in."

The next sound was a click and hang-up, then another call from Karen and another and another.

In her final message, Karen's voice seemed tense. "It's really important that I talk with you, Joanna. It's about that stuff at work I mentioned to you. Call me as soon as you get in, even if it's late."

Joanna quickly disconnected the machine and hurried back to the living room with it. She headed for the kitchen, motioning to Jake to follow her. "I want you to listen to something."

"What?"

"A phone call I got from Karen Rhodes yesterday."

Jake was at her side instantly. "What'd she say?"

"Listen." Joanna plugged the machine in and played the recording. She felt a chill run down her spine as she heard the voice of her friend.

Jake listened intently to the message. "What is this stuff at work she's talking about?"

"I'm not sure. She recently mentioned something to me about a research program that was bothering her. That was probably it."

"What research program?"

"She didn't say."

Jake shrugged. "I can't make much out of that."

"She was frightened, I can tell you that. That was not her usual tone of voice."

"She may be upset, but I wouldn't call that fright."

"That's because you didn't know her. And whatever it was, she was involved."

Jake looked at her quizzically. "I didn't hear her say that."

"She didn't in the phone call, but she gave me that impression when we talked." Joanna paused, thinking back to the conversation, trying to remember the exact words. "She'd mentioned the research and then she said, 'I'm—', and then she quickly substituted the words 'A lot of people are involved.' Karen always used that phrase to disassociate herself and her family name from something that might be derogatory."

"I think you're trying to make too much out of it."

"Damn it," Joanna said angrily. "Karen is trying to tell us something."

"Like what?"

"Something strange about research at the Institute. Something that involved her. Something that was wrong."

"And you're telling me that this somehow ties into her murder?"

"It might."

"How?"

"It just might."

"Look, I know you're trying hard. But let me tell you, it never works out this way. Nobody suddenly uncovers the big clue that solves the case. More often than not, we catch the bad guy because somebody squeals or talks too much. It's sad but true. Sherlock Holmes and Perry Mason exist in the movies, not in real life."

Joanna's face started to color. "Am I going to get another lecture from you, like the one this morning?"

"Would it do any good?"

"No. Because I'm not going to drop it regardless of what you say."

Jake gestured with his hands. He knew she was barking up the wrong tree, looking for something that wasn't there. If the girl was so frightened, she sure as hell wouldn't have gone to a dark rooftop at eleven-thirty at night. And if some kind of strange research was going on, why didn't she just go to the hospital authorities? She could have blown the whistle any time. And most importantly, nothing he'd heard could be connected to a serial killer. No, he decided, Blalock's notion would end up being a waste of time. But it would give him a reason to stay in frequent contact with Joanna Blalock, and that appealed to him.

"If you want to snoop around, fine. Do it, but do it quietly. And let me know if you turn up anything important."

Joanna smiled thinly. "You're really not so certain that Karen's message is unimportant, are you?"

Jake gestured again with his hands.

He turned and stood as a strikingly attractive woman walked into the living room. She was wearing faded jeans and an oversized football jersey. Her hair was dripping wet, her feet bare.

"Sorry to disturb you," she said. "I just want to get my suitcase."

"We're done," Joanna said, looking at Jake, who nodded. "Lieutenant Sinclair, meet my sister, Kate."

"It's a pleasure," Jake said, surprised when Kate extended a hand, more surprised by the firmness of her grip. "I was on my way out."

"Please sit and finish your drink." She said it as if she meant it, so Jake eased himself back down.

Kate sat on the edge of the couch next to Joanna. Her posture was erect, ankles crossed, knees together and tilted to one side. Sinclair studied her briefly. Kate could have passed for the doc's twin. She had the same soft patrician features and dark eyes. Even their hair was the same—light brown, bleached even lighter by the sun. The only difference was that Kate looked five years younger and her legs weren't as great. His gaze went to Joanna's legs. Fantastic.

"Kate just returned from an expedition in Guatemala," Joanna said, breaking the silence.

Jake nodded, caring less.

"How was the trip?" Joanna asked.

"Interesting," Kate said without enthusiasm. "But dangerous."

"Why so?"

"Looters." Kate ran long fingers through her wet hair, untangling it. "We were at a fabulous find called Rio Azul. It's an archaeological treasure beyond belief. And those bastards are going to destroy it."

"Won't the Guatemalan government help?"

"They try. But for every government official, there are ten looters. And the area of Rio Azul is unbelievable impossible to guard." She looked across at Jake, eyes sparkling. "Just think, Lieutenant, a metropolitan area the size of New York that existed over four thousand years ago."

Jake gave her a lopsided grin. He wondered if this was their usual conversation.

"How advanced where they?" Joanna asked.

"Easily on a level with the Egyptians in the time of the Pharaohs." Kate looked over at Jake's empty mug. "Another beer, Lieutenant?"

"No, thanks. I'm fine." *Two more minutes*, he told himself, *and I'm out of here*.

"What was your project?" Joanna knew that on large expeditions the work was divided into separate projects. Some archaeologists had expertise in buildings or agriculture, others in language, weapons, religion, and so on.

"I'm studying the ruling class."

Joanna's mind drifted, wondering what archaeologists would think if four thousand years from now they unearthed the body of Karen Rhodes. They would find a crushed skull and multiple fractures of the long bones. They would conclude that she was killed by some great force. And they would be right. But they would miss so much.

"Their king was called Kan-Xul," Kate continued.

"Good guy?" Jake asked awkwardly.

"So far. But he had some nasty friends."

"Oh?" Jake's interest picked up. "Like what?"

"We found a buried skeleton with a knife stuck in its ribs. Her jewelry was exquisite. She was probably a member of the royal family."

"How do you know it was a woman?"

"Bone structure," Kate replied.

"You can tell from the shape of the pelvic bones," Joanna said to Jake. Then to Kate, "Was she stabbed in the front or the back?"

"Back."

"Then the murderer was probably a woman."

Kate gave her a stern look. "Why do you say that?"

"Because a knife is a woman's weapon," Joanna explained. "And the overwhelming majority of backstabbers are female."

"I'm not sure I buy that," Kate said. "You've got to remember that this was four thousand years ago. Knives were the main weapon—for everyone."

"They had spears and hatchets, didn't they?"

"I suppose so," Kate said, still not convinced. "What do you think, Lieutenant?"

"Can't be sure," Jake muttered absently. He was thinking about a badly decomposed body found in a shallow grave in the backyard of a nice widow. It was loaded with arsenic, but they couldn't prove anything, not even the identity of the victim, although it was almost surely the widow's former husband. The widow was still living in Santa Monica, going to church regularly.

"Give us an educated guess," Kate urged.

Jake groaned inwardly, wishing he'd left when he had the chance. "What was the angle of the knife?"

Kate hesitated. "I'm not sure."

Joanna reached for a pen and held it in a horizontal position. "Was the handle straight—like this—or tilted?"

"Tilted up," Kate said at once. "But just a little."

"Then she got it standing up from behind," Jake said evenly. "And the stabber was about the same height as the victim. That's another point in favor of the killer being a woman." He pulled on his lower lip, still thinking about the grave in Santa Monica. "Where was she buried?"

"In the jungle outside the city."

"Lots of other bodies around?"

"Nope. It wasn't a cemetery, if that's what you're asking. That body was meant to be hidden."

"Were there any shovels?"

Kate smiled. "Two small ones buried on top of her."

"The killer was a woman," Jake said firmly. "A man would have lugged the body out into the jungle and dug the grave by himself. No witnesses that way.''

Kate stared at him with admiration. ''While you're at it, would you care to tell me the motive?''

''A man.''

''Are you serious?''

Sinclair nodded. ''After you exclude the nuts and crazies, most women kill for love or money.''

''Then she could have been killed for money.''

''Which probably belonged to a man,'' Jake said flatly.

Kate applauded lightly, amazed at his sharpness. ''Want to try one a little tougher?''

''Another time.'' Jake glanced at his watch. He hadn't fed his cat yet and the little bastard was probably getting meaner by the minute. He got to his feet, buttoning his coat. ''Dr. Blalock, I'll meet you tomorrow morning outside the Psychiatric Institute.''

Joanna showed Sinclair out. She came back to the wet bar, where her sister was mixing a brandy and soda. ''Interesting man,'' Kate commented.

''Because he's a cop?'' Joanna reached for a handful of ice cubes and placed them in a small towel, making an ice pack.

''No-o,'' Kate said slowly, ''because I didn't expect to find such a quick brain inside that good-looking head. He's a real hunk, isn't he?''

''I hadn't noticed.''

''Well, you should, because he was noticing you.''

''I don't think he's my type.''

Kate giggled. ''He's every woman's type. Strong and good-looking. And kind of bright, too.''

"And kind of opinionated. And a bit chauvinistic."

"So, he's an opinionated, chauvinistic, good-looking hunk. Do you agree?"

"I agree," Joanna conceded.

"I give him about a week."

"For what?"

"Before he asks you out."

Joanna smiled back at her sister. "He's still not my type."

"We'll see."

Joanna walked back to the couch and unzipped her skirt, letting it fall to the floor and stepping out of it. A silk slip still covered her thighs. She sat and stretched out, then placed the ice pack on the back of her head.

"Are you still getting those headaches a lot?" Kate asked.

"Not really. Just now and then."

"Liar," Kate said softly.

"Let's talk about Guatemala," Joanna said, the ice now numbing the painful area.

"I'd rather talk about Memorial Hospital. On the news tonight, I heard about that poor nurse. What happened?"

"She fell to her death."

"And?"

Joanna said nothing. She moved the ice pack down a little.

"The news reporter said that the police were called in. She also said that you did the autopsy." Kate studied her sister's face, waiting for a reaction. "Then I find you and the Lieutenant huddled together in the living room. Even to a naive twit like me that spells crime."

Joanna slowly nodded. "It was murder."

"I *knew* it," Kate said excitedly. She quickly sat down next to Joanna. "Tell me the details."

"I'm not sure you want to hear them."

"Try me."

Joanna sipped the remainder of her warm beer. She knew the full story would be out in a matter of hours, all the gory details included. "She was strangled, then thrown off the roof. Ten stories down."

"Was—was she dead before she hit the ground?" Kate asked hesitantly.

"No. She was alive, probably gasping for air." Joanna watched the color leave Kate's face.

"Oh, God!" Kate whispered, her eyes squinting with pain. "Do they know who did it?"

"Not yet." Joanna now wished that she had let Kate get the information from a television set. That way it was interesting but distant and impersonal. Up close, it was another matter.

Kate stared into space and wondered what the girl had felt, knowing that she was seconds away from death. "How old was she?"

"Twenty-five."

"Jesus." Kate shook her head sadly, now seeing a young girl fighting for her life, screaming, but nobody within hearing distance. "What in the world was she doing on that roof?"

Joanna shrugged, remembering that Jake had asked the same question. They had drawn a complete blank. A lot of guesses, but no answers. She glanced over at Kate. Maybe another woman would know. "You tell me."

Kate looked at her sister strangely. "I'm not sure I follow you."

"Let me ask you a question—completely out of context. Forget the murder."

the man was really well known. A mov

something like that."

"Why would he come to a psy

tal?"

"Maybe he was a patient."

"Who knows?"

shoulders. "Any other reasons?"

Kate nodded. "I a

people working in

"Right."

"Then ma

couldn't

kept s

time

on

J

hav

ulou

that

"M

_____ turkey."

Joanna remembered the weathered lounge chair and the semen stain on its cushion. "Why not go to some out-of-the-way motel?"

"There could be reasons."

"Like what?"

Kate ran a hand through her wet hair. "You understand that what I'm about to tell you does not reflect any personal experiences I've had."

Joanna smiled at her sister. *Jesus,* she thought, *this should really be good!*

"If you're Karen Rhodes you have to be very discreet about what you do. For example, if she were having an affair with a married man, she might not use a motel. He could be recognized. That's the last thing she would have wanted." Kate sipped her brandy thoughtfully. "Or maybe

e star or

chiatric hospi-

Kate shrugged her

ssume that there were other
the building."

ybe the man was a coworker who
et away to some motel. Maybe his wife
ch close tabs on him that there wasn't

'Particularly if the man had a wife who worked
with him," Joanna added.

"Oh, yeah. That would do it."

Joanna walked over to the wet bar for more ice
cubes. "What about a lesbian affair?"

"Nope. Two women can go home together at
night. No questions asked."

"So it had to be a man."

"A man she knew and trusted." Kate reached
for her drink as Joanna sat next to her. "Was I
helpful?" she asked.

"Maybe."

Kate sipped her drink, reflecting. Then she
shivered noticeably.

"Too much brandy?"

Kate shook her head. "I was thinking about that
skeleton in Guatemala and Karen Rhodes."

"What about them?"

"We really haven't changed much in four thousand years, have we?"

5

"I may have been wrong," Jake said to Joanna. "Dead wrong."

"About what?"

"I thought the girl might have been waiting for someone on the roof."

They were standing on the sidewalk across from the Psychiatric Institute, looking up at the mammoth structure. The morning was overcast and surprisingly cold. A northerly wind blew in gusts, making it even colder.

Jake had his hands in his pockets, shoulders hunched. "I checked the log on the helicopter landings the night before last. At exactly 11:25 P.M. they brought in that movie star with AIDS. The girl could have gone to the roof for a look."

Joanna glanced at the top of the Institute. "Not exactly a ringside seat."

"That doesn't matter." Jake turned his back to the wind. "People go to boxing matches and sit so far back the fighters look like ants. But they stay there until the end, believing they haven't missed a damned thing."

"The thrill of being a spectator, huh?"

"Something like that. How old was the girl?"

"Twenty-five."

"That's young enough to still be flakey. Maybe

she had a crush on him as a teenager. Maybe it lasted into her twenties.''

Joanna shuddered as she recalled the story she'd heard in the cafeteria earlier that morning. A nurse had told her that the movie star's once handsome face was now hideously deformed by angry, sarcomatous lesions.

''Dreams die hard,'' Jake said tonelessly. And now none of the pieces fit, he thought miserably. Last night he had a feel, a grasp of what might have happened on that rooftop. But today everything was hazy and out of focus. Loose ends dangled just out of reach. He hated them. Three dead women—a hooker, a divorcee, and a nurse—with no common thread to interconnect them except that they had all been murdered by a looney who liked to nibble on necks. ''We could stand out here all day chasing our butts and get nowhere. Let's go inside. Maybe we'll get lucky.''

''Where do you want to start?''

''With the people on the tenth floor.'' Sinclair patted his coat pocket out of habit, making sure his shield and ID were there. He looked over at the Institute. ''Give me a layout of the building.''

Joanna glanced up at the roof with its wire-link fence and for a moment a picture of Karen flashed into her mind. *Jesus! Why did you have to go to that rooftop? Why?* Joanna lowered her gaze to the bottom floor. ''The first two floors are used for administration. There are faculty offices and consultation suites on the third floor. The next six levels are patient wards, and the Brain Research Institute has the penthouse. There's an enclosed bridge that connects the Institute to the main hospital.'' Joanna pointed a finger, directing Jake's gaze. "The bridge goes from the lobby of the hospital to the second floor of the Institute."

"Is that bridge open at night?"

"Twenty-four hours a day. There are glass doors at each end. They're never locked."

"How long would it take to go from the hospital lobby to the roof of the Institute?"

"Five minutes, assuming a short wait for the elevator."

"And they have security guards patroling the floors?"

"Day and night. But if you're wearing a white uniform with an ID tag, they just nod and smile at you."

Jake paused, letting the information sink in. He looked over at the lower half of the Institute. "So, the first three floors would be empty at night?"

"Except for the cleaning crews."

"And on the tenth floor, the Brain—ah—Search—what the hell is the name of that place?"

"The Brain Research Institute. Call it the BRI. It'll save time."

"Yeah, the BRI. That would have been empty, too?"

Joanna moved her head noncommittally. "Maybe, maybe not. Researchers work funny hours."

Like cops, Jake thought. "What kind of patients do they keep here?"

"Mainly psychotics. People with manic depression, schizophrenia, disorders like that."

"Real wackos?"

"Some of them.".

"Who keeps an eye on them?"

"Nurses and aides."

"Can the patients wander around?"

"On the wards, yes. But not in the public areas of the hospital."

"Could they get to the elevators?"

"No. Each ward is sealed off by a locked door. Only the doctors and nurses have keys."

"So they're like prisoners?"

"For the most part."

Jake wrinkled his brow as a new thought came to him. "You told me that you used to work in the Institute, right?"

"Right."

"When was the last time you were in there?"

"Seven years ago."

"Do you think anything has changed?"

Joanna shrugged. "Probably not. But I can't be sure."

Jake looked up at the roof of the Institute, then over to the parking lot where Karen Rhodes's body had been found. His view of the parking lot was partially obstructed by the southeastern edge of the building. "I'm going to walk down the block a little so I can orient myself better."

Joanna nodded, her gaze now fixed on the Institute. Her mind drifted back seven years, to the last time she'd been in the building. She could still recall her conversation with Marshall Ullman, who was then chief of Psychiatry at Memorial.

"I've decided to resign from my residency immediately," Joanna had told him.

"Why?" the kindly old man had asked. He looked sick then and was to die of cancer eight months later.

"It's a rather long story, so I hope you will be patient with me."

"Take your time."

Joanna had hesitated, carefully choosing her words. She didn't want her story to sound any more bizarre than it already was. "After completing my internship last year, I went to El Salvador with Operation Hope. The village where I worked was heavily shelled by rebels and I ended up with a very severe concussion. I was flown back to San Francisco, where I was hospitalized for a long time. My roommate in the hospital was a young woman who had been badly injured in a car crash. She was very depressed, and as time passed and I got to know her better, I found myself becoming more and more depressed, too. I'd always been a happy, highly motivated person, so this bothered me a great deal."

"Did you consider yourself abnormal?"

"I wondered about it."

"When you were away from this depressed person, how did you feel?"

"Fantastic. Like a great weight had been lifted. One weekend I left the hospital on a pass. Those were two of the happiest days I'd ever known."

Ullman had smiled widely, believing that he had found the answer to her problem. "Well, there you are. There was nothing abnormal about your temporary depression. When we're around happy people we feel happy and when we're around sad or depressed people we feel depressed. And if you're confined to a room with a very depressed person, this effect will be exaggerated. Your problem was caused by a normal transference of emotion. It's a form of involuntary telepathy. Everybody experiences it at one time or another."

"That's what I believed. So I forgot about it until I started my psychiatric residency. And now it's returned. When I'm involved with depressed patients, I get depressed, and when my patients are manic, I become hyperactive. It only happens when I get to know severely psychotic patients, but once I'm away from them for a day or two, I'm suddenly myself again. It's happened time and time again. It's ruining my personal life and it's interfering with my professional duties, too.''

"Did you ever experience this before your hospitalization in San Francisco?''

"Never. I sometimes wonder if that mortar explosion in El Salvador was somehow responsible. I had a very severe concussion and was literally out of it for weeks.''

"Do you think the trauma may have altered some portion of your mind?''

"Who knows?''

The old man had sighed. "I've never come across anything like this in my entire career. I wish I had something to offer you.''

"Don't feel bad. I just wanted you to know why I've decided to leave. I've already chosen a new speciality. Things will work out fine.''

Joanna brought her mind back to the present as the detective approached.

"All right,'' Jake said, squaring his shoulders. "Let's go dig a little.''

They shared the elevator with the same patient and same attendant from the day before. She still looked spaced out and glassy eyed, off somewhere in another world. And she still smelled peculiar. Sinclair crowded himself into a corner, uncomfortable being so close to her.

The attendant abruptly stabbed at the floor selection panel. "Shit," he muttered. "Missed our floor."

It didn't seem to bother the woman.

Sinclair and Joanna exited at the tenth floor. The corridor was now busy, crowded with doctors and technicians moving back and forth. A low hum from a dozen different conversations filled the air.

"Give me a quick layout," Sinclair said.

"Laboratories and animal rooms to the right. Offices and conference room to the left." Joanna pointed down the corridor. "That's Hugh Jackson, the director of the BRI."

Sinclair studied the man wearing a long white coat. He had a medium build, with a face that had once been very handsome. The features were sharp, the nose aquiline, the jaw firm and jutting. But there were deep lines and early age spots, although the man was not yet sixty. The skin along his jawline and neck sagged badly. His neat gray hair was a toupee. Animated, hands gesturing, he was talking to a technician.

"I've seen that face before," Sinclair said, searching his mind.

"Probably in the society section of the newspaper," Joanna said, voice low. "Along with his wife."

"Yeah," Jake nodded, remembering. "They do a lot of work with charities."

"She's heavily involved," Joanna said, straight-faced. "That means she writes a check for ten thousand dollars and goes to a fashion show at the Beverly Hilton."

"Ten large is heavy involvement."

"Not to Hugh Jackson. His family owns half of Sacramento." Joanna waved to Jackson, who waved back. "Come on and I'll introduce you to him."

"Joanna," Jackson said expansively, "how nice to see you again!"

"Same here," Joanna said, shaking the man's hand. "You're looking well."

"It's the vitamins Marci gives me," Jackson grinned. "Good for all parts of the body."

Except the hair, Jake thought.

"Hugh, I'd like you to meet Lieutenant Sinclair from the Los Angeles Police Department."

"It's a pleasure, Lieutenant," Jackson said warmly and extended his hand.

Jake shook it, noticing the age spots. He thought about flashing his shield but decided not to. "Dr. Jackson, I'm here investigating the Karen Rhodes murder."

Jackson winced, shaking his head. "Dreadful. I still can't believe it."

"Did you know her?" Joanna asked.

"Of course," Jackson said, as if it should have been taken for granted. "She was—"

"Dr. Jackson," Jake interrupted quickly, "is there some place we could talk privately?"

"My office." Jackson led the way into a modest-sized room that was expensively decorated. The carpet was dark brown and obviously new; the walls were covered with a light gray grasscloth. Jackson gestured to two wingback leather chairs that were placed in front of a mahogany desk. He waited for them to sit, then eased himself into a massive swivel chair—the kind judges used, Jake noted.

"Coffee?" Jackson asked.

"No, thanks," Joanna said.

"Now, you were saying that you knew the

girl," Jake began, taking out pocket pad and pen.

"And her family," Jackson added.

"When did you first meet Karen?"

"About two years ago, when she first came to work at the Institute."

"Did you have frequent contact with her?"

"I rarely saw her until—oh—" Jackson pondered for a moment, rocking in his chair. "Say seven months ago. We had an opening for a research nurse and she expressed a great interest."

"What kind of research?" Joanna asked quickly, remembering Karen's phone message.

Jackson hesitated, studying her. "May I ask what your role is in this investigation?"

"I was asked to show the lieutenant around the Institute."

"In an official capacity?"

"They didn't issue me a badge, if that's what you are asking."

Jackson chuckled, then laughed—a deep, hearty laugh. "I'm relieved to hear that."

Jake wondered what was so funny about a badge. He felt a twinge of anger, but pushed it away.

"You were asking about the research," Jackson went on, his face more serious now. "We were studying a new class of drugs. They were antidepressants that had very few side effects. The drugs were to be given to patients in a double-blind fashion. We needed nurses to help us study the subjects and chart the results. Karen applied for the position and was promptly accepted."

"Was it a full-time job?" Joanna asked.

"Oh, no," Jackson said, reaching for a pipe. "It required maybe six hours a week. She would then meet with the staff every ten days or so to go over the results."

"How many different drug studies was Karen involved in?"

"She worked on two of my projects, both dealing with antidepressant drugs. And I know she also assisted Richard Abels on a newly discovered tranquilizer." Jackson rocked back in his chair, concentrating. "Of course, there may have been other projects I was unaware of."

Bullshit, Joanna thought, smiling pleasantly at Hugh Jackson. *You know everything that goes on in this Institute—who's working on what with whom, the results of every research project, and its cost down to the last dollar.* "Do all of your drug studies involve human subjects?"

"Oh, yes. Of course, we also do a fair amount of preliminary studies in animals to look for side effects and toxicities."

"Was Karen involved in that as well?"

"Not that I'm aware of."

"But you said she worked with Abels?"

"That's correct."

"And isn't virtually all of his work done on animals?"

"I can assure you he also does human studies," Jackson said, an edge to his voice. "May I ask the purpose of all these questions?"

"Just getting a little background." Jake broke in quickly. Enough time wasted, he thought.

"Of course, I want to be as helpful as I can," Jackson said, his voice now even.

Joanna asked, "Did Abels—"

Jake cut in again. "I think it might be a good idea to hold some of these background questions until later. I'm certain Dr. Jackson has a very busy schedule."

Joanna's face reddened, stung by Jake's rudeness. She clenched her jaws tightly and looked away.

"It has been rather hectic today," Jackson said, his face impassive. But inwardly he was delighted with the way the detective had put Joanna in her place. He detested pushy women, particularly those in medicine.

Jake turned a page in his writing pad. "When was the last time you saw Karen Rhodes?"

"At our staff meeting a week ago."

"Who else was there?"

"Four other faculty members. We're all involved in these studies."

"And these people all knew Karen?"

"Oh, yes. Perhaps not as well as I did. But they knew her."

Jake tapped his pen against the pad. "Would there be a reason for Karen to meet with any of the others in your absence?"

"Not that I could think of. A phone call or a chat in the hall, perhaps. You should probably ask them."

"So there would be no reason for her to be up here two nights ago?"

"None." Jackson lit his pipe, sucking hard to get it started. "And had she been up that night we would have certainly seen her."

Sinclair straightened up. "At 11:00 P.M.?"

Jackson nodded. "We were all here. Five faculty members and one technician."

"Why so late?"

"We had no choice," Jackson said, striking another match. "We were studying a marvelous new tranquilizer. It seemed to combat anxiety without causing sedation. Such a drug would make Valium obsolete overnight.'' He got his pipe going; the smoke was spiraling up. ''Anyway, the last group of monkeys responded very strangely to the agent. They became more excited rather than less so. We had to give them repeated injections of a drug to finally calm them down. The experiments ended shortly after eleven-thirty.''

The phone on Jackson's desk buzzed. He excused himself and answered it.

Well, well, Jake thought, *maybe we're about to get lucky.* Maybe somebody saw something. The crazy bastard who wacked Karen Rhodes wouldn't have stayed on the roof, not even for an extra minute. No way. Murderers—even the nutty ones—don't stick around to admire their work. He would have gotten out of there fast. And he had to go through the BRI to reach the stairs or the elevators. Jake looked at Joanna and got an icy stare in return. He wondered what the hell was wrong with her.

''Sorry,'' Jackson said, placing the phone down.

''You told me that the experiments ended shortly after eleven-thirty, right?''

''Correct.''

''Can you recall where you were between eleven and eleven-thirty?''

Jackson thought for a moment. ''Mostly in the animal room.''

''Were others in the room about the same time?''

Jackson gestured with his hands, and dead pipe ashes flew. ''There was a lot of coming and going, people sticking their heads in the door to see how the monkeys were doing.''

''Was someone in that room at all times?''

"The technician who gave the injections."

"What about the other four staff members?"

"Like me. Coming and going."

"What time did you finally leave the building?"

"At 11:45 P.M.," Jackson said promptly. "I was on the elevator and remember looking at my watch."

"Between eleven and eleven-forty-five, did you see anyone up here who shouldn't have been here? Any strangers?" Jake asked, hoping against hope, knowing that the killer was not stupid. Crazy maybe, but not stupid.

"No."

"You're absolutely positive?"

"I would have certainly remembered. Had I seen a stranger, I would have called security immediately."

Sinclair jotted down a note. "Does anybody on the staff ever go up on to the roof?"

"The technicians sometimes go there to sunbathe during lunch."

And maybe to screw at night, Jake thought. And then he remembered what he'd forgotten. *God damn it! I didn't ask Joanna if she could determine how old or how new that stain was.* "How many technicians work here?" .

"Six."

"All women?"

Jackson shook his head. "Two men."

"How many of them were working two nights ago?"

"Just one. Rudy Whalen."

"Is he here today?"

"He should be."

Jake wrote a note to himself about the stain on the lounge chair, then turned a page in his notebook. "Give me the names of everyone who was up here the night of the murder."

"Myself and Rudy Whalen and four staff members. Richard Abels, Julian Whitmore, and Mark and Sara Harrison." Jackson waited for Sinclair to write the names down. "They're all here today, except for the Harrisons."

"Where are they?"

"At the Psycho-Pharmacology meeting in San Diego."

"When did they leave for this meeting?"

"Two nights ago—just after we finished the experiments."

"At eleven-thirty at night?" Jake asked, scratching the back of his neck. "That's kind of late to start a trip, isn't it?"

Jackson nodded. "They had made plans to leave earlier, but like the rest of us, they stayed until the experiments were over. San Diego is only an hour and a half away."

Jake scribbled another note to himself. "When are they expected back?"

"Tomorrow evening."

Jake looked at Joanna. "Any questions?"

"Nothing that can't wait," she said coldly.

Jake closed his pad and stood. "I'll start with Richard Abels."

They walked toward the far end of the corridor, which was quiet now, just as it had been the day before. Joanna stayed a few steps behind, still upset with Jake for rudely interrupting her when she was questioning Jackson. She had listened to Karen's phone message over and over and was more convinced than ever that her friend was badly frightened about something at the Institute. Something that involved her. Approximately eight hours after she made the phone call, Karen was murdered. And Jake was ignoring it. Well, he might ignore it, but she wouldn't.

They came to a closed door. The sign on it read: DO NOT DISTURB—EXPERIMENT IN PROGRESS.

Jackson tapped lightly on the door and waited. Then he tapped again, more firmly.

The door cracked. A section of face looked out. "What?" It was more a growl than a voice.

"Richard," Jackson said softly, "this is Lieutenant Sinclair from the police department. He wants to ask some questions about Karen Rhodes."

"We're in the middle of an experiment," Abels said curtly. "Come back later."

Jake moved forward, putting his foot in the door. He flashed his ID and shield. "We won't take up much of your time."

"Shit!" Abels said disgustedly. "Well, come in and get done."

The room was surprisingly large. To Jake it looked like the control center of the Strategic Air Command. On the walls were giant video screens, all with blue backgrounds and white images. Some showed computerized pictures of the brain, others showed a brain with a grid superimposed over it. A flashing red dot danced around one of the screens.

They walked between machines humming with activity, panel lights blinking away.

"I'll need a few minutes to finish this run," Abels said, less angry now.

"Take your time," Jake said.

"I plan to." Abels was a slender man in his mid-forties with a wiry build and curly red hair. His face was narrow and white, freckled over the nose, with a small, tight mouth. He wore jeans and a polo shirt.

Jake watched Abels walk over to an opened area fifteen feet away. The detective leaned over to Joanna and spoke in a low voice. "Is that guy a doctor?"

Joanna nodded. "A neurologist and a psychiatrist."

"Jesus!" Sinclair murmured, feeling sorry for any patients who might get referred to Abels.

"You may as well come closer," Abels shouted. "You won't see anything from there."

In the center of the opened area was a table. Atop it was a monkey seated in a little chair. His head and trunk and extremities were clamped in iron bands, rendering him totally immobile. His eyes were wide open and pathetic. He showed Jake his teeth.

Jake felt a wave of nausea and looked away, then slowly looked back, fascinated by the gruesome spectacle. The top of the monkey's skull had been removed, exposing its brain. It glistened in the light, dome-shaped, full of grooves and convolutions. Two electrodes were stuck into the brain, like poles in the sand.

"Let's try area twenty-two again, Julian," Abels said.

Julian, who was sitting behind a switchboard, pushed a button. There was no sound.

The monkey's left arm jerked. He shivered, making a chattering noise.

"And again," Abels said flatly.

The monkey's arm jerked, less than before. He chattered more loudly, showing all of his teeth. Eyes so pathetic.

Jackson stepped in between Jake and Joanna

and spoke softly. "They're experimenting with a new anti-epilepsy drug. It's quite remarkable. One dose a day, no side effects."

"Okay," Abels said. "Put it in the bank."

Jackson pointed to the big screen. The red dot zeroed in on the exact area of the brain that had been electrically stimulated. Numbers flashed and were immediately fed into a computer.

"Let's take a break, Julian," Abels said and walked over to the group. "Now, what can I do for you?"

Hugh Jackson said, "Perhaps I'd better wait outside."

Jake nodded and waited for him to leave. "I'm Lieutenant Sinclair from—"

"You already showed me your badge," Abels said sourly.

Jake took a deep breath, willing himself to stay calm. "—from the Los Angeles Police Department. I want to ask you some questions about Karen Rhodes."

"Ask away."

"Did you know her?"

"Not really."

"Have any contact with her?"

"I saw her at some of the weekly staff meetings." Abels shrugged his shoulders. "I thought her name was Carrie."

"Did you ever speak with her?"

"I may have asked her a question or two, but we never had a conversation, if that's what you mean."

The monkey made a chattering noise as its left arm convulsed briefly. Abels glanced over, unconcerned. "Minor seizures sometimes occur after the experiment is over. They're of no importance.''

Except to the poor monkey, Jake thought. He turned his body so that he couldn't see the animal, not even in his peripheral vision. ''Were you here the night she was murdered?''

''Yes.''

''Where?''

''Hell, I don't know,'' Abels said tensely, scratching at an armpit. ''In and out of the rooms, walking around.''

''Let's narrow it down to between eleven and eleven-thirty. Can you recall which room you were in?''

''Mainly this one.''

''Alone?''

Abels shook his head. ''Julian was here, too.''

Jake glanced over at Julian. He was seated fifteen feet away, but he was concentrating, trying to overhear. ''But you must have spent some time in the corridor.''

''Some.''

''Did you see anybody in the hall who was unfamiliar or who shouldn't have been there?''

''No.''

''You're positive?''

''I'll swear to it if that's what you'd like.'' Abels looked over at Joanna, wondering why she was held in such high regard at Memorial. She was a pretty fair pathologist—he'd give her that—but her research was mediocre. As far as he was concerned, she was just another female physician, taking the place of a male who could do the job better. ''Are you now a member of the police department, Joanna?''

''Just showing the lieutenant around.''

"Very productive," Abels said sarcastically. "It'll look good on your curriculum vitae."

Disgusting little shit, Jake thought. "What time did you leave?"

"I left around eleven-thirty that night. And that's only an approximation."

"Based on what?"

"When I was driving home I listened to the twelve o'clock news on the radio."

Jake jotted down the information. "Would you ask your colleague to step over?"

Abels turned to Joanna, grinning. "Do you have any questions, Inspector?"

"Only one. Which of your research projects was Karen involved in?"

"None that I know of."

"Oh? We were told she was involved with work being done on a new tranquilizer."

"Who told you that?"

Jake leaned in. "Just answer the question."

Abels's face stayed impassive, but a vein bulged out on his temple. "She could have assisted us. You'll have to ask Julian. He's in charge of the tranquilizer project."

"We'll do that."

"Anything else?" Abels glared at Joanna.

"No." She smiled sweetly, wondering if the rumors that Abels was into kinky sex were true.

"Tell your partner to step over here." Jake turned away and looked at the monkey. The eyes. He envisioned Abels strapped in a chair, half his skull off, electrodes in place. And the monkey off to one side pressing the button.

"Lieutenant, I'm Julian Whitmore." He extended a hand with long, delicate fingers.

Sinclair shook it, noticing the glossy nails. Julian's grip was firm, firmer than need be.

"I couldn't help but overhear your questions to Richard. If you like, I can give you a quick capsule of my answers."

"Fire away," Jake said.

"I knew Karen Rhodes. We had coffee together on a number of occasions. We shared a number of mutual interests, particularly music and the ballet. I saw her last three days before her death. We had coffee in the cafeteria, chatted. She seemed fine." Julian Whitmore paused to rub an eyebrow. "On the evening she died, I was here in the Institute. I spent most of my time either in this laboratory or the animal room. I left at exactly eleven-thirty. The reason I know the precise time is that I was hurrying to a friend's party. It was important for me to get there before midnight. I saw no one unfamiliar in the corridor or in the elevator."

"Who was the friend who had the party?" Sinclair asked.

"Martin Fairchild. He's an artist who lives in Hollywood. At exactly midnight his friends were giving him a surprise gift. That's why I was hurrying to get there."

"Did you make it on time?"

Whitmore nodded. "With two minutes to spare."

Sinclair obtained Martin Fairchild's address and jotted it down. "Did you see Karen Rhodes socially?"

"How do you mean?"

"Did you date her?"

Whitmore, handsome with his sharp features and wavy brown hair, grinned shyly. "Oh, no.

The only time I saw her away from the Institute was at the Music Center. We chatted briefly. Nothing more.''

"I see.'' Jake was almost certain that Whitmore was homosexual. The glossy nails, the mannerisms, the Hollywood address where the party was held. But so what? The police shrinks were convinced that the serial killer was not gay. "On these coffee breaks you had with her—what did you talk about?''

"Mainly cultural affairs. The symphony, ballet, things like that.''

"Did she ever discuss her personal life?''

"Never,'' Whitmore said promptly. "She was a very private person. I think Karen would only confide in people she had known for a long time.''

"Was she usually happy?''

Whitmore thought for a moment. "Outwardly, yes. But I sometimes sensed that there was a sadness there. Deep and well covered.''

"But she never spoke about it?''

"No.''

Jake closed his notepad. "Thanks for your time.''

Jake and Joanna walked out into the corridor. Hugh Jackson was waiting for them.

"I trust Dr. Abels was cooperative,'' Jackson said.

"He was just a little bit more obnoxious than usual,'' Joanna commented.

"Richard can be difficult,'' Jackson agreed. "But he's also incredibly brilliant. One has to weigh the talents against the flaws.''

As they walked down the hall, Jake asked, "What flaws?''

"I'm afraid Richard has a bit of a temper that he doesn't control as well as he should."

"Has he been involved in any fights or brawls?"

"Some screaming and shouting matches," Jackson said carefully, "but no violence to my knowledge."

Joanna looked at Jackson. "What about that clipboard incident last year?"

"There was no real violence involved," Jackson said defensively.

"Tell me about it," Sinclair said.

Jackson sighed. "Richard became angry with one of the technicians and threw a clipboard at her. It struck her on the leg. He claimed it slipped from his hands."

"Was that the end of it?"

"No," Jackson said, stopping in front of a closed door. "The technician's husband confronted Richard and threatened to break his arms. Richard refused to back down and they nearly came to blows."

"On the patio in front of the Institute," Joanna added.

"Fortunately, cooler heads prevailed," Jackson went on. "Richard received a reprimand. The technician was moved to another laboratory in the hospital."

Cute, Jake was thinking. They tap Abels on the wrist and throw the technician on her ass. "What's in this room?"

"Rudy Whalen," Jackson replied, "the technician who was here the night of Karen's death."

They entered a large room that was lined with giant, floor-to-ceiling cages. The air was filled with a disagreeable mixture of aromas—sweet disinfectant and stale urine. In one of the cages a man stood with his arm held out in front of him, bent at the elbow. A huge padded glove covered his hand and forearm.

A screaming monkey flew at him—all teeth, arms, and legs. The monkeys in adjacent cages let out high-pitched shrieks, as if they were rooting for their mate. The animal attacked the man's glove with fury, his long incisors biting into it. In a fraction of a second the man had the monkey by the back of its neck, rendering it virtually immobile. The handler carefully examined the animal, then threw it across the cage and quickly exited.

"Pierre ain't too happy today," Rudy Whalen announced to the visitors.

"Rudy," Jackson said, "this is Lieutenant Sinclair from the police department and Dr. Blalock. They're here investigating the death of Karen Rhodes. They'd like to ask you some questions."

"Sure," Rudy said, peeling off his glove.

Jake looked up at him, thinking that this was one technician Abels wouldn't throw a clipboard at. Whelan was a huge man at six feet five and two hundred forty pounds. He had the heavily muscled shoulders of a weight lifter. His biceps stretched the short sleeves of the T-shirt he was wearing. He was in his mid-twenties with a crew-cut, deeply tanned skin, and a boyishly handsome face that belonged on a marine recruitment poster. "You were here on the night Karen Rhodes was murdered?"

"Yes, sir," the technician answered, looking away from Jake's eyes. Rudy's expression was even, but sweat was breaking out on his neck and back. He hated cops and feared them. Where he came from—in the East San Gabriel Valley—cops kicked the shit out of people and asked questions later.

Jake detected the technician's uneasiness and decided to run his name through the computer and see if he had a file. Just a hunch. "Do you spend all of your time in this room?"

"Just about."

"Let's narrow it down to between eleven and eleven-thirty that night."

"I never left the room."

"Not even to use the john?"

"I peed in here," Rudy said without hesitation.

"But Dr. Jackson told me that people were coming into this room every five seconds."

"They were. I just locked the door and peed in the sink."

Hugh Jackson rolled his eyes upward and shook his head. "You don't make that a practice, do you, Rudy?"

"No, sir."

Jake asked, "Did you know Karen Rhodes?"

"No, sir."

"Ever see her?"

Rudy shrugged his massive shoulders. "I don't even know what she looks like—looked like."

"What time did you leave here that night?"

"Close to midnight." Rudy reached for a log-book and flipped pages. "I made my last observation on Pierre at 12:05 P.M. Then I left."

"Was anybody up here when you were leaving?"

"No, sir. Everybody was gone."

Jake studied Rudy's tan and heavily muscled arms. Plenty strong enough to throw a body twelve feet, he decided. "Do you ever go up on the roof?"

"No, sir."

"Not even to get a little sun?"

"Naw," Rudy said easily. "I catch my rays at the beach."

Jake nodded, then looked over at Joanna.

"Do you have any notations in your logbook between 11:25 and 11:35 P.M.?" Joanna asked.

Rudy flipped a page. "At 11:30 P.M., I wrote that Pierre was nice and calm, awake but not making any noise."

"Do you remember who else was in the room at that time?" Joanna asked.

Rudy thought for a moment, a decided effort. He slowly shook his head. "I can't be sure."

Joanna glanced at Rudy's elbows. "Ever do any wrestling?"

"Some," Rudy said, expanding his chest and standing even taller. "I'm trying to get on the pro circuit, but it's a bitch."

"Lots of competition, huh?"

"It's all fixed," Rudy said disgustedly. "You either know the right people or you—"

Pierre, the monkey, started screaming and raising hell and his mates joined in.

"Chow time," Rudy explained.

They left the animal room and headed for the elevators.

"If there's anything else I can do, please let me know," Jackson offered.

"I want to question the Harrisons as soon as they get back," Jake said.

"They'll be here tomorrow evening at eight o'clock. We're having an important lecture then at the Institute. I'm certain they'll be back for it."

"I'll see them the following morning at ten o'clock."

"They'll be here," Jackson assured him. "And again, if I can be of any help, just yell."

Jake and Joanna rode the elevator down in silence. Joanna was still fuming over Jake's rudeness. It had stung so badly, particularly since it occurred in front of Hugh Jackson. At times like this, Joanna wished she were a man. Then she could tell Jake Sinclair to blow it out of his ass or go fuck himself. But she knew she was incapable of that kind of language and could never pull it off even when she was furious. On the other hand, she wasn't about to let him get away with it. Before the day was over, they would have it out and Jake would understand that his rudeness would not be tolerated in the future.

They got off at the sixth floor and walked over to a locked door with a Plexiglas window.

"Are all the wards locked like this?" Jake asked.

"Right. No key, no entrance." Joanna pushed the visitor button on the wall.

"Who has keys?"

"Doctors, nurses, attendants."

A rotund, middle-aged black nurse peered out of the window. She waved, remembering Joanna from the days when she was a resident in Psychiatry. The door opened.

"Well, well," Lucy Barnett beamed. "Look what the wind blew in. How have you been?"

"I've been fine. What about you?"

"Pretty good, all things considered."

Joanna gestured to Jake. "Lucy, this is Lieutenant Sinclair. He's here to investigate Karen's death."

"That poor child." Lucy shook her head sadly. "Only a crazy man would do something like that."

Jake smiled to himself, wondering if the nurse knew how right she was. "I'd like to ask you some questions. I hope this is not an inconvenient time."

"It wouldn't matter if it was. Every charge nurse got a call this morning from the dean's office. We were told to instruct our staffs that you were coming around and to make ourselves available." The charge nurse looked away as her lower lip quivered. "That phone call wasn't needed. Everybody here is going to help you as much as we can. Because they all loved Karen. There wasn't a sweeter girl on the face of this earth, I'll tell you that."

Joanna felt her eyes becoming moist. She cleared her throat. "Did you work with Karen the day before yesterday?"

"For a little while. My shift was over at three o'clock, but I had to stay until four. One of the paranoid schizophrenics got a little violent. It took some time to calm him down."

"How violent?" Sinclair asked.

"Kicked over a table, threw a chair at one of the attendants."

"How did you calm him down?"

"I didn't. Karen did. She walked right up to him and told him to cut it out. Just like that. And the patient starts crying and Karen leads him back to his room." The nurse took out a handkerchief and gently blew her nose, her eyes still on Jake. She wondered how fast the police would have responded and how thorough their investigation would have been if the victim had been a black girl from Watts rather than a white girl from Bel Air.

"Wasn't that kind of dangerous?"

"She knew how to handle him."

Joanna asked, "Did Karen seem to be her usual self?"

"Sweet as ever."

"Was she worried about anything?"

"Not that I could see."

Jake looked around, now aware of the audience nearby. There were two other nurses, two attendants—both big and well muscled—a ward clerk, and a scattering of aides. Jake decided to address the entire group. "Did any of you work with Karen Rhodes her last day?"

One attendant stepped forward, and the ward clerk timidly raised her hand.

"The rest of you can go back to your work." Jake walked over to the attendant. He was a big, well-built man in his early thirties with dark, Mediterranean features. "What's your name?"

"Alex Pappas."

"You work the three-to-eleven shift that day?"

"No. The seven-to-three shift. But I stayed late helping with the psychotic patient."

"The guy who threw the chair?"

"Yeah. The damn thing just missed me."

"Did you try to take him down?"

"I was getting around to it, but you have to be careful with the ones who are really crazy. They can be double strong."

"Karen Rhodes handled him without any problem though, right?"

Alex nodded his head with admiration. "She could do magic."

"Did you notice anything unusual about her though?"

"No. She was her usual self."

"Thanks for your time," Jake said, turning to

the ward clerk. Her name tag read "Paula Coe."

"When did you see Karen?"

"About two forty-five that afternoon, when she first came to work."

"Did you talk to her?"

"Oh, sure."

"What'd you talk about?"

"I just said hello."

Sinclair sighed to himself. "Did you notice anything unusual that day?"

"Not really. Except for the visitor."

"What visitor?" Sinclair asked promptly.

"A little old lady who was on the wrong floor."

"Was she the only visitor?"

Paula nodded. "The only one on my shift."

"What about on the evening shift?"

"Let me check the logbook." Paula hurried over to the desk, flipped through pages, then came back. "There were no visitors on the three-to-eleven shift."

"Thanks." Jake made a mental note to have all the visitor logbooks checked, all charge nurses questioned. He walked back to Lucy Barnett. "How long has the paranoid been a patient here?"

"About a week."

"And he was walking the streets before then?"

"No. He was transferred here from another hospital where he'd been a patient for a month."

"What hospital?"

"In Bakersfield." The nurse looked up at Jake, shaking her head. "You're on the wrong track, Mr. Detective. The man who did this to Karen is not sick crazy, he's mean crazy. There's a big difference."

* * *

Outside, the day was turning brilliant with a bright sun and only scattered clouds. The wind had died down to a soft breeze.

"How did you figure Rudy for a wrestler?" Jake asked.

"The heavy calluses on his elbows," Joanna told him.

"Do they get them on their knees, too?"

"Sometimes. But if you find calluses on the knees in southern California, it usually means that the person is a surfer."

"From rubbing on the board, huh?"

"Right."

Jake nodded and added the new facts to his memory bank. Calluses on the elbows—wrestler; on the knees—surfer.

Joanna kicked at an imaginary object on the ground, trying to find the right words. "Lieutenant, I didn't appreciate your rudeness when I was questioning Hugh Jackson."

"You mean the way I cut you off?"

"Exactly," Joanna said sharply.

Jake took a deep breath and exhaled loudly. *Be nice,* he told himself. *You still need her.* "All right, let's get it straight, once and for all. Your best friend gets murdered and you find out she's left you a phone message. The message says that she's worried about something at the Institute. You put two and two together and come to the conclusion that the murderer is walking around in the Institute. Right?"

"It's possible."

"Possible, but it won't wash. It doesn't fit with the facts. You're ignoring the fact that we've got a serial killer on our hands. A real wacko. He doesn't give a damn about any research. And then there are his first two victims. The little hooker and the young divorcee. Were they part of this medical research, too?'' Sinclair shook his head vigorously. ''It just doesn't fit. And you start questioning these doctors as if they're prime suspects.''

''It didn't bother you at all that Abels lied?''

''When?''

''When he said that Karen wasn't involved in his research?''

''Christ!'' Jake groaned. ''I don't like the little bastard either. But he told you that Julian Whitmore handled the work on the tranquilizer.''

Joanna smiled thinly. ''Richard Abels won't let anybody handle his research projects. He's genuinely paranoid. He doesn't trust anyone.''

''I hope you're not planning on questioning Abels again.''

''No. It's Julian Whitmore that I want to talk with.''

''I'd be careful if I were you. You can get into all sorts of trouble by stepping on the wrong toes.''

''I'll handle it.''

''That's what I'm worried about.''

''Will you need me anymore?''

''I'll let you know,'' Jake said, looking at his watch. ''I've got to run and meet with the helicopter pilot who flew the AIDS patient to Memorial. Maybe he saw something.''

''Good luck,'' Joanna told him. ''But I wouldn't be too optimistic. That roof was pitch black at midnight.''

''You never know.''

Jake walked away, glancing back at the Institute. He could still see the monkey with no skull. And its eyes.

From a window high up in the Institute, a figure in a darkened room cracked the drapes and peered out. He focused in on Lieutenant Sinclair and Joanna Blalock as they parted company. They were going to cause trouble. He was convinced of that. Better start thinking of ways to deal with them.

6

"You want to talk or screw?" the prostitute demanded.

"Well, maybe both," the fat man said.

"It's going to cost you more. Time is money, honey."

"All I got is twenty dollars."

"Get lost!"

Edward watched the pair from the shadows of an alley in West Hollywood. He kept his eyes on the hooker as she turned away in a huff and walked down the sidewalk, swinging her buttocks in an exaggerated fashion, trying to attract customers from the passing cars. The prostitute was tall and slender with a big Afro. She was wearing a skimpy rabbit-skin coat and short pants, despite the chilly night air. Edward had selected her to be his next victim.

This was not the first time Edward had seen the prostitute. He had noticed her the night he killed the teenaged hooker. His First Event. That's what Edward called his outings. Events. Edward could still remember the wonderful sensation of the little whore's heart pumping wildly as he held the knife deep in her chest. Her youth had flowed from her to him, filling him with power and vigor, like a marvelous transfusion. Edward felt his penis throbbing.

His mind drifted back to the night he'd picked up the teenaged prostitute and taken her to a sleazy hotel in Hollywood. When he could not sustain an erection, she had laughed and refused to return his money. She also called him some very unpleasant names. He was embarrassed and belittled and seething with anger, but all he did was slink away like a beaten dog. Hours later he returned, and after paying her double the usual rate, he took her back to the motel where he performed well. Two orgasms. Then he had a third when he killed her. He had pinned her against the bathroom wall, compressing her windpipe with a powerful hand. She sucked hard for air, trying to make a sound, perhaps to scream. Then he stuck a six-inch blade into her upper abdomen and directed it upward, under the sternum, until it reached the girl's heart. The teenager struggled for her life, desperately gasping for air and at the same time trying to move her body away from the terrible pain in her stomach. Edward held on, using just the right amount of force on the girl's windpipe. He did not want her to pass out. He wanted her to see death coming. Slowly he pushed the knife into the girl's left ventricle and her heart began to beat wildly as if attempting to expel the metal intruder. Edward felt wonderful. He could feel her vitality and youth passing out of her and into him, the knife acting as a conduit. And his timing had been perfect. The moment of her death coincided with his final orgasm.

The second Event wasn't Edward's fault, either. The victim had brought it upon herself. He had accidentally bumped into her while turning down an aisle in a West Los Angeles supermarket. His arm went up reflexively and his hand landed on her left breast. His hand stayed there as he lost his balance momentarily. He apologized profusely, but she called him a pervert and yelled for the store manager. He left the market hastily, the woman's screams and invectives following him out the door.

A week later, Edward was driving past a laundromat in the late evening and saw the woman leaving with a bundle of clothes. He quickly made a U-turn, parked his car and followed her down a narrow alley. Edward hurried up behind her and, as she turned, he chopped the side of her neck firmly, karate style. The attractive brunette dropped to the ground, stunned and only semiconscious. Quickly he was on top of her, ripping open her blouse and tearing through her bra. Edward took out a highly sharpened knife and gently stabbed at the woman's left breast. She moaned. Then he turned the blade and carefully began slicing skin away. Blood gushed as the woman let out a high-pitched scream. Edward plunged the knife into her chest repeatedly, quieting her, then grabbed her purse and watch and ran. Later he threw everything into the sea from the Santa Monica Pier.

The next day he read the newspaper account of the woman's death. The police believed she had been killed for her purse and watch. The woman was survived by a nine-year-old son.

Edward took in a deep breath of the cool night air, again thinking back to the death of the teenaged prostitute. It had been wonderful to feel her die, to feel her life ooze away. Then he had bitten her gently on the shoulder, just breaking the skin.

He had done it to the attractive brunette as well. Both had tasted nice and soft with a hint of salt. Edward loved the intimacy he felt with his victims, particularly at the moment of death.

His muscles now began to ripple beneath his black leather jacket. He felt strong and vibrant, all of his senses heightened. Hot blood was surging through his body, soon to be concentrated in his genitals. That was the sensation he was waiting for. It signaled the onset of the Event.

"What are you looking at, motherfucker?"

Edward spun around and faced a mean-looking black man wearing a long fur coat and a white fedora. He had rings on every finger.

"You better talk quick."

Edward spotted a discarded whiskey bottle nearby. In a split second he grabbed it by its neck and smashed it on the pavement. Then he held it up, jagged edges pointed at the man, and moved a step forward into the dim light.

The pimp was reaching for his knife when he saw Edward's face—or at least part of it. The lips were drawn back in a snarl, exposing teeth, more animal than human. The mouth uttered a low-pitched growling sound. But it was the eyes that made the pimp back up. They glared at him like some wild beast peering out of a cave. The pimp had seen eyes like that before. In prison. Those eyes belonged to crazies who would cut your tongue out with a razor and laugh while they did it.

The pimp backed away slowly, then whirled around and ran into the darkness.

Edward turned his attention back to the hooker, who was leaning into a car window, talking to a potential customer. The woman was perfect for

Edward's needs. He planned to strangle her, then let her drop from a great height, just as he'd done with Karen Rhodes.

Tonight's Event—Edward's Fourth Event—had one purpose: to distract the police. Their thinking would have to change with the death of the black whore in Hollywood. They would surely see the similarities between the deaths of Karen Rhodes and the black hooker. And they would have to believe that a serial killer was stalking the streets of Los Angeles, picking his victims at random.

Edward smiled broadly, enjoying the game he was about to set into motion.

Tires screeched as the car pulled away. The hooker had lost her customer. She sighed wearily and began walking down the sidewalk. Edward pulled up the collar of his leather jacket and put on a Los Angeles Dodgers baseball cap, bringing the bill well down over his forehead. Quickly he snapped on a pair of latex gloves and placed his hands in his pockets, concealing them. Edward moved out of the shadows and trotted after the prostitute.

The prostitute heard the footsteps behind her and turned. She studied the guy for a moment, but it was the baseball cap that caught her attention. The last undercover cop to bust her was wearing one of those damned things. "You looking for me?"

"Sure am."

"What do you want?"

"A little action."

The whore hesitated, now looking around the area for unmarked police cars. She wondered if he was wearing a wire and if she was being set up. She decided to play this one very carefully. ''What you got in mind?''

''You know.''

''I ain't no mind reader.''

Edward did not like the delay. The longer he was out in the lighted street with the whore, the more chances of a witness seeing them now and remembering it later. ''I'll pay fifty bucks.''

The hooker nodded. He had said the magic words.

''You follow me.''

''Where are we going?'' Edward asked, playing stupid.

''To a hotel around the corner.''

Edward followed five paces behind the prostitute, his eyes fixed on her body. She was taller than he'd thought, with the thin but well-muscled arms of a woman who worked out with weights. Probably strong, he thought, and fairly agile. But it wouldn't help her. Her throat would be crushed before she knew it.

The whore felt uneasy about this customer. He wasn't a cop, she was certain of that. It was something else, but she couldn't put her finger on it. He was kind of creepy and she wondered if he was kinky, maybe into sado-masochism. She wasn't going to put up with that kind of shit. The hooker patted her handbag. She always carried some protection with her.

As they approached the hotel, Edward glanced up to see if it had a fire escape. It didn't. Good, he hummed to himself. He didn't want anything to break the whore's fall.

The hotel lobby was small, with worn-out furniture and a threadbare carpet. The air stank with the stench of stale cigar smoke. An old man was sitting upright on a couch, sound asleep. He looked more dead than alive. As they passed the front desk, the night clerk glanced up at the whore, then stuck his face back into the *Los Angeles Times*. Edward turned his head away, like an embarrassed customer.

Entering the elevator, Edward noticed the stairs leading up, and next to them the fire exit. Perfect. That was how he would leave without having to pass the front desk again. He watched the whore punch the floor button, again measuring her height and strength. It would be easier if he could somehow neutralize those attributes without arousing her suspicions. Otherwise she might be able to put up a fight and scream and maybe draw a crowd. But how could he do it? How? She was street smart and probably tough as hell. As the elevator jerked to a stop, he still didn't have an answer to his problem.

Moments later they entered a hotel room with forty-year-old fittings and furniture. The bed had brass rails and a mattress that sank in the middle. The spread was so worn one could see through it. An ugly radiator was near the window; an overhead fan slowly rotated. The walls were paper thin and the sounds of a couple arguing next door came through clearly.

The hooker sat on the side of the bed and began to wriggle out of her rabbit-skin coat. As she twisted, her handbag slipped from her grasp and fell to the floor, its contents spilling out. An opened wallet. Lipstick. A wire brush. She saw the edge of the brass knuckles protruding and held her breath.

Edward's eyes were focused on a photograph in the opened wallet. It showed the hooker and a small child, all smiles. Jesus, the whore was a mother, he thought disgustedly. Well, she won't be one much longer. Edward felt as if he was about to do the child a favor. The people at Social Services would find the child a new home, a far better one than she was leaving.

The prostitute knelt down and began shoving the contents back into her handbag, hoping he hadn't seen the brass knuckles. They were her only form of protection. She was strong for a woman, but most men could overpower her. However, it was another story when she was wearing brass knuckles. One hit could do real damage. The last guy she used them on ended up with his forehead split open. She closed her handbag, not locking it.

"Stay on your knees," Edward said softly.

"For what?"

"Women on their knees get me excited."

She watched him carefully, knowing that something was amiss. His eyes now had a strange glaze. This was not some ordinary john. The hooker's hand slowly moved to her handbag.

In an instant Edward was on her, hands gripping her neck. She tried to get off her knees, but it was impossible. He was powerful and above her, pushing her down, his grip even stronger now.

The prostitute clawed at his arms, her nails digging into the sleeves of his leather jacket. Her head began to swim; images were becoming fuzzy. Desperately she reached down and groped for her handbag, fumbling with it for a moment, then finding the brass knuckles and slipping them on. She lashed out at him, the metal knuckles pummeling the back of Edward's neck and shoulders, each blow bruising and painful.

Edward ducked his head to protect his face, and when he did, his grip loosened.

The hooker sucked in fresh air; now revitalized, she managed to throw a vicious punch that smashed into Edward's chest. It took his breath away, and for a moment he was blinded by the terrible pain.

She swung again, this time missing. Edward saw his chance and went for her exposed neck. His grip was on the mark, quickly finding her larynx, and in a split second her windpipe was crushed.

Edward backed off and watched the hooker squirm on the floor, gasping for air that would never reach her lungs. He rubbed at his neck and shoulders, but it was his chest that bothered him most. It felt like he'd been hit by a sledgehammer. He wondered if a rib was broken.

Edward walked over to the window and opened it. The whore was still squirming on the floor, hands on her throat, eyes bulging.

Edward got on his knees and kissed the woman's neck. He began to gently nibble on it, barely breaking the skin. She tasted sweet, much sweeter than he had anticipated. He bit down harder, now feeling as if he were part of her, as if they were one.

"Want to take a ride? A real fun ride?" Edward asked softly. He waited, watching until he thought he saw her nod. "Good."

He picked her up like a sack of potatoes and tossed her out the window.

7

Dr. Mary Bailey held the dental cast up. "This is a model of the killer's teeth."

"Is there anything distinctive about them?" Joanna asked.

"Not really. Their alignment is fairly good. One of the central incisors is chipped." Mary placed the dental cast under an illuminator that projected an image of the teeth onto a wall screen.

Joanna studied the image. "I don't see the chip."

"I'll show it to you." Mary Bailey reached for a pointer and walked over to the screen. She was a tiny woman, barely four foot eleven, with small, delicate features. As a dental student she had been kidded mercilessly because she had to stand on a box to work on patients. It didn't bother Mary. She knew she would never practice dentistry, but instead would go into research. Now a full professor at Memorial, she was a world authority on the human bite. Mary pointed to a central incisor. "Here's the chip."

"I still don't see it."

"That's because you're not a dentist."

"I've never considered that a disadvantage." Joanna adjusted the focus, still not detecting the deformity. ''Is it unique enough to identify the killer?''

''Hardly.'' Mary reached for a cigarette and lit it, inhaling deeply.

''I'd like a photograph of the dental cast to include in my report on Karen Rhodes.''

''I can't do that.''

Joanna looked at Mary Bailey oddly. ''Why not?''

''I just can't.''

''That's not a very good reason.''

''I'm sorry. It's the best I can do.''

''Do you realize that this is a coroner's case?''

''It doesn't matter.''

''The hell it doesn't,'' Joanna said sharply. She considered having Mary Bailey served with a court order, but decided against it. Too complicated, too much paperwork. There was an easier way. She pushed her chair back and stood. ''I'll have Lieutenant Sinclair from Homicide give you a call. Perhaps he can convince you otherwise.''

''You're working with Sinclair too?''

''Of course,'' Joanna said, straightfaced.

''Why the hell didn't you say so?'' Mary mashed out her cigarette and gestured for Joanna to sit back down. She walked over to a partially opened door that led to a reception area and closed it. Then she came back and sat next to Joanna and spoke in a low voice. ''What I'm about to tell you is absolutely confidential, not to be included in your report. Okay?''

''Okay.''

''The reason I can't give you photographs is because the impression wasn't obtained from Karen Rhodes's body. It was gotten from bite marks on the first two victims. The bite on Karen was more of a chew. It was impossible to get a decent impression.''

Joanna furrowed her brow, puzzled. ''Then why are you showing me this dental cast?''

''Because I believe the chew mark was made by the same person who nibbled on the other two women. For example, the chew mark on Karen also showed a chipped central incisor.''

''That doesn't sound like very solid evidence.''

''It wouldn't stand up in court, if that's what you mean.''

''Does it concern you that the other two victims had bites and Karen had a chew mark?''

''A little,'' Mary conceded. ''And there were other differences as well. The initial two victims were stabbed to death, not strangled like Karen. But the dental evidence strongly suggests it was the same person who killed all three women.''

Joanna stared up at the ceiling, thinking about Karen and what she was doing on the rooftop at eleven-thirty at night. She had to be meeting someone. But who and why? ''Sinclair told me that the bites on the victims represented a form of intimacy. Is that your opinion as well?''

''Yes and no,'' Mary Bailey said carefully. ''I was at the meeting when the police shrink gave us his profile of the killer. I don't buy all of it. To them, the word *intimacy* has sexual overtones. It implies that these were sex murders. I'm not convinced of that.''

''I'm not either. Karen was certainly not sexually assaulted.''

''You mean, no vaginal trauma?''

''Right.''

''That doesn't mean much. Most of the biters are impotent.'' Mary lit another cigarette and began blowing smoke rings. "I don't think these are sex murders for two reasons. First, the number of bites. In most sex murders, the victim is bitten an average of three times. Our victims had only one bite. And then there's the nature of the bite. Most love bites have a suck mark, a bruised center. We don't see that here."

"So you don't buy the intimacy angle?"

"I didn't say that. I said it wasn't sex, at least by current definition."

"Are you telling me that the bites represent some crazy form of intimacy?"

"Crazy to us. Not to him."

"But he does get pleasure from it, right?"

"More than you could imagine."

"Jesus." Joanna shuddered.

Joanna took the elevator down three floors, then walked across the enclosed bridge that connected the Dental Institute to Memorial Hospital. A group of students were just behind her, chatting and laughing loudly. Joanna tuned them out, her mind now totally preoccupied by the information she had obtained from Mary Bailey. The differences between the three victims bothered her. Two stabbed and bitten, one strangled and chewed. The mark of a serial killer was consistency—she knew that. They rarely varied, always performing as if they were programmed to commit the same act over and over again.

Joanna considered the possibility that there were two killers on the loose, one of whom was inside Memorial. But that theory would never hold up. The dental evidence said otherwise. So it had to be one man, a serial killer. And somehow he lured Karen up to the rooftop. But how?

And how could all this be connected to the strange research that had frightened Karen?

Joanna turned into a wide corridor and walked past the autopsy room. Directly ahead she saw Arnold Weideman, the chief of Pathology, chatting with a technician. Weideman looked over and saw Joanna, then abruptly turned away. Joanna glanced at the old man's back as she passed by. There had been a time when the two of them got along well. When Joanna first arrived at Memorial, she and Weideman had worked together on several sensational murder cases. Weideman—who considered himself a forensic pathologist, although he wasn't—had been in the media spotlight for the first time in his life and enjoyed it immensely. As time passed, however, Weideman became more of a liability than an asset to Joanna. He would rush to talk with the press, often prematurely, and on occasion gave out distorted information that Joanna would later have to retract. Joanna began working alone and eventually set up a forensic division within the Department of Pathology, much to Weideman's dismay. The spotlight shifted to Joanna and Weideman returned to obscurity. He felt betrayed, used. As chief of Pathology, Weideman tried to make Joanna's life as unhappy as possible. He doubled her administrative duties, gave her numerous teaching assignments, appointed her to tedious committees, even attempted to cut back on her secretarial help. For the past year he had avoided having any conversations with Joanna.

Joanna walked into her office and began to shrug out of her long white coat.

"You're late," said Virginia Hand, a middle-aged secretary with frizzy blond hair and designer glasses.

"For what?"

"The slide review with Dr. Rodman."

Joanna slapped her forehead. "Damn! I forgot."

"I think he's still waiting for you."

Joanna slipped back into her white coat and hurried out, heading for the room where the microscopes were kept. The house staff called it the Show and Tell, the place where all slides were reviewed and final diagnoses given. Joanna had been scheduled to meet with Rodman thirty minutes ago to go over the slides on Karen Rhodes.

David Rodman jumped to his feet as Joanna entered the room. She motioned him to sit back down. "Sorry I'm late."

"No problem."

Joanna pulled up a stool close to the microscope. "Shall we begin?"

"I—ah—we've already reviewed the slides," Rodman said hesitantly.

"Who is we?"

"While I was waiting for you, Dr. Weideman came in and asked why I was sitting around. I told him I was waiting for you. And then he starts asking me what time you were supposed to be here—and—and all kinds of shit."

"And what did you tell him?"

"That you were due here shortly." Rodman unwrapped a stick of gum and began to chew angrily. "Screw him! I'm not a timekeeper."

"I hope you didn't tell him that."

"No." Rodman grinned nervously.

"And then he reviewed the slides with you?"

"Only after telling me that residents shouldn't

be sitting around doing nothing. That it was up to the faculty to make certain all of our time was used efficiently."

Up his, Joanna thought, but remained silent. Her stomach twisted uncomfortably. She hated the relationship she had with Weideman. The slights, the backstabbing, the overt hostility. But it wasn't her fault, it was his, and if she had to live with it she would. Her gaze went to a box of slides next to the microscope. On top was stenciled in the name KAREN RHODES. The thin slices of tissue mounted on the slides were all that was left of her friend. "Did the slides show anything unexpected?"

"Nope."

"I'd still like to go through them quickly."

"Sure." Rodman reached for a slide and placed it under the microscope. "Do you remember when you were asking me some questions about Karen Rhodes's personal life?"

"Yes."

"Well, I heard something interesting in the cafeteria last night." Rodman hesitated for a moment, choosing his words. "Of course, it's secondhand information, so I don't know how accurate it is."

"Secondhand, from whom?"

Rodman hesitated again, now wishing he hadn't brought the subject up.

"I don't want names. Just general categories."

"Nurses," Rodman said promptly. "I heard one of them saying that Karen really wasn't Miss Goody Two-Shoes. Apparently this nurse was skiing up at Sun Valley a few months ago and happened to see Karen in one of the outdoor hot tubs. It was late at night and Karen was in the tub with a French skier—both of them were nude. They were really getting it on."

Joanna looked at him strangely. That wasn't the Karen she knew. Nude in an outdoor hot tub at a ski resort? No way! "And you believe that story?"

"Hell, I don't know what to believe anymore."

"That's not what I meant. This nurse you're talking about, is she straightforward, or is she likely to exaggerate and lie?"

Rodman thought for a moment. "She's been around the track a few times. I'd tend to believe that what she said was what she knew."

"Is that the end of the story?"

"No. Another nurse mentioned that Karen was sleeping with Bobby Hannah in the residents' on-call room. On a regular basis."

"Do you believe it?"

Rodman shrugged. "I'm not so sure. This second nurse is a real cow and talks just to hear the sound of her own voice." He nervously began strumming the tabletop with his fingers. "She also mentioned some gossip she'd heard. Again, I don't know if it was true or not."

"What is it?"

"Don't quote me as the source of this information."

"I won't."

Rodman exhaled loudly. "She said that Karen and Bobby Hannah got their kicks by nibbling on one another."

By 6:30 P.M. the cafeteria in the Psychiatric Institute was crowded with doctors, nurses, and other staff. A few patients with their visitors sat off to one side, as if separated from the professionals by some invisible curtain. Joanna picked up a small cucumber salad and coffee, then scanned the big room until she saw Julian Whitmore sitting alone at a corner table. She waved and walked over to him.

"Is that all you're having?" Julian asked, watching her unload the tray.

"I had a large lunch."

Julian went back to his apple pie covered with whipped cream. "I hope this won't take too long. I've got to be at the Music Center by eight tonight."

"What's on?"

"Vivaldi."

Joanna nodded, remembering that Vivaldi was Karen's favorite composer. "I only need a few minutes of your time. In particular, I want to know the research projects Karen was involved in."

"Are you still working with the police?"

Joanna moved her head ambiguously. "They are gathering as much background information as possible."

"Okay. Fire away."

"Tell me about her research projects."

"There were two that I knew about. She was the research nurse on a new tranquilizer that Richard Abels and I were studying. It's a remarkable drug in that, unlike other tranquilizers, it has very little sedative effect. The second project she worked on dealt with a new class of antidepressants or mood-elevators."

"Were you involved in that as well?"

"No. That study belonged to Hugh Jackson and, to a lesser extent, Richard Abels."

"Hugh Jackson controls all the research, doesn't he?"

Julian hesitated, his eyes narrowing noticeably. He pointed at Joanna with his fork. "If you want specific information about Hugh Jackson, I suggest you ask him."

Joanna sipped her coffee, wondering if she'd touched on a sensitive area. But what? Her question about Hugh Jackson was innocuous enough. Wasn't it? She made a mental note to think about it later. "I'm not interested in specifics about Hugh. I just wanted to know if he'd be aware of all research projects that Karen participated in."

"I suspect he would. Hugh has a hand in virtually all the research projects, and the staff likes it that way. You see, Hugh is quite brilliant and he greatly improves whatever research he becomes involved with. And he's very generous, usually giving other investigators more credit than they deserve. He's loved by most, admired by all."

"And he sees patients too?"

Julian nodded. "They love him, too. God knows where he finds the time to do it all."

"Did he and Karen get along well?"

"Yes, indeed. She was absolutely thrilled to work with him on the mood-elevator study."

"Tell me about this mood-elevating drug."

"My knowledge of this project is indirect, mainly what I've heard from others." Julian finished off his pie and pushed the plate away. "It's a very potent mood-elevator, but apparently it has some unpleasant side effects."

"Such as?"

"Hyperactivity, and, at high doses, visual hallucinations."

"How'd you learn about these side effects?"

"Karen told me. She loved to talk about drug

research. She'd talk forever to anyone who'd listen."

Joanna squinted her eyes. "Karen never impressed me as a very talkative person, particularly about professional matters."

"No, no!" Julian held up his hands, palms out. "I think you've misinterpreted what I said. She loved to talk about research to those of us involved. I think it made her feel like she was one of the investigators—you know—a scientist. I can assure you that outside of this institute she talked to no one."

Joanna bit down on a slice of cucumber and chewed slowly. She wanted to carefully phrase the next question. "Did Karen ever express concern about any of the research?"

"How do you mean?"

"Was she bothered by it? Did anything upset her?"

"Oh, yes," Julian said promptly. "She was really bothered by one of the animal experiments. Several monkeys had been injected with the new tranquilizer and instead of calming down they went wild. They shrieked and screamed and banged up against the cages ferociously. Karen was in the animal room at the time and was really frightened by it. She literally ran out of the room."

"When did this happen?"

"About a month ago."

"Has the drug been given to humans?"

"Yes. But of course at much lower doses than the monkeys received."

"Were there any adverse effects in the human subjects?"

"Some. But nothing like that."

"Are you sure?"

Julian nodded emphatically. "Positive. But if you'd like to look at the data I'll be glad to show it to you."

"I'd really appreciate that," Joanna said and pushed her chair back.

They rode the elevator up with a group of nurses. With her peripheral vision, Joanna watched Julian Whitmore as he dabbed at an eyebrow. He was exceptionally handsome. She wondered again about his sexual orientation. She couldn't be certain. But so what? His sexual preference was his business. As far as she was concerned, Julian was a friend, someone who was more than willing to help. The nurses got off on the sixth floor, Joanna and Julian on the tenth.

The Brain Research Institute was quiet and totally deserted. They walked to the far end of the corridor and into a small, well-appointed library. The walls were lined with shelves filled with bound journals and textbooks. Off to one side were racks holding recently arrived publications and periodicals. In the center of the room was a big conference table with research protocols stacked upon it.

"Here we are," Julian said, opening a thick volume entitled *Tranquilizer DP-18*. He quickly flipped through the pages and stopped at the section on side effects.

Joanna glanced at the list of adverse reactions seen in fifty patients who took the drug.

Gastrointestinal (nausea, cramps, diarrhea)	7%
Cutaneous (rash, pruritis)	6%
Cardiovascular (tachycardia)	2%
Central Nervous System:	
Drowsiness	5%

Hyperactivity	1%
Headache	2%
Blurred vision	1%

"I thought you said the drug didn't cause drowsiness?" Joanna said.

"It doesn't. Five percent is nothing. That means only one in twenty noted drowsiness." Julian looked up at the wall clock. "Have you seen enough?"

"I'd like to scan the rest of the protocol, if that's all right."

"Sure. I'm going to my office and make a few phone calls. Then I'll close up shop. Okay?"

"Fine with me." Joanna waited for Julian to leave, then quickly thumbed through the protocol. There were four pages that dealt with side effects, describing each in detail. She carefully read them, looking for any hint out of the ordinary. The adverse effects on the central nervous system were almost negligible. Five percent of the patients taking the drug became drowsy, but so did three percent of those who took a placebo. Joanna, dispirited, pushed the volume away.

She sighed wearily, wondering where to go next. The problem was that she didn't know what she was looking for. Only that it was something that had frightened Karen, something to do with research. And it sure as hell wasn't a bunch of screaming monkeys.

Her gaze went to another thick protocol just to her left. It was entitled *RD-ME 42*. She guessed that RD stood for research and development, ME for mood elevator. The principal investigators were Hugh Jackson and Richard Abels. She flipped through the pages until she came to a section that listed adverse reactions. They were numerous, particularly those associated with the central nervous system. Hyperactivity (8%), excitement (10%), visual disturbances (6%), increased libido (9%), personality changes (10%). Someone had underlined personality changes. Joanna heard the conference room door opening and quickly closed the volume.

Hugh Jackson stood in the doorway, staring down at her. "May I ask what you're doing here?"

"I was looking at the research Karen was involved in," Joanna said, trying to keep her voice steady.

"I see." Jackson's face was impassive, but his neck veins were bulging. "Did you seek permission to do so?"

"Julian said it would be all right."

"Julian is not the director of this institute. He doesn't have that authority."

"He told me that the research project was his."

Jackson walked over and glanced down at the protocol in front of Joanna. "So you have reviewed the tranquilizer data?"

"That's correct."

"And what did you find?"

"Nothing."

"Are you satisfied that nothing god-awful is going on up here?"

"Well, I didn't review all the protocols."

"And you're not going to." Jackson took out his pipe and lit it, sending up plumes of smoke. "Most of the protocols on this table deal with drugs that don't belong to us. They belong to pharmaceutical companies who have entrusted us with their drugs, to test them and see what their benefits and toxicities are. The information is strictly confidential. Furthermore, the patients taking these drugs are listed in these protocols and there is no way we will allow anyone to see those lists. This institute has assured the patients and their families of absolute privacy regarding their participation in these drug trials. We will not break that agreement.''

''I'm not asking to see those lists, Hugh.''

''Then what is it you're looking for?''

Joanna hesitated. ''I can't reveal that at this time.''

Hugh Jackson rolled his eyes upward. ''When you can, please let me know. Then I can give you the information and we can all get on with our work.''

The door opened and Julian entered. Hugh Jackson gave him a stern look. ''I'd like a few words with you.'' Jackson turned back to Joanna. ''Finish your review if you like. Make no notes, copy no names. Then please leave.''

Jackson led the way out, with Julian a step behind. As the door closed, Joanna ran over and pressed her ear against it, concentrating her hearing. She heard Jackson's voice, muffled and angry, the words unintelligible. The voices became fainter as the men walked away.

Joanna sat on the edge of the table, angry with herself. *So stupid,* she told herself, *so dumb to get caught red-handed. I didn't have to come up here tonight. I could have used Julian. He would have given me all the information I wanted on his research and he would have reviewed the other protocols as well. He was close to Karen, a friend. He would have done whatever I asked. Stupid! Now I'm persona non gratis in the BRI.*

She glanced down at the thick protocols on the table and wondered whether she should go through them. Why bother? I don't even know what I'm looking for. And besides, if something terrible were going on, no one would be stupid enough to describe it in the research protocol. I should have thought about that too before I came up here tonight.

Joanna walked into the hall and went to the elevators. Down the corridor she saw Richard Abels and a nurse going through the door that led to an amphitheater. They were followed shortly by Hugh Jackson, who glanced at Joanna and quickly turned away.

Joanna thought back eight years to the last time she had been in that amphitheater. She was giving a talk and the slide projector broke down. Without slides, her presentation had been dreadful. She pushed the elevator button impatiently.

A door near the elevator opened and a cleaning woman wrestled with her equipment, trying to squeeze it all through the partially opened doorway. Joanna hurried over and held the door. The cleaning woman nodded her thanks and continued down the corridor.

Joanna was about to close the door when she peeked in. In front of her was the darkened projection room that looked down on the amphitheater. She saw the ceiling lights above, heard voices coming from below. Impulsively, she stepped into the room, crouching low, and closed the door quietly. She peered through the little window. Richard Abels and a nurse were sitting in the first row.

Hugh Jackson stood next to a woman seated at the front of the amphitheater. They were facing the projection booth.

"How do you feel?" Jackson asked.

"Sexy," the woman said in a low, husky voice.

"What does that mean?"

"I'll give you three guesses." The woman was dressed in a black cocktail dress and wore a single strand of pearls. Her legs were crossed and the dress came up to the mid-thigh level. She wiggled in her seat and the dress crept up higher. "Make that one guess."

As Joanna studied the woman, her eyes widened in disbelief. It was the same woman she and Sinclair had seen in the elevator of the Psychiatric Institute—the thin, middle-aged woman with unkempt hair and a strange odor. Now, she looked totally different. Her makeup was exquisitely applied, her hair fluffed and hanging down to her shoulders. She uncrossed then recrossed her legs, her dress riding up even higher. The woman looked down at her thigh and seductively ran her hand along it.

"Shouldn't you cover your thigh, Cybil?" Jackson asked.

"I can't. It's so hot. I'm burning up inside." Cybil stood and began to dance around Hugh Jackson, her pelvis rotating and swaying in a provocative manner. She threw her hands into the air and pranced toward the far end of the room.

Joanna raised up from her crouching position for a better view. Her shoulder hit an overhanging shelf and a telephone fell to the floor, making a loud thud. Joanna froze.

"What the hell was that?" Abels asked.

"I'm not sure. I think it came from the projection booth," Jackson replied. "You'd better take a look."

Joanna replaced the telephone and bolted out of

the projection room. She ran past the elevators, glancing up at the overhead panel. Both were on the sixth floor and heading down.

Across the corridor Joanna saw the fire escape and dashed for it. She was in the stairwell, quietly closing the door, as footsteps sounded in the hall. Joanna pressed against the wall, not moving a muscle. The footsteps came closer and closer, then the door suddenly opened. Joanna was behind the door, trying not to breathe. She heard a second set of footsteps approaching.

"Anybody there?" Jackson asked.

"No. And I don't hear anyone going down the stairs, either."

"Call Security. Have them come up immediately."

The door closed.

Joanna waited until she no longer heard voices or footsteps. She took off her high heels and went down one flight slowly, silently. She stopped and listened again. All was quiet.

Joanna broke into a full run, taking the steps two at a time.

8

"I don't believe it," Jake said to Joanna.

"I saw it with my own eyes. The female patient we saw on the elevator had been transformed into a very sexy lady."

Jake thought back to the skinny woman with the unpleasant odor. "Are you sure it was her?"

"Beyond any doubt."

"And she also did a little dance, huh?"

Joanna nodded, wishing again that she hadn't accidentally knocked the phone to the floor in the projection booth. She wondered what would have happened next. "It's very, very strange, isn't it?"

"I think it's kind of miraculous."

"This type of miraculous transformation occurs only in the movies. It doesn't happen in real life, not in a matter of days."

Jake shrugged. "Maybe they gave her one of those mood elevators you told me about. She went from sad to happy. It happens."

"You're missing the point."

"That's because you haven't made one." Jake took out a handkerchief and mopped the perspiration from his brow. The day was overcast and humid, the temperature near ninety degrees. He felt sweat soaking through his shirt. "Let's just hope we can find something important by going through the dead girl's things."

They were standing in front of a two-story English Tudor home located in the fashionable Brentwood area. The house belonged to Marissa Shaw, a nurse at the Psychiatric Institute. She had inherited it two years ago when her parents were killed in an airline crash outside of Dallas. The mortgage payment, taxes, and upkeep came to twenty-five hundred a month. There was no way she could afford that on a nurse's salary, so she took in roommates. Karen Rhodes had lived in the house for the last two months of her life.

"So you know Marissa Shaw, huh?" Jake asked.

Joanna nodded. "She once dated one of my residents."

Jake stuck a finger behind his collar and pulled it away from his neck. "Do you want to do the questioning?"

"I'll get more out of her than you will," Joanna told him. "She'll trust me and be more open."

"Okay," Jake said equably. "You do the openers. But don't push. Be nice and friendly and let her do the talking."

Joanna rang the bell. They heard a small dog yapping inside, a female voice shushing it.

The chains came off the door and it opened.

"Hello, Joanna," Marissa Shaw said in a soft voice.

"Hi, Marissa," she said, taking her extended hand. "This is Lieutenant Sinclair from the police department. We'd like to ask you some questions about Karen."

"Lieutenant." Marissa nodded, stepping aside. "Please come in."

They went into a big, comfortable living room. The couches and chairs were upholstered in a thick, gray fabric, worn but usable. The furniture was oak, old and nicely polished. A brick fireplace was off to one side, a bay window looked out on a manicured lawn. Big throw pillows were everywhere.

"Can I get you something to drink?" Marissa asked.

They politely declined, but Jake was dying for a beer.

They sat on a sofa facing Marissa, who was in an overstuffed, highback chair. The dog was yapping away in the kitchen.

Jake thought he detected a faint aroma of marijuana, but couldn't be sure. He briefly studied the shapely woman across from him. She was in her early thirties with sharp features, dark eyes, and a slender straight nose. Auburn-colored hair flowed down to her shoulders. She had the kind of good looks that would last a lifetime, Jake decided.

"We know how upset you must be," Joanna began, "so we'll make our stay as brief as possible."

"It's like a nightmare," Marissa said, speaking as though she were in a trance. "I still don't believe it."

"When did Karen move in?"

"About two months ago." Her voice was so soft that Joanna and Sinclair had to concentrate their hearing.

"Is that when you first met her?"

Marissa shook her head. "I met her a few months before that. We worked together on one of the wards at the Institute."

"Was it your idea or hers that she move in?"

Marissa thought for a moment. She curled her legs under her, hands clasped around a knee. She was wearing jeans and an oxford-blue shirt. "Mine, I think. I mentioned that one of my roommates was moving out and I needed someone to take her place."

Joanna paused, wondering why Karen, a girl with millions, would want to share a house with others. "What kind of person was Karen? Of course I knew her, too. But we would like your opinion."

"Sweet and thoughtful." Marissa reached for a cigarette and lit it. Her hand was steady. "When I first met her she seemed so reserved, almost shy. But as I got to know her, I realized that she was just a private sort of person—one who picked her friends carefully."

"Do you think her family background had a lot to do with that?"

"I'm certain of it," Marissa said promptly. "She felt like her family name was a responsibility. In public she always acted like someone was watching her, writing her biography."

"Was she this way in private as well?"

"Exactly the same. She was very careful. It was like the smallest indiscretion on her part might find its way into the newspapers." Marissa looked over at the bay window, her eyelids heavy from lack of sleep. She had barely slept since Karen's murder, but the night before had been the worst. She had been awakened by a terrible nightmare in which she saw Karen falling through space, her hand outstretched, screaming for help. And now Marissa saw the horrible image again. She shuddered to herself and took a deep drag on her cigarette, forcing her mind back to the questioning. What was the question? Oh, yes. Karen's family. "I think she really felt that her family name was a burden."

"You make her sound almost Victorian."

"I think she would have been happier if she had been born a hundred years ago."

"The restraints would have been the same."

"But she would have had a lot of company."

"So she felt like she was different?"

"She *was* different," Marissa said matter-of-factly. "She was bright, beautiful, worth a hundred million, with a father who one day will be president of the United States. I think that's a little different, don't you?"

Joanna nodded. She felt that Marissa was telling the truth, but she also felt that the nurse was holding back, being very careful. Too bad Jake was present, she thought. Women talk much more freely when men aren't around. "Was she a good nurse?"

"Excellent."

"Did she enjoy the research work she did in the BRI?"

"Loved it. When the drugs they were testing proved to be effective, she'd get very excited. She'd keep me up all night talking about it." Marissa smiled for the first time. "You'd think that she had invented the damned drug."

"Did you work in the research program as well?"

Marissa nodded. "It was an easy extra fifty dollars a week."

"Did you two work on the same projects?"

"Sometimes. It varied."

"What kinds of drugs were being tested?"

"Antidepressants, mood elevators. That kind of thing." Marissa stifled a yawn, her eyelids beginning to droop again. *I shouldn't have taken that Valium pill*, she thought. *I should have waited*.

"Did she get along well with the people in the BRI?"

Marissa hesitated. "She thought Hugh Jackson was God and Julian Whitmore was his son. But she couldn't stand Abels or Mark Harrison."

"Why?"

"Abels tried to come on to her a few times. She told him to buzz off, but he persisted." Marissa shivered to herself. "He must be the ugliest man in Los Angeles. Easily the most obnoxious."

Joanna looked away, thinking how stupid Abels had been to lie. But then, maybe he had a reason. "So she never went out with him?"

"Are you kidding?" Marissa scoffed. "He even called her up at home once. She was furious."

Jake wetted his lips. He couldn't wait to question Abels again. The little shit!

Jake felt beads of perspiration on his upper lip and brushed them away with a finger. The room was very warm and close, the air still and heavy with cigarette smoke. But Jake's nose still picked up the scent of marijuana. He watched Marissa fighting her fatigue, straining to keep her eyelids up. Goddamn drugs. He wondered if she were a doper, hooked on that shit, and whether it had affected her memory.

"What about Mark Harrison?" Joanna asked. "Do you know him?"

Joanna shook her head.

"He's an absolutely gorgeous man," Marissa said, her voice lower, almost husky. "Very, very handsome. And very, very married."

"Did he come on to her, too?"

"In subtle ways. She told him to get lost."

Joanna grinned. "Now she doesn't sound so reserved and shy."

"I'm using my words," Marissa said easily. "Karen would have said something like, 'No, thank you, I'm not interested.' "

"Did she date anyone special?"

"Bobby Hannah," Marissa answered, then looked at Jake. "He's a resident in surgery at Memorial."

"How long did they go together?" Joanna asked.

"For two or three months." She took a final drag from her cigarette and extinguished it. "I could never understand the relationship. He's kind of aggressive and loud. Out of character for her."

Joanna patted her hair in place, thinking. "Opposites attracted to each other?"

"Maybe."

"How close were they?"

"Very. For a while."

"Did he spend nights here?" Joanna asked and saw Marissa's face harden for a brief second.

"Not to my knowledge."

"Did they sleep together?"

"We never discussed it," Marissa said sharply.

Bullshit, Joanna thought. "When did they break up?"

"About five months ago."

Marissa reached for another cigarette, then decided against it. Her throat was already raw and irritated from smoke, and all the talking was making it worse. She felt Jake's eyes on her and stared back at him, wishing they'd finish and get the hell out and leave her alone.

"Who left whom?"

"He dumped her," Marissa said, her voice tinged with bitterness.

"She must have talked to you about that," Joanna said quickly.

"Not really. She just said he was becoming too demanding, that he always wanted things his way. And when she refused, he walked." She lighted another cigarette, inhaled deeply. "He's the type of man who never looks back. The next night he was probably out with someone else."

"What kind of demands did he make?"

Marissa opened her mouth, hesitated, searched for the right words. "You've got to understand the sort of person Bobby Hannah is. He believes that alcohol was invented for him to drink, women for him to play with, gall bladders for him to remove. Everything for him. Other people just didn't matter."

Joanna watched Marissa drag repeatedly on her cigarette, the puffs more rapid than before, more nervous. Something was bothering the hell out of her. "What were the demands?" Joanna persisted.

The dog started yapping in the kitchen again, scratching at the door.

"Is it that important?" Marissa asked.

"It might be."

Marissa took a deep breath and exhaled audibly. "He wanted her to be more open, more aggressive, more spontaneous."

"Give me an example."

"He was on call late one night and insisted that she meet him in the house staff lounge. You know, where the residents sleep. She refused and he didn't talk to her for a week.'' Marissa shook her head, lips tight. "He can be a real bastard.''

"So it seems," Joanna said sympathetically. *And Karen and Bobby were sleeping together, weren't they, Marissa? Why did I have to drag that information out of you?* "Was she badly hurt when he split?''

"Crushed would be a better word. She couldn't eat, couldn't sleep. If I mentioned his name she'd start to cry.''

"Did it affect her work?''

"Uh-uh. In public you'd never know. People like the Rhodeses do their crying in private.''

"Did she finally break out of it?''

"With help," Marissa nodded. "She went to a psychiatrist.''

"Who?''

"Jeremy Brock.''

Joanna waited for Jake to jot the name down. She knew Brock well. He was a superb psychiatrist who limited his practice to the most difficult cases. He would have ordinarily referred simple problems, like Karen's, to a younger associate. But maybe he made an exception for Karen Rhodes. "For how long did she see Brock?''

"A couple of months." Marissa ran her hands through her hair, fluffing it in place. "Gradually she got over it. As a matter of fact, for the past two months she seemed more lively than ever. Full of spark and spunk. You've got to give Brock credit. He really turned her around.''

"Did she take medications?''

"Nope. Just the usual therapy—you lie on the couch and let's sort your problems out.''

"How do you know she didn't take medication? Did she tell you that?''

Marissa thought for a moment. "No. She told me that they explored her feelings in depth. She never mentioned pills, so I thought—"

"I see." Joanna thought back to Karen's handbag—it hadn't contained any pills. Maybe she kept them in her medicine cabinet. "How deep was Karen's depression?"

"Like I told you, she was really crushed."

"Did she ever talk about suicide?"

"Never to me."

"During the last few weeks of her life, was she happy?"

"As far as I knew."

"Was she dating anybody new?"

"No."

"Did you see Karen on the day of her death?" Joanna asked.

Marissa nodded. "We had lunch together, then shopped for an hour in Beverly Hills."

"Did you notice anything unusual about her?"

"No."

"Did you two make any plans for later when she got off work?"

Jake's ears pricked up. It was a good question, one that he might not have asked.

"No," Marissa said. "Just the usual 'See you later.' "

"Can you think of any reason why Karen would have gone up on the roof of the Institute?" Joanna asked.

"Jesus, no! Not at eleven-thirty at night."

"How about during the day?"

Marissa shrugged. "For what?"

"How did you learn that Karen had been murdered?"

"I got a call from a friend in the ER."

"Who called you?"

"Nancy Evans, the head nurse."

"So you were home at the time?"

"Asleep in my bed."

The dog started barking loudly, scratching at the kitchen door. Then it began whimpering.

"Excuse me," Marissa said. "I've got to let Fudge out."

Joanna waited for her to leave, then leaned over to Jake. "Are there any points you want me to concentrate on?"

"Ask her if *she* ever dated Bobby Hannah," Jake said in a low voice.

"Do you think she did?"

Jake nodded. "She knows too much about him. Her information isn't just from girlie talk."

"Why do you think Karen moved in? Hell, she could have bought her own house."

"A lot of women don't like to live alone." Jake sat back, pleased that he had let Joanna do the initial questioning. She was smooth and nice, and with people like Marissa Shaw, smooth and nice worked better than tough and nasty. A lot better.

Joanna leaned over again. "What do—?"

Jake held up a hand as Marissa Shaw came back and seated herself. "Sorry about the interruption," she apologized.

"No problem," Joanna said. "You were saying that Karen appeared to be reasonably happy?"

"I thought so."

"Did she still see Bobby Hannah on occasion?"

"They met for coffee a few times."

"At the hospital?"

Marissa nodded.

"At night?"

Marissa nodded once more. "But she never

dated him again. At least that's what she told me."

Joanna leaned back, glancing at Sinclair, both with the same thought. Did Karen go to the roof of the Psychiatric Institute to meet Bobby Hannah? Possible, Joanna thought, remembering her conversation with Kate. Bobby Hannah was someone Karen Rhodes knew and trusted and probably still loved. "Was she still sleeping with him?"

Marissa's eyes flashed. "You'll have to ask Bobby Hannah about that."

"Did you ever date Bobby Hannah?"

"We dated for a while," Marissa said, now stirring restlessly.

"Were you two serious?"

"For a little while."

"When?" Joanna asked, smiling inwardly and reminding herself never to underestimate Jake Sinclair.

"A year ago. Maybe longer."

"Is he a violent type of person?" Joanna asked evenly.

Marissa straightened up, suddenly understanding what Joanna was driving at. "No, no," she said quietly. "He's loud and aggressive, but I don't think he would ever be violent."

Joanna turned to Jake. "Do you have any questions, Lieutenant?"

"Just a few. But first I'd like to open a window, if it's all right with you, Miss Shaw. It's a little stuffy in here."

Jake walked across the living room to a sliding glass door and opened it. Outside the air was still muggy, the day overcast. Too many loose ends, Jake thought, too many threads, none of which tie together. Except maybe for this Bobby Hannah, who was screwing Karen Rhodes in and out of the hospital and maybe on the rooftop of the Institute. And maybe he was screwing Karen and Marissa Shaw at the same time, maybe a threesome. But so what? There was no law against that. And remember, the guy who iced Karen Rhodes also iced two other women who were in no way connected with Memorial Hospital.

Jake's eyes suddenly narrowed. How do you know the other two victims had no connection to Memorial? They could have been patients or even frequent visitors to a sick friend. Better check it out. Wackos and looneys, he reminded himself, were everywhere, even in and around medical centers.

He slowly walked back and sat on the sofa. "Miss Shaw, tell me a little more about Dr. Abels," Jake said.

"Creepy," Marissa shivered. "He's the type who's got to touch you when he talks. Do you know what I mean?"

Jake nodded. "Did he ever ask you out?"

"Once," she said, making a face. "I told him to get lost."

"Did any nurses date him?"

"There was a Filipino nurse he tried to do a number on," Marissa said. "He made a move on her in his car. She had a police whistle in her purse and blew the hell out of it."

"Did he ever hit anyone you know of?"

"He threw a clipboard at one of the technicians. Her husband was going to kill him."

"What happened?" Jake asked innocently.

"They quieted it down. Abels is a genius, so they let him get away with murder."

Sinclair smiled thinly.

Marissa suddenly realized what she had just said. "I didn't mean it that way."

Jake scribbled a note on his pad. "You said Karen thought Hugh Jackson was God. Why'd she think that?"

"Because he's kind and brilliant. He's the sort of person who goes out of his way for others."

"And Julian Whitmore?"

"Nice guy."

"Did Karen ever date him?"

Marissa's eyes narrowed. "Hardly!"

Jake closed his notepad. "Do you have other roommates here?"

"Just Peggy Collins. She moved in about six weeks ago."

"Did she know Karen well?"

"Not really. Peggy works the eleven-to-seven shift at the Institute. Karen worked three to eleven. Their paths didn't cross that much. When one was awake, the other was asleep."

"Could we talk with Miss Collins?"

"Of course," Marissa said, getting to her feet. "She's asleep in the downstairs guestroom. I'll get her for you."

"Take your time," Jake told her. "We'd like to look at Karen's room."

"It's upstairs. The end bedroom on the right."

"Has anyone been in there since Karen's murder?"

"No, no one," Marissa said softly, the sadness suddenly coming back. She looked over at Joanna. "I haven't called the family about Karen's things. I thought it was too soon."

Joanna nodded. "Wait another week," she said gently.

Marissa's lips began to quiver, tears welling in her eyes. She shook her head, trying to keep her composure.

Joanna touched her shoulder. "You really helped us. More than you know."

Marissa reached in a pocket for a Kleenex. "Sorry," she whispered, dabbing at her cheeks.

"We'll be upstairs for a few minutes," Joanna said quietly.

Jake led the way up a flight of stairs. Several of the steps were cracked, the railing in need of repair. On the wall was a small but obvious water spot.

The door to Karen's bedroom was standing open. The room was modest in size with bed, dresser, wall mirror, and a cushioned rocking chair. A built-in closet was packed with clothes. Everything was neat and feminine.

"Let's start with the bathroom," Jake said.

Out of habit, the detective checked the tub first, then the toilet and the tank behind it. Next he went to the basin and the counter beside it. There were rows of assorted perfumes and cosmetics. The medicine cabinet was filled with the usual toiletries. Sinclair removed three pill bottles and studied their labels. He held them at arm's length, trying to read the fine print.

Jake handed a bottle to Joanna. "What's this?"

"Naprosyn," she told him. "It's an arthritis drug, but it also works for menstrual cramps."

"And this?" Jake passed over another bottle.

"Valium." Joanna noted the prescription date and counted the pills. "She was prescribed thirty of them in January. There're twenty pills still in the bottle."

"Not exactly a heavy user," Jake remarked, giving Joanna the last bottle.

"Birth control pills." Joanna placed the bottles back in the cabinet and followed Jake into the bedroom.

On top of Karen's dresser was an expensive-looking antique clock and a framed photograph of a distinguished middle-aged couple. Joanna recognized the man—Senator Alexander Rhodes.

Sinclair began rummaging through the drawers. He examined pantyhose, nighties, T-shirts, tennis shorts, and polo shirts. The middle drawer was filled with bras and panties. At the bottom he found some undergarments that looked like they came from Frederick's of Hollywood. The hidden bras and panties were scanty, erotic, black with frilly lace.

Sinclair held them up; he could easily see through the material. "Maybe she wasn't so shy," he said aloud.

He kept digging through the lingerie, finding two marijuana cigarettes and a color photograph of Karen and a handsome young man. They were on a beach, tanned, arm in arm. The young man's left hand was on her buttock, inside her bikini.

Jake sniffed the marijuana. "Did you check her blood for drugs?"

Joanna nodded. "We found nothing."

Jake handed the photo to her. "Do you recognize the man?"

Joanna studied the picture, then shook her head.

"It's not Bobby Hannah, is it?"

"No."

Jake pocketed the photo. He got down on his hands and knees and checked under the dresser and under the bed. He turned the mattress, found nothing. The night table contained nosedrops, Kleenex, and a paperback romance novel.

Jake grinned at Joanna. "Where's her jewelry?"

"Maybe she didn't keep anything here."

Jake pointed to the closet. "It's going to be in there. Everybody hides stuff in their closet."

Jake went back down on his knees with a grunt. He began sorting through rows of shoes and slippers. Behind them was a tennis racket and cans of balls. He opened the cans and examined them. Nothing. Near the corner of the closet was a box containing new Gucci loafers. He held them up, shook them. Out came a velvet bag. In it were a pair of half-carat diamond earrings, a gold necklace, a diamond and sapphire bracelet. "Never fails," Jake muttered, putting the jewelry back in place.

Next he went through the clothes that were hanging—dresses, blouses, skirts, jackets. In the inner pocket of a sportscoat he found eighty dollars in twenties. "A treasure chest," he commented.

The top shelf was packed with sweaters, shirts, hats. Under a stack of cashmere sweaters there were two leather-bound volumes. The words "My Diary" were engraved in gold lettering on the front of each volume.

Jake quickly flipped through the pages, noting the dates. The diaries were for the past two years. "We're missing this year's edition," he said sourly.

Jake started another search, beginning in the bathroom, then heading back to the dresser, bed, mattress, and closet. He found nothing. He began a third go-around.

Joanna sat in the rocking chair and perused Karen's diary. Each day took up one side of a page. She wrote about what she had done, how she felt, what she wished for. Joanna read about a day in Karen's life from the year before.

May 16

I love him so much, but he seems almost afraid of me. It's like he doesn't want to get too close, become too involved. He sees it as a trap, a loss of his independence. I don't want his freedom. That's his main attraction. He's totally free. God, I wish I could be like that!

Isn't that crazy? I've got everything in the world, yet I want more. But my Aunt Beverly says that's an affliction all women have. They want more. I guess that makes me a woman.

Joanna closed the diary. She felt she was prying, reading the private thoughts of someone who never intended for anyone to see them. But then again, Joanna thought, Karen was a murder victim and every detail of her life would be carefully examined, all secrets uncovered. The one thing she strove for in life would be denied her in death—privacy.

"It ain't here," Jake said irritably.

"We'd better find it," Joanna said, getting to her feet. "These diaries will tell you more about the girl than a thousand witnesses."

"And maybe—just maybe—it'll tell us what the hell she was doing up on that roof." Jake looked around the room, glanced behind the mirror, checked the floor and walls for hiding places. "Where is that damned thing?"

"She might have taken it home," Joanna suggested. "You know, to her parents' house."

"I don't think so. Too personal." Jake reached for the diaries. "Did you find anything interesting in these books?"

"Not really. There's one passage from last year about a guy she was in love with."

"Bobby Hannah?"

"Probably. It sounded like him."

Jake looked at his watch. "Would Hannah be in surgery now?"

"I can find out." Joanna picked up the phone and dialed the operator at Memorial, who connected her to the department of surgery. She spoke briefly with the house-staff secretary and hung up. "Bobby Hannah left this morning to participate in a surgery workshop in Anaheim. He's not on call tonight, so he's not expected back until tomorrow morning."

Jake took out his notepad and jotted down the information. He glanced at the top of the page, where earlier he had scratched through the names of Mark and Sara Harrison, the researchers who had been in the BRI the night Karen was murdered. They had departed later that evening to attend a conference in San Diego. Instead of returning to Los Angeles as scheduled, they had crossed the border into Mexico for a holiday. Jake had reached them by phone at the hotel on Rosarita Beach. They had seen nothing unusual the night of Karen's death. No strangers, no nothing. Jake closed his notepad. "Let's go talk to the other roommate. I'll handle this part of it."

Downstairs, Peggy Collins was waiting for them. She was a wisp of a woman, just five feet tall, with short brown hair and a cute pixie face.

She was twenty-four years old, but she still had to show her ID in bars.

Marissa did the introductions. The women were perched on the edge of the couch, not relaxing against the back cushions. Joanna and Jake sat opposite them in chairs.

"Miss Collins," Jake began, "I understand you moved in about six weeks ago?"

"That's right." Peggy's voice was high, pleasantly toned.

"Did you get along well with Karen?"

"Oh, sure." Peggy smiled at her roommate. "She and Marissa are my two favorite people."

Jake nodded, noting that the girl spoke about Karen as if she were still alive. "Did you two do things together?"

"On our days off we'd go to the movies, shopping, things like that."

"How often did you do that?"

"Just occasionally. We had different work schedules."

"Was she happy the last few weeks?"

"She seemed that way to me." Who wouldn't be happy with all that money? Peggy asked herself. Millions and millions. Jesus!

"Was anything bothering her?"

"Not that I knew about." Peggy paused, little furrows appearing in her forehead. "There was one thing I remember."

Jake leaned forward. "What was that?"

"One of her contact lenses was giving her a lot of trouble."

Jake sighed and leaned back. "Was there anything major?"

"No."

"Do you know Dr. Abels?"

"Ugh!" Peggy squinched up her nose.

"Did he ask you out?"

"Once."

The dog started barking and raising hell out on the lawn and Sinclair waited for it to quiet down. He wondered how many women Abels had approached for dates. More than a thousand, he guessed. The little shit was probably playing the odds. Ask out enough women and eventually one of them will say yes. "And what happened?"

"I told him I was going with someone."

"Were you?"

"No."

Jake studied the girl. She was acting so nonchalant, unconcerned. "Where were you the night Karen was murdered?"

"At work," Peggy Collins said, her voice an octave higher.

"How did you find out she was murdered?"

"I heard about it at the hospital." Peggy wrapped her arms around her shoulders. "I didn't believe it at first. I guess I still don't."

"Can you think of any reason why someone would want to kill her?"

Peggy shook her head, shivering to herself.

"Was Karen frightened of anybody?"

Peggy's eyes widened. "There was one patient who gave her the jitters. He was a psychotic who believed he was God. He thought all nonvirgins should be sacrificed to cleanse the world."

Looney Tunes time, Jake thought. "Did he threaten her?"

"Not really. It was just scary the way he'd stare at her. He had one of those triangular faces that looked like the devil." And he was hairy and smelled bad and liked to expose himself, Peggy remembered.

"Was he a big man?"

"He wasn't that tall, but he had broad shoulders and was very strong. Even the attendants were kind of frightened of him."

"Because of his strength?"

Peggy nodded. "And because he once attacked one of them."

"What happened?" Jake leaned forward.

"He just grabbed an attendant and threw him across the room. Right out of the blue for no reason."

"Was the attendant hurt?"

"Just bruised."

Jake took out his notepad. "What's the patient's name?"

"Murray was his last name."

"Is he still at the Psychiatric Institute?"

"I'm not sure. He was supposed to be transferred to the state hospital at Camarillo."

Jake looked over at Marissa. "Did you know this patient?"

"Never heard of him."

Jake jotted down the patient's name and underlined it twice. His eyes went back to Marissa Shaw. "Did Karen take any trips during the last six months?"

"She went to Palm Springs on a few weekends," Marissa said. "Her family has a big house there."

"Did she go to any islands?"

Marissa lighted another cigarette, the smoke burning her already irritated throat. She had promised Karen never to mention her trip to Martinique. Karen had had such a great time, drinking and making love in the sun, forgetting for a brief moment that her last name was Rhodes. She had made Marissa swear never to tell. But what difference did it make now? "About three months ago she went to a Club Med in the Caribbean."

"Which one?"

"I think it was Martinique."

Joanna said, "Karen didn't seem like the Club Med type." *And she never told me about it*, Joanna thought.

"She wasn't," Marissa agreed. "But her shrink thought it would be good for her to get away and meet new faces."

"Did she enjoy it?" Joanna asked.

"She thought it was great," Marissa said and silently asked her dead friend to forgive her for breaking a sworn oath. *But I won't give them any details*, she promised, *only the bare outlines*. "You see, it was away from California and nobody knew anything about her or her family background."

"Did she meet anybody special there?" Joanna asked, thinking about the photo in her drawer.

"Some guy named Denny. I think he was from Florida." Marissa smiled to herself. His name was Jean-Claude and he was from Paris.

"Did she ever see him again?"

Marissa shook her head. "Karen wrote him a letter. He never answered."

"Did Karen keep a diary?" Jake asked, the leather-bound volumes on his lap.

"Religiously," Marissa said promptly.

"Every day?"

"Like clockwork."

"Did she ever let anyone read her diaries?"

"God, no!" Marissa smiled. "If someone came

within five feet of those things, she'd look at them strangely."

"How long had she been keeping a diary?"

"For years, she told me. She started when she was at some girls' school in Italy."

"So she was writing in it right up until the time of her death?"

"Absolutely."

"I found the volumes for the past two years," Jake said evenly. "But the book for this year is missing. Do you have any idea where it might be?"

Marissa and Peggy looked at each other. If a signal passed between them, Jake didn't see it. The women shook their heads.

Jake thought about searching the house, but that would require a warrant. "It's important," he said with gravity. "Where else could it be?"

"It should be here," Marissa said evenly. "I saw her writing in it a few nights ago."

"Where?"

"Upstairs in her bedroom. She liked to write in her rocking chair."

"I want you ladies to look for that diary." Jake handed each a card. "If you find it, call me."

"Should we search her room as well?" Marissa asked.

"Look everywhere." Jake stood and nodded to the nurses. "Thanks for your help."

Outside the air was dead still and even more humid. A small gray terrier was lying on the lawn, tongue out, breathing fifty times a minute. Next to him was an old shoe he had been playing with.

Jake bent down and offered his hand to the dog, then began scratching the terrier's stomach. "No hits, no runs, no errors."

"If only we could find that diary!"

"I wouldn't get my hopes up too high. Any other thoughts?"

"The psychotic would fit the bill," Joanna said.

"You think so, huh? Do you think they also let him out on a pass a couple of times so he could kill the other two women?" Jake stood and stretched his back. "You've got to remember that we're dealing with a serial killer."

"I'm aware of that."

"I'm not so sure." Jake brought his hands up to his temples. "It's like you've got on blinders. You keep focusing on Karen Rhodes and forgetting the other victims."

"That's because I knew Karen."

"I know," Jake said sympathetically. "For completeness sake, go ahead and check out the psychotic. Find out if and when they transferred him to Camarillo."

"There are a number of other things I need to discuss with you," Joanna said, thinking back to the gossip that Bobby Hannah and Karen liked to bite each other.

Jake checked his watch. "I've got to run. Maybe we could do it later . . . over dinner?"

Joanna studied Jake Sinclair's handsome features. His teeth were so white she wondered if he'd had them capped. "Is this going to be social or professional?"

"Both."

"I probably shouldn't," Joanna said, and immediately regretted saying it.

"Why not?"

"Because I try not to mix business and pleasure."

"Want to think about it?"

"Yes," she said softly.

As they walked to the car, the automatic sprinkler system went on. A hose started spraying water. The terrier barked, now angered, and dashed over to the hose. He stalked it for a minute, growling, then clamped it in his teeth, pulling and jerking. The predator finishing off its prey.

Jake watched. He had the uneasy feeling that he had overlooked something. Something obvious. And important. He kept his eyes on the terrier as he searched his mind, thinking back.

"By the way," Joanna said, "did those helicopter pilots see anything?"

"Nothing," Jake said, his concentration broken. He tried to reach for the thought again, but it was gone.

9

Joanna knew there was trouble the moment she walked into the dean's office. Simon Murdock was sitting on the edge of the desk, arms folded across his chest. In a wingback chair next to him was Arnold Weideman. Murdock rose as Joanna entered. Weideman didn't bother.

Murdock gestured to a chair and waited for Joanna to sit. "I'm afraid we have a bit of a problem, Joanna."

"More than a bit," Weideman added gruffly.

"This morning I received a call from Richard Abels," Murdock went on. "He was very upset about your rummaging through the research protocols in the library at the BRI. He feels it's a very serious matter and so do I."

"And so does Hugh Jackson," Weideman said. "He came to my office first thing this morning to complain of your behavior. I've been a friend of Hugh's for twenty years and he's the most even-tempered man I've ever known. But you've certainly managed to rile him up, Dr. Blalock. Congratulations."

"Wait a minute!" Joanna said defensively. "I didn't steal into that library and begin flipping through all the research protocols. I'd spoken with Julian Whitmore about his project and it was he who invited me into the library and showed me the protocol."

"He had no such authority," Weideman snapped.

"Of course he did," Joanna said promptly. "The research project belonged to him. He was listed as one of the principal investigators."

Weideman asked, "Do you know who the other principal investigator was?"

Joanna thought for a moment. "Richard Abels, I think."

"Correct. Did you obtain his approval as well?"

"No."

"Why not?"

"Because I didn't feel it was necessary."

"No, no. The reason you didn't ask Abels is that you knew he would not give you his permission."

Joanna clenched her jaw, trying to stay calm, but her cheeks began to color. "You can ask me any questions you wish, but don't answer them for me."

Weideman's face reddened. He turned away, shifting his considerable bulk. "And as a matter of common courtesy, Hugh Jackson's permission should have been obtained as well."

"Why?"

"Because he's the director of the BRI."

"I don't buy that," Joanna said evenly. "If someone wanted to review my research, I certainly would not expect that person to ask for *your* permission."

Weideman looked as if he were about to explode. His face reddened even more and was now punctuated with tiny spider veins on his jowls and his bulbous nose.

Simon Murdock quickly interceded. "Let's not say anything we'll regret later."

"Impertinent," Weideman muttered under his breath.

Joanna kept her face impassive, but screw you, she thought.

"Please, please," Murdock pleaded, gesturing for calm. He felt a stab of pain in his temples, the start of a migraine. "Excuse me for a moment while I take my medication."

He walked over to a wet bar at the far corner of the room and slowly poured a glass of water, taking as much time as possible. He needed to find a way to settle the dispute without causing too much damage. Joanna would have to be reprimanded to the satisfaction of the others, but not enough to upset her severely. All of the people involved were important to Memorial. Jackson and Abels were world-renowned scientists who brought fame and large amounts of grant money to Memorial. Joanna Blalock was a superior forensic pathologist and, although young, she was already making her mark. In addition, forensic pathologists were in short supply. Weideman was not really of much use now. He had done all he was going to do and would retire in another two years. But he had some very powerful friends. Murdock swallowed a tablet and sipped water.

"Are you all right, Simon?" Joanna asked from behind him.

"Yes, fine." Murdock walked back to the desk and sat in his swivel chair. He rocked gently, letting more time pass, allowing tempers to cool further. "I think we're dealing with a major misunderstanding here. Joanna felt she had acted properly by obtaining Julian Whitmore's permission before she reviewed the protocol. Others, including myself, feel that she should have asked for Abel's permission as well." Murdock nodded to Weideman, who nodded back his approval. "I don't think any great crime was committed. Nevertheless, research is very serious business and no one likes to see his work or ideas meddled with. And Joanna, you've meddled where you shouldn't have. That's why Hugh Jackson and Richard Abels were so upset—with some justification, I might add."

"With a lot of justification," Weideman grumbled.

Joanna held out her hands. "Am I to be led away in handcuffs?"

"That's not amusing," Murdock said.

"I'll tell you what's not amusing—to be brought in here and lectured to as if I were some student."

"That's how you've behaved," Weideman snapped.

Joanna glared at Weideman, detesting the man and his manners. She turned to Murdock. "Doesn't anyone care that Karen Rhodes was murdered at the Psychiatric Institute? Doesn't anyone give a damn? Or are we just going to be concerned with proper protocol?"

Murdock blinked rapidly. "Are you saying that some research at the Institute had something to do with Karen's death?"

"I don't know."

"So it's a wild goose chase?"

Joanna hesitated, trying to decide how much she should tell them. "No, it's not. Karen mentioned to me that something strange was going on at the Psychiatric Institute."

Murdock stiffened in his chair. "Like what? Give me particulars."

"Karen was murdered before she could give me any details."

"And, of course, if something was amiss, you were the only person Karen would confide in. Right? She wouldn't have come to me or to her grandfather, who happens to sit on our board of directors. Is that what you're saying?"

"I'm saying that something strange was going on at the Institute. That's all."

"You're also pointing a finger at a very fine institution and intimating that some of our staff may have been involved. Is that your intention?"

Joanna realized that she had now dug herself into a deep hole. She wished she had kept her mouth shut. "I'm not accusing anyone. I'm simply telling you what Karen told me. And the next day she was murdered. If you were in my place, wouldn't you want to know what that strange research was all about? I think so."

Murdock nervously strummed his fingers on the desktop. "Were the police informed of this?"

"Yes."

Murdock groaned audibly. "And what was their response?"

"You'll have to ask them."

"Unbelievable," Weideman hissed, pretending to be more upset than he was. Good, he kept thinking, she's putting the noose around her own neck. It'll make the hanging so much easier.

Murdock made a mental note to do quick damage control. He would ask the chief of police whether they took Joanna's story seriously. He hoped not. But if they did, he would have to tactfully smooth it over. And pray that it hadn't been leaked to the press. He looked over at Joanna, his expression impassive. She was very good, an asset to the faculty. But now he wondered if she were becoming a liability. Someone who might bring discredit to Memorial. Maybe Weideman was right—get rid of her before she caused real trouble. Murdock cleared his throat. "Did the police ask you to investigate the research protocols at the Institute?"

"They wanted as much background information on Karen as possible."

"I see." Murdock rubbed at his temples as his migraine worsened. He wondered how difficult it would be to find a replacement for Joanna. "I think it best that we leave all matters pertaining to Karen's murder up to the police. Under no circumstances do I want faculty used in their investigation, and that includes you, Joanna. Understood?"

"Yes."

"I will so inform the police." Murdock got to his feet. "I know you have a busy day, Joanna, so I won't keep you any longer."

Murdock waited for her to leave, then slammed his fist into an open palm. "God damn it!"

"Do you think that she'll keep her nose out of it?" Weideman asked.

"If she knows what's good for her, she will."

"I'm not so sure she does."

Murdock nodded and reached for the phone. "I'd better alert the people in the Institute."

Joanna trudged wearily into her apartment, slamming the door behind her. She sat down heavily in an overstuffed chair and lay back and kicked her shoes off. Slowly she stretched out, muscles aching, her joints creaking pleasantly.

"Joanna? Is that you?" Kate Blalock's voice came from the bathroom.

"It's me."

"I'll be out in a second."

Joanna waited for the noise of the shower to stop, then said, "Run a hot tub for me, would you?"

"My pleasure."

Joanna slumped into the soft chair and glanced down at the newspaper on the coffee table. The murder of Karen Rhodes was still a front-page story. The news media were having a field day, digging into every aspect of her past and her background. The latest revelation was that Karen's roommate at a posh girls' school in Italy had been dismissed for using marijuana. An unnamed source had indicated that Karen was also involved, yet had received no punishment. Joanna remembered the joint Sinclair had found in Karen's dresser and wondered how much it had cost the Rhodes family to buy off the Italians and hush things up. But all the Rhodeses' money and power could not quiet the media now. If anything, it would spur the bastards on.

Kate walked into the living room, still dripping water, a towel around her. "Guess what?"

"What?" Joanna smiled up at her younger sister. Physically they resembled each other so closely, yet in every other way they were so different, as if they had come from different generations.

"I met a gorgeous stockbroker who lives across the way."

"You don't waste any time, do you?"

"And he's got a friend who lives upstairs."

Joanna sighed wearily, knowing what was coming next. "I hope you didn't include me in your plans."

"Just for drinks."

"I'm really tired."

"Come on," Kate urged. "It might be fun."

"I've had a very long day and I've got to get an early start tomorrow."

Kate gave her sister a long, sharp look. "You're going to end up an old maid, aren't you?"

"No."

"Like hell! You're beautiful and you've got a great body. And you're so wrapped up in your work you don't leave time for men."

"Not true," Joanna said calmly.

"Come on. When's the last time you were serious with someone? Tell me."

"It's been a while."

"Like years, maybe?"

"All right, all right." Joanna held up her hands in mock surrender. "Invite your two new friends over for drinks."

"I already have. They'll be here in ten minutes."

"Christ!" Joanna growled, pushing herself up from the comfortable chair.

Joanna stopped in the bathroom to turn off the faucet and let the hot water run out of the tub, then went into her bedroom. She stripped off her clothes, throwing them into a corner, and began to select an outfit for the evening. Just drinks, Kate had said. But that will probably mean dinner out. She decided to keep it casual. Jeans, silk blouse, loafers. If her date didn't approve, too damn bad!

He could leave and she could return to her nice, hot tub.

Joanna snapped on a new bra and studied herself in the mirrored closet door. Her body was still damn good, slim and well proportioned, but there was some sag in her abdominal muscles that wasn't there a year ago. She turned and gazed at her profile in the mirror, sucking in her stomach to remove the small paunch. Not bad for a thirty-four-year-old broad. She smiled. ''An old maid, huh?'' Joanna said aloud. She was still smiling, but the thought bothered her. And with each passing year it bothered her more. She wanted marriage and children but rarely met men who measured up to her standards. And when she did, they were either married or intimidated by her brains. Except for one. Four years ago. A handsome, bright, adventuresome attorney whom she fell for like a ton of bricks. But two months into the relationship, Joanna discovered that he was hooked on cocaine—badly hooked. He chose the drug over her.

Her mind drifted to Jake Sinclair. Kate was right. He was a good-looking hunk. And probably a lot brighter than he wanted the world to know. For some reason, she remembered the way he walked. Soft, effortless steps, like a giant cat. Joanna shook her head. She couldn't envision herself next to a cop.

The doorbell sounded. Joanna turned away from the mirror and hurriedly dressed.

Minutes later she walked into the living room. Only one man was there. Kate introduced her to Will, the stockbroker. He was a slender man in his late twenties with curly brown hair, fashionably dressed in drab, ill-fitting clothes. Joanna smiled as he extended his hand and she saw the manicured nails and the Rolex watch.

"David should be here shortly," Will said to Joanna.

"Who's David?"

Will looked at her oddly. "Your date."

"Oh."

Kate took Will's arm. "Come on and help me mix the martinis. Your friend has exactly five minutes to get his buns down here."

"Sometimes he's a little forgetful," Will said somberly.

Great, Joanna groaned to herself. This should really be a fun evening.

She sat down in the overstuffed chair, resting her head back. Her ears tuned in on the conversation at the wet bar, where Kate and Will were discussing the proper amount of vermouth for the martinis. Next they talked about a musical group called Kool and the Gang and their latest release. Then they chatted excitedly about the fact that the Rolling Stones were planning one last tour before disbanding.

Joanna loved having her sister visit and the longer she stayed the better. Kate was the only real family Joanna had left. Their father had died years ago in an auto accident and their mother was institutionalized with Alzheimer's disease—now she was little more than a vegetable, recognizing no one. The once happy family life Joanna had known back in the Bay Area seemed so long ago, like a part of another world.

The doorbell rang. Joanna quickly got to her feet. "I'll get it."

She walked slowly to the door, making sure her

blouse was tucked in firmly and patting her hair in place.

Joanna opened the door and looked up into a pair of thick glasses. "You must be David."

He nodded, studying her intently. "Are you the pathologist?"

"I am."

"So much for preconceived notions."

"What did you expect?"

"A tough-looking woman wearing a blood-splattered apron."

"Are you disappointed?"

"Nah!" David's smile was huge and made her smile back.

Kate called out from the bar. "Eureka! I've made the perfect martini."

"I'd better check," David said gravely. "The younger generation don't know their elbows from their asses when it comes to martinis."

Joanna watched him move to the bar, where he tasted the mixture, deemed it superb; he came back with two long-stemmed glasses, handing one to Joanna.

"Your sister has two wonderful qualities. She's beautiful and she makes a damned good martini."

Joanna sipped her drink, nodding. "I take it that you hold those two qualities in high esteem?"

"They're near the top of my list. Just behind punctuality and virginity."

Joanna chuckled softly, studying David over the top of her glass. He was in his late thirties with long, unkempt brown hair that almost reached his shoulders. His corduroy coat was well worn and smelled of stale tobacco. With his thick glasses, Joanna thought he looked like an assistant professor at some junior college. But he obviously had a wonderful wit.

"Do you mind if we sit? I detest drinking while I'm standing."

"David," Kate called out, "we forgot the olives."

"I prefer lemon peels."

Joanna turned on the sofa, now looking at David's well-tanned complexion. On his neck was a healed, two-inch surgical scar. Probably a biopsy site, she guessed, for an enlarged lymph node.

"See anything interesting?" David asked, catching her stare.

"I was wondering where you got your tan," Joanna lied.

"On the Baja coast in Mexico."

"Do you go there often?"

"Once a year. That's where I go to do my first drafts."

"Are you a writer?"

"Yes." David finished his drink in a gulp. "Best martini I ever had. Can you make them as well as your sister?"

"Better." Joanna sipped her drink. It was good, not great. "What do you write?"

"Books."

"Fiction or nonfiction?"

"It's fiction, but there's some truth in it."

"I would guess you write mysteries."

"Nope."

"Horror stories?"

"In a way. But not about ghosts and witches."

"What kind of horror do you write about?"

"War."

"Have I read anything you've written?"

"Probably not."

The phone rang behind the wet bar. Kate picked it up, then called to Joanna. "It's Detective Sinclair, Sis."

"I'll take it on the other phone." Joanna excused herself and hurried into the bedroom, closing the door behind her. She sat on the edge of the bed and stared at the phone, wondering if Jake wanted to come up for another talk. Or maybe it was about that dinner date. She hoped for the latter.

Joanna picked up the receiver. "This is Dr. Blalock."

"Sinclair here. I'm down at the morgue and we need your help."

"What have you got?"

"A strangled woman."

"Was she pushed off a roof?"

"Probably shoved out of a window."

Christ, Joanna thought, another one! "Who's been assigned to the autopsy?"

"Nagura. He's just finishing up now and says there are things you ought to see."

Joanna nodded reluctantly. She didn't want to go to the damn morgue—not tonight. But she knew that important things got lost or misplaced after an autopsy was finished, particularly at the county morgue. In one case, she remembered, the body itself was lost. "I'm on my way."

She grabbed a leather jacket and her handbag and walked back into the living room. The men were debating whether to order take-out Chinese or go to a nearby Thai restaurant. Kate was opting for pizza.

"I'm afraid I've been called back to the hospital," Joanna said.

"Oh, no!" Kate groaned disappointedly. "How long will you be?"

"Too long."

David asked, "Can I walk you to your car?"

"Please don't bother. Enjoy your martinis."

Outside the night air had turned chilly with a light mist. Joanna zipped up her bomber jacket and hurried through the garden toward the parking area. She heard a sound in the bushes behind her and stopped to look. Seeing nothing in the shadows, she continued on her way.

Edward crouched low behind a thick hedge of shrubbery and watched Joanna walk into the garage. He smiled to himself, noting the bomber jacket and jeans she was wearing. So she plays at night.

Good.

So do I.

Forty-five minutes later, Joanna walked into the Los Angeles County Morgue. Its autopsy room was immense and well lighted, with a dozen dissecting tables arranged in rows of two. All the tables were scrubbed down and empty except for the one nearest the door, where Sinclair and Robert Nagura waited. There was a third man present whom Joanna didn't recognize. He was short and stocky with a raspy cough.

"Thanks for coming down, Doc," Jake said, then pointed to the stocky man. "I don't think you've met my partner, Lou Farelli."

Farelli nodded, watching Joanna peel off her leather jacket, her breasts pushing against the well-fitted silk blouse. Farelli forced himself to look away.

Joanna snapped on a pair of latex gloves and

took a magnifying glass from her handbag. "Give me a quick summary."

Sinclair looked down at the black prostitute, split wide open from pubis to sternum, her chest and abdominal cavities totally eviscerated. "She was a hooker who took a six-story fall night before last. The responding officers noted that she had bruises on her neck and was wearing brass knuckles. Foul play was suspected." He nodded to Robert Nagura, the acting coroner.

Nagura cleared his throat. "She had abrasions and black-and-blue marks over the anterior aspect of her neck. The larynx was completely crushed by some powerful force. There were freshly abraded areas on the fingers of the right hand— beneath the brass knuckles—indicating she put up a fight. Other than that, she had the usual trauma associated with a six-story fall."

Joanna looked down at the prostitute's hands. "Where are the brass knuckles?"

Nagura pointed to a small table nearby. Farelli reached over and picked up the plastic envelope containing the brass knuckles and handed them to Joanna.

Joanna held the brass knuckles under a light and carefully examined the weapon with a magnifying glass. The front of the knuckles was clean. But there was material embedded in the back, where the knuckles would have touched the prostitute's fingers. Joanna gently scraped the material from the knuckles onto a sheet of paper. "Get me a microscope."

Within a minute, a binocular Zeiss microscope was set up in the autopsy room and Joanna was intently studying the scrapings from the brass knuckles. "There's a small sliver of skin here."

Nagura asked, "Is it from the hooker?"

"I don't think so. The sliver is white and she was black." Joanna moved the slide on the microscope and increased the magnification. "There are two other materials present. One is black and looks synthetic, maybe from clothing. And the other—here's a big piece, a very big piece." She moved to a lower magnification and reached for a small set of tweezers. At length she said, "It's latex."

Sinclair moved in closer. "Can you put it all together?"

"I can guess."

"Then guess."

"Just one more thing." Joanna pushed away from the microscope and examined the hooker's fingers and hands, then searched diligently under the fingernails, finding nothing. Using her magnifying glass, she examined the knees and noted the fresh abrasions and the carpet fibers embedded in the skin. "I think the prostitute was on her knees when she was attacked. She fought like hell, using the hand with the brass knuckles. She made contact with the garment the killer was wearing, something black."

"A sweater?" Sinclair offered.

"I don't think so. The black material wasn't a fiber. Maybe plastic or leather. We'll know more after analysis. The prostitute also made contact with something the killer was wearing that was made out of latex."

"A condom?" Nagura guessed.

"Maybe, but I doubt it. It's too thick. A pair of latex gloves is more likely." Joanna thought for a moment, then nodded to herself. "The killer has her by the throat. She swings at his arm, hitting whatever garment the killer is wearing. Then she strikes his hand, ripping through the latex gloves and taking a silver of skin.''

Jake was thinking that latex gloves meant no fingerprints. But he'd still have to go over the whore's hotel room with a fine-tooth comb. Shit! There would be fingerprints in that room dating back thirty years. ''Is that sliver of skin going to help us?''

''Maybe, but I wouldn't bet on it.'' Joanna pulled her gloves off and discarded them. ''If there is enough tissue, we can do a DNA analysis that will stand up in court every bit as well as a matching fingerprint. The problem is that I don't think the sliver will be large enough to analyze.''

''But you'll try.''

''I'll try.''

Jake sighed resignedly. ''I wish to hell we had some kind of physical make on this guy.''

''We do. He's big, strong, and white, and he wears latex gloves when he kills. He also has a chipped central incisor.''

''But no face.''

''Not yet.''

Jake escorted Joanna back to her car. The temperature outside had dropped even lower, and now a light rain was falling. As they walked along a narrow sidewalk, their arms touched and rubbed. Both felt the electricity between them.

Jake stared at the front of Joanna's bomber jacket, fantasizing that she had nothing on underneath it.

''Are you going to ask me out to dinner, Jake?''

''I already did.''

''I mean, again.''

He smiled. "We'll do it this weekend. I'll call you."

"Why not tonight?"

Jake hesitated, just long enough to curse his compulsive behavior. "Because I've got to get to that flea-bitten hotel where the hooker was murdered. Maybe the night clerk remembers somebody. Maybe we'll get lucky."

"Something interesting happened at the hospital today."

"What?"

"I don't talk well on an empty stomach."

Jake grinned mischievously. He reached out and touched the tip of her nose with one finger. "Then it'll just have to wait."

10

"You'd better take your dinner break now," the charge nurse said.

"What?" Marissa Shaw looked up from the chart she was reading.

"You'd better take your dinner break now," the charge nurse said again. "They're going to stop serving in the cafeteria soon."

Marissa glanced at the wall clock and reached into a drawer for her purse. It was 7:30 P.M. and everything was quiet on the 6 East Ward of the Psychiatric Institute. Most of the patients were in bed; a few were in the solarium watching a giant television screen.

"You don't look well," the charge nurse said, studying Marissa's face. "Are you sick?"

Marissa shook her head. "Just tired."

"Are you still thinking about Karen?"

"I guess."

"Go get some dinner. You'll feel better."

Marissa took out a ring of keys and opened the door leading to the elevators. She closed the door behind her and waited for the lock to snap back into place. She smiled at the charge nurse through a Plexiglas window, then turned away. The smile quickly faded from her face.

The lobby of the Psychiatric Institute was

packed with staff and visiting psychiatrists. A volunteer at the front desk was handing out stick-on name tags for the visitors to place on their lapels. Marissa wove her way through the crowd, passing a big poster announcing that the evening's guest lecturer was a Nobel Laureate. She nodded to a security guard at the door and walked out onto the patio.

The sky was red and gray and blue, day turning into night. A full moon was rising.

Marissa sat on a low brick fence and nervously lit a cigarette. Her eyes went back to the crowd of psychiatrists in the lobby. They were all well dressed, obviously affluent, pleased—she knew—to be members of the prestigious clinical staff. *What would they do*, she wondered, *if they found out what was really going on in the Institute? What would they do if they had read Karen's diary? Nothing*, she decided. *They would hush it up, make believe it never happened, and go along their way. Just like I'm going to do.*

Marissa shook her head angrily, again feeling as if she had been betrayed. *Damn it, Karen! Why did you have to keep a diary? Why did you have to write about everything in your life? Why did you have to write about me? If anyone had read your diary it would have been so embarrassing for both of us. Nurses—you and me—involved in something so stupid and risky. Nurses, for chrissakes! And I didn't even know about it. But you did, and you wouldn't tell me. Why?*

Marissa dragged on a cigarette and nodded to herself. She knew why. Because Karen was too embarrassed, too afraid Marissa would talk about it and ruin Karen's precious family name.

Marissa shuddered, thinking about the embarrassment and humiliation she herself might have faced. Thank God that Joanna Blalock didn't see the diary! She would never have kept it quiet. She would have demanded a complete investigation.

The goddamned experiments! They were so dangerous and at times so uncontrollable. My God! They had experimented on humans in a way that no medical university would have allowed. Psychotics were used as guinea pigs. And so were some normal people.

Marissa wondered again if she had done the correct thing when she made the phone call and told him about the diary. Only hours ago she had discovered it under her bed with the dog's toothmarks all over it. Fudge had somehow gotten hold of it and dragged it into Marissa's bedroom to play with. Ten minutes after reading the diary she phoned him.

Marissa had expected him to be upset about the diary, but he wasn't. He calmly explained that the protocols for all experiments had been reviewed and approved by Memorial's Human Use Committee. He admitted the experiments had risks, but he suspected that Karen had exaggerated the dangers in her diary. Marissa still wasn't convinced, so he offered to meet with her and go over the diary, explaining what was done and why. They agreed to meet in his office at 11 o'clock tonight, after Marissa's shift was over. All of the research physicians involved in the experiments would attend the meeting.

Marissa looked at her watch, then quickly crushed out her cigarette and headed for the parking lot. The sky was now a dark blue with streaks of red from the setting sun. A few cars were still pulling into the lot, fewer yet were leaving. Marissa heard a sound behind her and quickly looked around. A woman got out of a car and hurried toward the Institute. Marissa walked on, finally reaching her five-year-old BMW. She climbed into the car and locked all the doors. After turning on the overhead light, she took the diary from the glove compartment and began reviewing it, marking those passages that concerned her most.

Four cars behind Marissa, Edward was crouched in the shadows next to a paneled truck. He was wearing a black leather jacket and latex gloves. His breathing was faster than usual, his heart thumping, as he came closer to the moment of the kill. He so enjoyed the Event, and his enjoyment would be even greater tonight because he planned to do her a little differently. He didn't want to kill another nurse—it was too dangerous. But he would change things just enough to confuse the police even more.

Edward kept his eyes focused on the light in the BMW. What the hell was she doing? Unlike his other outings, this Event was on a tight timetable. He had to do it before eight o'clock or not at all. Shit! Edward cursed silently. He was already behind schedule.

Marissa read the last entry in Karen's diary. She brushed a tear away as her mind drifted back to the last conversation she had had with Karen. They had just finished lunch at Nieman Marcus. Karen was stirring her coffee aimlessly, her thoughts obviously elsewhere.

"Is anything wrong?" Marissa had asked.
"Not really," Karen had said.
"Come on. What is it?"
"Just everyday things."

"Maybe you should get away for a while."

"Maybe." Karen had shrugged.

"Why don't you go back to a Club Med?" Marissa suggested. "It really did you a world of good last time."

"I'd just take my problems with me."

"What problems?"

Karen shrugged again. "Maybe you're right. Maybe I should go again."

"Maybe I'll come with you."

"Really?"

"Sure. Which one should we go to?"

"Let's try Cancun in Mexico."

"Great!"

"Margaritas and sunrise tequilas," Karen said dreamily.

"And Kaopectate," Marissa added.

They had laughed, good friend enjoying a light moment.

Ten hours later Karen was dead.

Marissa looked at her watch. It was almost eight and she had to return to the ward. She switched off the overhead light and closed her eyes to say a silent prayer for Karen. Marissa made the sign of the cross and climbed out of the BMW. Placing the diary on the roof, she leaned over to lock the car door.

The karate chop was perfectly placed. It caught Marissa high on the cervical spine, just below her head. She felt no pain. There was a flash of light, a sensation of falling, then blackness. She didn't feel the powerful hands tear through her uniform and rip her pantyhose apart. She was oblivious to the fingers that entered her vagina and rectum. Edward moved his fingers back and forth forcefully and roughly, making certain that red marks and abrasions would appear near the orifices.

He leaned over and licked her lips and breasts, trying to resist the overwhelming urge to bite into flesh. He wanted to taste her so badly. Edward moved down to her thigh and kissed the inner surface, nibbling ever so gently. His penis was throbbing now, an orgasm starting.

Quickly he took a thick rope from his pocket and placed it around her neck, then pulled with all of his strength, crushing her windpipe.

He held her to the ground, watching as she jerked and sucked for air.

Marissa's eyes opened and for a brief moment she was aware. She tried to struggle, but consciousness faded. Her brain, now depleted of oxygen, sent out a final barrage of impulses. Her arms and legs suddenly stiffened and convulsed, flapping against the pavement. Slowly, the muscles relaxed and then she was still. Absolutely still.

Edward kissed her lips softly, tasting her wonderful sweetness. Then he pushed her body underneath the car and walked away, the diary tucked under his arm.

11

David Rodman tried not to look at the corpse of Marissa Shaw, but his gaze kept drifting back to her face. She hadn't changed since he first met her three years ago. So pretty, so wonderful to be with. And now she was lying on an autopsy table, her torso split open from sternum to pubis, her organs eviscerated. Only her face seemed real.

Rodman turned his attention to the end of the table where Joanna Blalock was examining Marissa's lower extremities with a magnifying glass. For the third time. He wondered what was so important about Marissa's legs. On his examination, there was nothing remarkable except for the abrasions near the vagina.

Joanna straightened up and stretched her back, then extended the magnifying glass to Rodman. "Would you like to go over her again?"

"No. I'm ready."

"Good. Now describe the positive findings and using those findings construct a story that will tell us exactly what happened to Marissa Shaw last night."

Rodman approached the table and stood at an angle so he didn't have to look at Marissa's face. "The patient was strangled to death by a rope, probably made out of hemp or some similarly coarse material. I base this on the fact that the indentation made by the rope had irregular margins. Furthermore, there were numerous fibers embedded in the skin. The killer was probably very powerful in that the indentation marks were very deep and in places had totally abraded through the skin, rupturing small blood vessels and causing blood loss. The rope made a crisscross mark on the anterior aspect of the neck, indicating that the victim was attacked from the front. Thus, she may have known the killer."

"Maybe. But then again, maybe not."

Rodman wrinkled his brow, now unsure of himself. "Surely, she was strangled from the front."

"Yes. But was she initially attacked from the front?"

"I would assume so."

"Don't assume. Begin with the proposition that she could have been attacked from the front or from behind and then find evidence to tell you which is true."

Rodman's lips moved, but made no sound. He was thoroughly confused.

"Think back to the autopsy on Karen Rhodes," Joanna prompted him.

Rodman quickly moved to Marissa's head and lifted it, then swept her hair up, exposing the posterior neck. There was a distinct bruise mark at the base of the occiput. "A goddamn karate chop."

"Exactly. Now tell me what happened again."

Rodman stared into space as all the pieces of evidence began to fall into place. *Goddamn it*, he cursed himself. *When will I learn to think like Blalock, to be compulsive and meticulous and to accept the obvious as fact only when everything else has been excluded?* "Let me retract my earlier statement. She may or may not have known the killer. Marissa went to her car and stopped, maybe to reach for her keys."

"Her car key was in the door."

"Then she was probably unlocking her car door when he karate-chopped her from behind. Now, she's down, dazed for sure, maybe unconscious. He takes out the rope—no, no—he wouldn't do that yet. He starts to assault her sexually, then—"

"How can you be sure he sexually assaults her before he strangles her?"

"I can't. It's just a guess. But most sex murderers like to get their kicks before they kill the victim."

"Good," Joanna said approvingly. "Go on."

"He's very rough with her and that accounts for the abrasions around her vagina and rectum. Maybe he's a sadist. Who the hell knows? But he induces a lot of pain and she begins to resist, so he strangles her."

"How do you know she resisted?"

"Scrapes on her elbows."

Joanna gave him a thumbs-up sign. "You're getting there, Rodman. Slowly—I'll be the first to admit that. But you're definitely getting there."

David Rodman beamed.

The door to the autopsy room opened and Arnold Weideman entered, followed by Harry Crowe, the diener of the morgue.

Weideman skipped the usual amenities. "Have you finished the postmortem exam?"

"Not yet," Joanna said.

Weideman glanced at the eviscerated corpse,

then at the organs in stainless steel pans. "It looks to me as if you're very near completion."

"I'm not. It'll be at least an hour more."

"Then let me have your preliminary findings."

Joanna shook her head. "I can't do that. This is a coroner's case and I've been instructed not to release my findings to anyone."

Weideman's face colored, his neck veins bulged. "Now you look here, young lady. I'm meeting with Simon Murdock in fifteen minutes and I demand—"

Joanna held up a hand, palm out. "You can demand all you want. I won't release my report to you or anyone else until I'm authorized to do so by the appropriate authorities."

Weideman slammed his fist down on a metal table. An empty pan fell off and hit the tile floor, then rattled around loudly.

Joanna stiffened at the sudden noise, but willed herself to stare back at Weideman and not back down.

There was a long, awkward silence. Nobody moved.

Harry Crowe's eyes darted back and forth between Weideman and Joanna. Hesitantly, he took a step forward. "If you want to remove the corpse, Dr. Weideman, just tell me so. We can get the new pathologist to do the examination. Yes?"

Joanna's eyes widened. "What new pathologist?"

"That's not your concern," Weideman said tersely.

Harry Crowe wetted his lips. "You want me to remove the corpse?"

Joanna glared at the diener. "Harry, if you so much as touch the body, I'll call the police."

"That don't bother me none," Harry said, unfazed.

Joanna smiled thinly. "There's a big, tough cop out in the parking lot at this very moment. His name is Jake Sinclair. If you move the body, I'll call him. And believe me, Harry, he'll bother you plenty."

Harry looked up at Weideman, who gestured with his head. The diener backstepped to his earlier position.

Weideman said, "I'll expect a final report on this autopsy in one hour."

"I won't do it," Joanna said firmly. "If you want the findings, you'll have to obtain written authorization."

Weideman's face began to color again. "I hope you realize your days are numbered in this department."

Before Joanna could respond, Weideman spun around and stormed out of the autopsy room, Harry Crowe a step behind.

Rodman watched the swinging doors and waited until they became motionless. "What a bastard," he said quietly.

Joanna looked down at her tightly clenched hands and slowly relaxed them. Her nails had torn through the palms of the latex gloves. She stripped them off and reached for a new pair.

"Do you really think he'll try to push you out of the department?" Rodman asked.

"I'm not going to worry about it," Joanna said lightly, hiding her concern. Although Weideman was scheduled to retire in a year, he was still a very powerful man at Memorial. She wondered if Weideman had recruited a new forensic pathologist behind her back. That would be his style.

Joanna snapped on a new pair of latex gloves and with effort pushed Arnold Weideman out of her mind. She looked down at the rope marks on Marissa's neck. "So you're convinced she died by strangulation?"

"Absolutely."

"Did you find any clues that might tell us who did it?"

"Not really. The blood on her neck was probably Marissa's, but we'll have it typed out."

"Do you think she was killed by the same man who murdered Karen?"

"I think so, but I can't be sure. Both were strangled to death, but he used a rope on Marissa."

"Why a rope?"

Rodman shrugged. "Who knows? Maybe he hurt his thumb and couldn't do it barehanded."

Joanna nodded approvingly. She hadn't thought of that. Rodman really was blossoming into a forensic pathologist.

"Of course," Rodman went on, "if we could find a bite mark, there'd be no question as to who did it."

Joanna's eyelids narrowed. "I hope you haven't mentioned that bite mark on Karen to anyone."

"Not to a soul."

"Keep it that way. It's the killer's signature. If he's going to continue to kill young women, we want him to continue biting them."

"If it's his signature, how come he didn't bite Marissa?"

"He did. You just didn't see it."

Rodman sighed audibly and reached for the magnifying glass. He examined the soles of her feet and her heels, then the legs, knees and thighs, front and back. Approaching the groin he saw the abrasions leading to the vaginal area. A few scabs, some deep scratches. He continued up to her lower abdomen.

"You just missed it."

"Will I need a speculum to see it?"

"No."

He went back to the abrasions and focused in. Just lateral to the labia majora, he saw superficial teeth marks. Insane, Rodman thought, absolutely insane.

"What do you think?" Joanna asked.

"I think he left his calling card."

"Can we make a dental cast?"

"Probably not. The marks are very superficial."

"But we should try."

"Yeah. We should try." Rodman walked over to a small stool and sat down heavily, slumping up against the wall. He peeled off his gloves and let them fall to the floor. He tried to remember back to the last time he'd seen Marissa alive.

Joanna studied the pensive expression on his face. "What's wrong, David?"

Rodman glanced over at the body, then down at his gloves on the floor. "Marissa and I were once close."

"When was that?"

"When I was an intern. Three years ago."

"What kind of a person was she?"

David gestured with his hands. "Lively. Fun. Pretty. Honest as hell. Too honest."

"Did you two live together?"

"I wanted to, but she preferred the arrangement we had. At the time, I was on call thirty-six out of every forty-eight hours and she was working the three-to-eleven shift at the Psychiatric Institute. It was a strain just to see each other a few times a week. I thought it would be great to move in together, but she didn't think it would work."

"What finally happened to the relationship?"

David hesitated, now wishing he'd never started the conversation about Marissa.

"If it's none of my business, just say so."

David shrugged. "It doesn't really matter now, does it?"

Joanna remained silent.

"I thought we were a pair, Marissa and I. God knows I loved her at the time. The thought of marriage had even crossed my mind. Then one night I stopped by her place unexpectedly and saw her walking up the driveway, arm in arm with another man. I was crushed. It was like someone had kicked the wind out of me. The next day I confronted Marissa and I've got to tell you that I was furious as hell. She told me that she cared about me, but that she cared about someone else, too. She wasn't ready to settle down and she didn't want to be tied to one person. She wanted her independence. And that was the end of our relationship." And there were other things she had said, David reminisced to himself. Almost without emotion—like a woman reading off a shopping list—Marissa had told him that she was tired of doing the same things over and over, that she wanted more passion and adventure in her life. And then she smiled, telling him what a nice guy he was. David had walked away without saying anything, her words still stinging, his eyes misting up.

"You never talked to her again?"

"I thought about calling her a hundred times."

"But you never did?"

David shook his head. "I called once."

"And what happened?"

Rodman rubbed his temples, remembering the call and the pain that came with it. "A man answered the phone. I recognized his voice and hung up."

"Who was it?"

"Bobby Hannah."

Joanna blinked, but kept her expression even. "How long ago did you make that call?"

"Three years ago."

"And how long did the relationship between Marissa and Bobby last?"

"As far as I know, it never ended."

"I have trouble believing that."

"Why?"

"Because six months ago Bobby and Karen Rhodes had a very serious relationship."

Rodman smiled thinly. "You don't know Bobby Hannah very well, do you?"

The sunlight in the parking lot was so intense that Joanna had to shade her eyes with both hands. Uniformed policemen and plainclothes detectives seemed everywhere, scouring every foot of the roped-off lot. Marissa's BMW sat alone and off to one side, its doors, hood, and trunk opened. Jack Sinclair stood at the rear of the car, barking orders to a uniformed cop. He spotted Joanna in his peripheral vision and waved her over.

"You tell that television reporter to stay behind the tape," Jake was saying. "And if she crosses it again, I'm going to run her little buns out of here. You got that?"

"Yes, sir," the uniformed cop said.

"Then do it."

Joanna moved next to Jake, her back to the sun. "Any clues?"

"Nothing, nada," Jake said hoarsely. "The nurse comes to work at three and leaves for dinner at seven-thirty. Nobody notices anything unusual. The Institute is having a symposium in the auditorium and a couple of hundred people are there. Still nothing unusual. Marissa walks out to her car for who knows what reason. She gets wacked out and then pushed under the car. She doesn't come back from dinner and the staff gets worried. They search for her, even send a security officer to check her car. The security guy doesn't notice that the key is in the car door, doesn't look underneath the car. Nobody knows where she is. At 6:45 A.M. an orderly drives into the lot and parks next to Marissa's car. He sees her purse and reaches down for it. He spots the body. Like I said, nothing, nada. What about the autopsy?"

"The victim was definitely strangled, but this time with a rope."

"What kind of rope?"

"Coarse fiber, probably hemp or a similar material. Some of the fibers were obtained from her neck wound and are being analyzed now."

"A rope, huh?" Jake said, more to himself than to Joanna. For a moment he considered the possibility that there were two killers. No, he decided, it was the same guy. Too many similarities. "Why a rope on this one?"

"I can think of three possibilities. He changed his method either to amuse himself or to throw the police off. Or he somehow injured his thumbs and couldn't use them forcefully."

"What's the most likely reason?"

"Number two. He's trying to throw you off his trail."

"How do you figure that?"

Joanna's eyes narrowed as she thought back to the autopsy findings, to the deeply abraded areas around the vagina and rectum. *The killer left those marks for me to find. Clever bastard!* "The sexual assault was so crude and obvious. There were scratch marks and abrasions around the vagina and rectum that were meant to be noticed. And he took his usual nibble amid the abrasions, in an attempt—I think—to hide the teeth marks. My chief resident missed the bite mark and I can tell you he's very good."

But not nearly as good as you, Jake thought. "This guy—your chief resident—has been told to keep his mouth shut about the bites?"

"Oh, yes. And he will."

Sinclair looked up at the sky as a helicopter approached. His gaze went over to the roof from which Karen Rhodes was pushed, then down to Marissa Shaw's car. The killer had to be intimately familiar with Memorial, Jake was thinking. He had to know how to find his way to that rooftop and he also had to know that the parking area would be full of cars last night. Ordinarily that lot would have been deserted at 7:30 P.M. and the killer would have never tried anything in a lighted, empty parking area. No, no. He was too smart for that. He knew there was a lecture by a Nobel Laureate at eight o'clock and he knew the lot would be packed with cars, giving him damned good cover. Who is this wacko? A looney patient? Maybe a past or present employee gone mad? Jake reached for a cigarette and remembered that he'd stopped smoking two years ago.

The nicotine urge passed and he brought his concentration back to the killer. But he still couldn't put it all together. How did the three non-hospital victims and the murders of two nurses fit together? The only real common denominator was that all five victims had bite marks. The killer's signature. "The last thing we need is for the press to find out about the bites."

"To be honest, Jake, I don't think the killer could stop biting his victims even if he wanted to. A newspaper story wouldn't be much of a deterrent."

"Maybe. But I'll give you another reason to keep the biting away from the press. If it ever got out, we'd see a dozen copycat murders in a week. And I'm not just talking about the wackos either. Let me give you an example. A guy has been waiting five years to kill his wife so he can marry his girlfriend without dividing up the family assets. Well now, he says, as he reads the story in the newspaper. He then strangles his wife and bites her neck, chewing on it to mess up the teeth marks. We chalk it up to the serial killer and he dances off into the sunset with Miss Culver City."

"Everything is airtight on my end, but I can't guarantee you that something won't leak out of the department."

Jake squinted an eye. "I'm not following you."

"While I was performing the autopsy on Marissa, the chairman of my department came in and demanded that I give him my findings."

"What would he want them for?"

"Probably for some press conference. He loves the limelight, but unfortunately he has no grasp for what is important forensically. He'd happily tell the press everything, including the bite marks, if given the chance.''

Everybody wanted to be a hero and stand in the spotlight, Jake thought. Everybody but old cops who wanted things nice and quiet until they got their pensions. ''I hope you told him to shove off.''

''I did. But he is chairman of Pathology and I can't be sure he won't find a way to read my autopsy report.''

''What's his name?''

''Arnold Weideman.''

''I'll take care of it for you.''

''How?''

''I'll talk to my friend, Mortimer Rhodes.''

Joanna stared at him incredulously. ''Your friend, Mortimer?''

''Yeah. The chief got tired of answering the old man's phone calls, so he appointed me to speak with Mortimer on a regular basis. We talk every day and I keep him informed of our progress or lack thereof. He's a pretty decent fellow and believe me when I tell you he won't take any crap from Weideman or anyone else at Memorial.''

''You're amazing, Jake,'' Joanna said and watched him smile and expose those gorgeous white teeth.

''I have my uses.''

''I never doubted that.'' Joanna smiled back at him and felt her face beginning to color. She brought a hand up to shade her eyes and cover the blush.

A uniformed cop ran up. ''Lieutenant, the press wants to know if you're going to make a statement,'' he said, breathing hard.

''Not now,'' Jake said, then glanced over at

Joanna. "How long did you think the rope he used was?"

"Approximately two and a half to three feet. And he broke the skin, so there's probably blood on it. If you find it, bag it without touching it."

Jake turned back to the uniformed cop. "Get a dozen men and check out all the storm drains and trash bins in a four-block radius. You're looking for a piece of rope made out of hemp. It probably has blood on it. If you find it, bag it without touching it."

The cop nodded firmly and hurried away.

Joanna said, "Even if you find the rope, I doubt that it will help very much."

"You never know. If there's some gooey blood on it, we might be able to pick up a fingerprint."

"But the killer wears latex gloves, remember?"

"Well, maybe he didn't wear gloves this time, since he used a rope rather than his bare hands."

"I wouldn't bet on that."

"Neither would I." Jake reached under his coat and adjusted his holster, touching the safety as always on his .38 police special, making certain it was on. "Have you got anything else for me?"

"A bunch of things. But it's going to take some time."

"You can tell me about them while we're driving over to Marissa's home. I want you to help me go through her belongings."

Jake changed lanes and turned off of Wilshire onto San Vicente Boulevard. "So Marissa was lying, huh?"

"Beyond any doubt," Joanna said.

"And your source is good?"

"Impeccable. He and Marissa were lovers three

years ago. He left when he found out that she was also seeing Bobby Hannah. So Marissa was lying when she told us that she began dating Bobby Hannah a year ago. And she lied when she told us that their relationship lasted only briefly. Of course, it's not the biggest lie in the world."

"It's big enough. If they lie about one thing, they'll lie about everything. Now we can't believe a damn thing she told us." Jake gazed out at the tree-lined boulevard with its wide, grassy center divider. The joggers were out in force, sleek in their multicolored warm-ups. He wondered if Karen and Marissa jogged so they would keep in shape and stay young forever. Although Jake never admitted it, he hated it when the murder victims were young. He figured that they'd never really had a chance with life. Children were the worst. Innocent and defenseless. Easy prey, their murderers the most vicious.

"Why would Marissa lie?" Joanna broke into his thoughts.

Jake shrugged. "Like I told you before, everybody lies. Presidents, mothers, friends. Everybody."

"But they usually have a reason."

"Like what?"

"Like I think Marissa had been seeing Bobby Hannah for the past three years, even when he was supposedly going with Karen."

"Do you think Karen knew?"

Joanna had asked herself the same question over and over again. How could Karen not have known? She wasn't that naive. Or was she? "Deep down she might have. But she'd never admit it to herself. Women are very good at deceiving themselves."

"What are you trying to say?"

"I think Marissa was lying to protect Bobby Hannah. I think she knew that Bobby and Karen were still sleeping together, right up to the time of Karen's murder."

Jake thought for a moment, trying to fit the pieces together. "You think Marissa lied because she believed that Bobby Hannah was somehow involved in Karen's murder?"

"I'm just guessing."

"Keep guessing," he urged.

"If I'm right, then maybe—just maybe—Marissa was killed because of something she knew. Or because of something she said."

"To Bobby Hannah?"

Joanna gestured with a hand. "Maybe."

"Do you have anything to back up that theory?"

"Suppose I told you that there was an interesting story circulating around Memorial, a story about Bobby Hannah and Karen getting their sexual kicks by biting each other?"

Jake turned his head slowly to Joanna. "How does this fellow spell his name?"

"H-a-n-n-a-h."

Jake pulled up to the curb outside the Brentwood home where Marissa had lived. As he and Joanna walked across the lawn, Jake could feel the neighbors' eyes looking at them from behind closed drapes. People were fascinated by murder—he knew that—but they were also repulsed by it and didn't want to get too close.

Peggy Collins met them at the door and led the way into the living room. Joanna and Jake sat on the couch, Peggy on a cushioned footstool across from them.

"This must be a terrible time for you," Joanna said softly.

Peggy nodded slowly. "It's like an awful nightmare that keeps going on and on."

"There are just a few questions Lieutenant Sinclair would like to ask you. Do you feel up to it?"

"I'll try." Peggy reached for a pack of cigarettes on the lamp table. "I hope you don't mind if I smoke."

"Not at all." Joanna watched the young nurse light a cigarette. There was a noticeable tremor in her hands and she looked like hell. Her cute pixie face was drawn and pale, her doelike eyes now bloodshot with dark rings beneath them.

Peggy inhaled deeply as she glanced nervously around the living room. "I've got to get out of this place. Everything here reminds me of death."

"Where will you go?"

"To San Diego, where my family lives."

"When do you plan to leave?"

"I'm going to clear out of this house today and spend the night at a girlfriend's apartment. Tomorrow morning I'll be on the San Diego Freeway heading south."

Jake took out his writing pad and obtained the address and phone number of the nurse's family in San Diego. He knew the neighborhood where her home was located. Nice, conservative, white. "That's not far from Mission Bay, is it?"

"Within walking distance. Have you been there?"

"A few times." Jake hated small talk, but the nurse was obviously tense and frightened and he wanted her to calm down. She would remember more that way. "You can get a good view of the whales passing by."

"I love to do that."

Jake nodded and smiled ever so slightly. The nurse nodded with him. "I need to ask you some questions. Just routine things."

"Okay."

"When did you see Marissa last?"

"Yesterday morning about eight o'clock. I'd just come home from the graveyard shift and we had some coffee together."

"Was anything bothering her?"

"Not that I could see."

"So she was in good spirits?"

"She seemed fine."

"What did you two talk about?"

Peggy hesitated, thinking back. "A guy I was dating. A surgical resident."

Joanna leaned forward. "Not Bobby Hannah?"

"No. He's a friend of Bobby's. His name is Don Dowling."

Joanna touched Peggy's arm reassuringly. "We don't mean to pry, but little things may be very important here. Things that seem unrelated to Marissa's death may be very helpful to the police. With that in mind, could you tell us in as much detail as possible about your last conversation with Marissa?"

Peggy used the end of her cigarette to light another. "I told Marissa that I hadn't heard from Don in over a week and I was concerned. She said not to worry about it, that surgical residents often behaved that way. I told her that I was really upset by his failure to call, so she said she'd ask Bobby about it."

"Bobby and Marissa were close friends, weren't they?"

"Sometimes I think they were more than just friends."

"Oh?"

Peggy nodded. "You know, the way they'd touch each other and laugh and talk about sex."

"Do you think they were sleeping together?"

Peggy inhaled deeply and slowly let the smoke out. She hated talking about the private lives of her former roommates. It was like rummaging through their personal effects. Her eyes scanned the living room with its polished oak furniture and bay window and fireplace. Once a cozy home, she thought. Now a house of death.

"Were they sleeping together?" Joanna asked again.

"Probably," Peggy said softly. "I remember the first time I saw Marissa and Bobby together in the cafeteria at the Institute. I had dinner with them and that's when they fixed me up with Don. Anyway, Marissa told me that if I was going to date a surgery resident, I better get used to meeting him in the linen closet or in the on-call room. Then Bobby said something like, 'If you're going to meet him in the on-call room, don't use the lower bunk. That one belongs to me and Marissa.' He said it like he was joking, but I knew he wasn't."

"When was this dinner?"

"About two months ago."

"Did Bobby ever come over to this house?"

"Not while I've been here."

"Did Karen know what was going on between Bobby and Marissa?"

"I don't think so," Peggy said evenly, but she thought otherwise.

Joanna leaned back and looked over at Jake. "Do you have any questions, Lieutenant?"

"Just a few," Jake said, waving a cloud of smoke away from his face. "What type of person is Bobby Hannah?"

"I don't know him well," Peggy said.

"Tell me what you do know."

"He can be funny and charming one moment and a real bastard the next."

"Does he have a temper?"

"I've never seen it, but Don says that Bobby has a real short fuse."

"Any fights, brawls, that kind of thing?"

"Not that I know about."

"One last question. You were telling us that surgery residents are on call a lot and have to meet their girlfriends in linen closets or in the on-call room. Right?"

"Right."

"Do they also meet in cars parked in the hospital lot?"

"God, yes! It's their favorite place."

Well, well, Jake thought, and maybe they do a little banging on the roof too. "We'd like to look through Marissa's things. Could you show us to her bedroom?"

Peggy led the way up the stairs and into a large, tastefully decorated bedroom. The furniture was French antique, the drapes linen and frilly, the bed canopied and covered with a large quilt. In the center of the bed lay Fudge, Marissa's terrier. The dog's eyes followed the trio as they entered the room, but her body remained motionless.

Peggy shook her head sadly. "Fudge hasn't moved since I got the phone call this morning. She knows something bad has happened."

Jake reached over and scratched the terrier's

ear. "Who is going to look after the dog when you leave?"

"I thought I'd take her with me to San Diego— if you think it's all right."

"It's a good idea. I think Fudge would enjoy watching the whales swim by."

Peggy smiled, nodding at the detective. "I'll be downstairs if you need me."

They searched the adjoining bathroom first. There were the usual cosmetics and body lotions as well as a variety of medicines, including birth control pills, tranquilizers, and pain relievers. On the way out, Jake picked up the bathroom scale and checked out its underside. Slowly he pried out a small cellophane envelope containing a white powder. He sniffed it, then tasted it with a wetted finger. He gave Joanna a sour look before flushing the cocaine down the toilet.

In the bedroom, Fudge's eyes followed Jake as he got down on hands and knees to look beneath the bed. He fished out a well-chewed slipper and a cookbook that had also been gnawed on. There was nothing atop the canopy, nor was there anything of importance in the closet that was packed with clothes and shoes and shoe boxes. Jake did not find hidden jewelry or money, so he went over it again. He still came up empty.

Jake walked over to the dresser and watched Joanna close the top drawer. "Anything?"

"A birthday card from Bobby Hannah. It reads, 'I'll always love you. Bobby H.' "

"When was her last birthday?"

"Last month."

Jake reached for the card and pocketed it. "Anything else?"

"Some bills. Water company, credit card, gas. And a receipt for some Xeroxing."

"How recent is the Xerox bill?"

Joanna studied the date. "Yesterday."

"What was copied?"

"It doesn't say."

"How many pages?"

"Forty."

Sinclair wrinkled his brow in thought. "Something to do with work?"

"Maybe. But they've got plenty of copy machines at the Institute."

He studied the bill, noting the address. "We'll check it out. Maybe somebody will remember something."

Joanna's stomach made a loud, growling sound. Her cheeks colored slightly. "Forgive me. I'm afraid I skipped lunch today."

"So did I. Want to get a bite?"

Joanna hesitated. "I'm so backed up with work that—"

"Too busy for food, huh?"

Her stomach rumbled again. "Aw, hell! All right. But I'm telling you up front, Jake, I detest fast food."

"Even chili dogs?" he asked solemnly.

"Oh, Jesus!"

Sinclair glanced at his watch. "Can your stomach hold out for another hour?"

"Probably. Why?"

"I want to make a quick stop at Memorial and have a little chat with Bobby Hannah."

"He may be tied up in surgery."

"Well then, he'll just have to untie himself, won't he?"

Peggy showed them to the front door, then

closed and locked it behind them. She ran up the stairs at full speed, vowing not to spend a minute more than necessary in a house that reeked of death. Her two roommates murdered within a week of one another. Both nurses, like her. Maybe the looney who did it was outside now, waiting for darkness. She glanced out of the window and saw the setting sun. It would be night soon. *I'll be out of here before it gets dark,* she promised herself, *even if I have to come back for some things tomorrow.*

She dashed into a small storage room and found her large, battered suitcase. As she jerked it from under a pile of boxes, the handle snapped off. "Shit!" she hissed and disgustedly threw the handle down.

Peggy glanced over at Karen's suitcases that were made of rich dark leather and engraved with gold initials. Then she spotted Marissa's large Samsonite, dented and scuffed, but still serviceable. She carried it quickly into her bedroom and placed it on the bed, opening it. In the lining was a folded, sealed envelope. She ripped it open and saw the photocopied pages and immediately recognized Karen's handwriting.

Peggy sat on the floor and began to read.

12

Jake Sinclair leaned against the counter at the nurses' station, a phone nestled between his ear and shoulder, and waited for the police operator to patch him through to Lou Farelli. He flipped through his writing pad, reviewing what Marissa Shaw had said about Bobby Hannah and wondering what was truth and what was lie. If she was sleeping with him, Jake thought, then all bets were off and everything she said was worthless. He could still remember a cold-blooded, savage hitman who used to hang his victims up on meathooks, then beat them to death with a crowbar. The killer's girlfriend, who he kicked the hell out of regularly, swore under oath that he was warm and cuddly. A real teddy bear.

The automatic door to a nearby surgery suite suddenly opened and a gurney was pushed through. Jake glanced over at the patient—a frail old man with his mouth opened, eyes sunken and rolled back. He looked more dead than alive. They wheeled him into the outpatient surgery recovery room.

There was a burst of static on the phone, followed by Lou Farelli's voice. "What's up, Jake?"

"I want you to put two men in Marissa Shaw's house tonight. Tell them no TV, no lights."

"You figure he's going to try to ice the third roommate?"

"Maybe. The Collins girl probably won't be there when you arrive. She's spending the night at a friend's."

"How are we going to get in?"

"Use one of your special keys. Also tell the guys to bring along some dog biscuits. The girl's got a pet terrier that does nothing but bark and whine."

"Got you."

"Did the search of the hospital area turn up anything?"

"Nothing. No rope, no gloves. No nothing. Our killer is real clever, ain't he?"

"Naw. Just real looney." Jake hung up, nodding to himself. The murderer was behaving exactly the way the police shrinks said he would. The wacko would never leave a murder weapon behind. He'd save the bloody rope as a memento, something he could touch and stroke, something that would let him relive the thrill of the kill over and over again.

"Lieutenant!" Joanna called out and waved him over.

Jake waited for a gurney carrying a small child with a heavily bandaged arm to pass, then walked to the far end of the counter where Joanna was talking with a nurse.

"Dr. Hannah will meet us in the lounge," Joanna said. "The head nurse will make certain we're not disturbed."

"We appreciate your help," Jake said.

The nurse nodded to Jake, her expression much softer now that she knew he was investigating the Memorial murders. A shiver ran down her spine. She had known Marissa Shaw and had had a passing acquaintance with Karen Rhodes. Both now dead, murdered, their throats crushed. She shivered again and glanced at the wall clock. Five o'clock. *I'll be out of here by six*, she promised herself, *before it's dark. And even then, I'll still have one of the security guards escort me to my car.* She checked her handbag for the can of Mace and wished she was brave enough to buy a gun, as some of the nurses had done.

Halfway down the corridor, Jake and Joanna moved to one side, letting a gurney pass by. The patient's nose was heavily packed with cotton, but bright red blood was seeping through and around the wadding. The patient was gagging, red spittle coming out of his mouth.

"Jesus!" Jake said in a hushed voice. "I don't see how they can let these patients go home in a few hours."

"It looks a lot worse than it is," Joanna explained. "And it's been clearly proven that these patients recover every bit as well at home as they would in the hospital. These outpatient surgery centers are also very cost efficient."

"I see," Jake said, not seeing at all. *Cost efficient, my ass*, he was thinking. All that meant was that it cost less to do the procedure, but he'd be willing to bet a grand that the insurance companies didn't lower their premiums a nickel and that the hospital still managed to jack up their prices so they made a nice profit. Only the patient, as usual, got screwed, being sent home prematurely to suffer and not be looked after.

They walked into the doctors' lounge and closed the door behind them. Bobby Hannah was standing at the rear of the room, pouring coffee into a Styrofoam cup. He was wearing green surgical garb, his mask pulled down around his neck. The front of his scrub suit was soaked with perspiration.

"Can I pour you some coffee?" Hannah asked.

"No, thanks," Joanna said. "Bobby, this is Lieutenant Sinclair. He's investigating the murders at Memorial and would like to ask you some questions."

"Sure. Fire away," Hannah said easily. He strode over to an old leather couch and sat down heavily, propping his feet up on a badly scarred coffee table. "Please excuse my feet, but I've been on them for five hours straight."

"No problem," Jake said as he and Joanna sat in director chairs directly across from Hannah. Jake took out his writing pad and flipped pages until he found a clean one. "When was the last time you saw Karen Rhodes?"

Hannah sipped coffee noisily. "About three weeks ago. I ran into her in the cafeteria. We talked for a few minutes before I got beeped."

"What'd you talk about?"

"Nothing really. It was a 'Hey, how are you?' and 'Nice to see you' type conversation."

"Did she seem upset about anything?"

"No. She was her usual self."

Sinclair jotted down a note, reminding himself to have all hardware stores around Memorial checked out. Not too many people bought hemp rope these days, he figured, and if somebody did, the store owner might remember.

Joanna picked up the questioning. "Did you make plans to see her again?"

"Nope. It was over between us."

"What caused you two to break up?"

"We just grew apart," Hannah said, then shook

his head, annoyed with himself. "Naw, that's not the reason. The real problem was that Karen had changed. She became so damn serious and began to look into the deeper meaning of everything. It was like everything we did had to be psychoanalyzed, and, of course, she was the analyst. I just couldn't put up with it anymore."

"Did you ever talk with her about it?"

"A dozen times," Hannah said promptly. "But she always had the same answers. Surgeons, she felt, were so egotistical that they couldn't see beyond their own images. But psychiatrists—well now—they were like the gods on Mount Olympus." Hannah flicked his wrist disgustedly. "The real change in Karen occurred when she became involved in those damn research studies at the BRI. That's when she really changed."

"You think the studies affected her?"

"Who the hell knows?" Hannah sipped the last of his coffee, then crumpled the styrofoam cup. "Everybody over there is weird. The psychiatrists are all nutty and the other people who work over there are either crazy to begin with or become that way after they've been over there for a while. I think it's something in the air they breathe. If you work over there long enough, you'll end up with a psychiatric diagnosis."

Jake leaned forward, interested. "Is that a fact or just your opinion?"

Hannah gestured with his hands noncommittally.

"His opinion," Joanna said quickly, but she knew there was a modicum of truth in Hannah's statement. Psychiatrists had a higher rate of suicide and mental illness than any other group in the medical profession. But that didn't mean that all psychiatrists were crazy, and it surely didn't mean that psychiatry somehow caused mental illness.

Jake shifted around in his seat, briefly studying Bobby Hannah. The doctor had a stocky build with broad shoulders and well-muscled arms. He had a triangular face with thinning blond hair and ice-blue eyes. Jake could understand why women found Bobby Hannah attractive. "Did you and Karen ever meet on the roof of the Psychiatric Institute?"

"No way! Why in the world would I want to go up there?"

"Did you ever meet her in your car in the parking lot or in the doctors' on-call room?"

Hannah thought for a moment, then grinned sheepishly. "In the parking lot once or twice."

"Did you two used to bite one another?"

Hannah's eyes flashed angrily. "No! Hell, no! Where did you get that from?"

Jake ignored the question. "Never?"

Hannah shrugged his shoulders. "We might have bitten one another's lips. Nothing beyond that."

"You sure?" Jake watched Hannah concentrating and wondered what he was thinking and whether he was trying to concoct a lie. So stupid to try that. Even the pros eventually screwed up when they attempted to string lies together. And this boy wasn't a pro. "Yes or no?" Jake persisted.

"We may have nibbled on one another, but nothing—"

"Where? Arms? Stomach? Neck?"

"Ar—arms," Hannah said hesitantly.

"Never on the neck?"

"Never. That would show, and neither of us wanted that."

Sinclair nodded at the logic. Hannah and the nurse were in the public eye. The last thing they wanted was a love bite on the neck for their patients and colleagues to see. "Do you remember where you were between eleven and eleven forty-five the night Karen was murdered?"

Bobby Hannah sighed sadly. "I was on call in the hospital. When I heard the news I ran to the ER. But they had already pronounced her."

"Did you talk with anyone in the ER?"

"Luther."

Sinclair jotted a note in his writing pad, then glanced over at Joanna. "Do you have any questions?"

Joanna asked, "Bobby, can you think of any reason why Karen would go to the rooftop of the Psychiatric Institute?"

"At eleven-thirty at night? God, no!"

"Were you on call last night?"

"No. I returned from Anaheim in the late afternoon and made rounds quickly. I left here about six o'clock last night and didn't return until this morning."

"When did you learn about Marissa's murder?"

"I heard a—" Hannah's voice broke and he cleared his throat. "I heard about it in the OR this morning."

Joanna thought back to Marissa's bedroom and the birthday card from Bobby Hannah. "Were you close with Marissa?"

"Yes, but that was in the past too. But we stayed good friends."

"When did you see her last?"

"Three or four weeks ago. I took her to dinner for her birthday."

"Did you send her a card?"

Hannah nodded sadly. "Yeah. She loved those damn things."

The door opened and a nurse looked in. "Dr. Hannah, we're ready for the herniorhaphy in Four."

With effort Hannah got to his feet. "Will you need me any further?"

"No. Not for now." Jake watched him leave and waited for the door to close, then turned to Joanna. "What do you think?"

"Bobby Hannah and Marissa were more than just good friends. I'm certain they were lovers."

"Why?"

"Remember the birthday card Bobby sent to Marissa?"

"Sure." Sinclair reached in his coat pocket and took out the card.

"Read it."

"I'll always love you. Bobby H."

"That's not something you write to a good friend, is it?"

Sinclair sighed wearily. "Why in the hell would he lie about that?"

Joanna smiled sweetly. "Everybody lies. Presidents, mothers, friends. Everybody."

Jake smiled back at her. "There may be hope for you yet."

Joanna could feel her stomach rumbling. "Jake, I'm starving."

"We're almost there."

They had just left the freeway and entered San Pedro, a small coastal town at the southern edge of Los Angeles County. It was 8:30 P.M. and a light, chilly rain was falling. The streets were deserted.

Joanna studied the neighborhood as they drove through it. The area was mainly downscale with pizza shops, minimarts, and gas stations. All closed. Up ahead she saw a boarded-up store with graffiti spray-painted on the door, and next to it the rubble of a demolished building.

They turned into a narrow street and stopped in front of a small white building with no distinguishing features except for a neon sign that spelled out "Mandrakis" in fancy script.

"Here?" Joanna asked, giving Jake a peculiar look.

"Here," he said, and opened the door.

The restaurant was much larger than it seemed from the outside. There were thirty small tables covered with red-checkered tablecloths and arranged in a horseshoe around a hardwood dance floor. At the far end was a bandstand. The musicians sat on the edge of the stage, smoking cigarettes. Joanna couldn't spot the kitchen, but the air was filled with spicy, exotic aromas.

A heavyset man with a protuberant abdomen and black hair that was streaked with gray limped over to them. He stopped in front of Sinclair and stared at him. "You've been away too long, Jake. Too long. Shame on you."

Jake nodded guiltily.

The heavyset man grabbed Jake in a bearhug, patting his back. "You come more often, you son of a bitch."

With effort Jake managed to disengage. "Joanna Blalock, meet Dimitri Mandrakis."

Joanna extended her hand. Dimitri bowed, kissing it, his eyes never leaving her face. "You're beautiful."

"Thank you." Joanna blushed.

Dimitri grinned at Sinclair. "She's too beautiful for you, Jake. Way out of your league."

"I know."

Dimitri led the way to a choice table next to the dance floor. He limped badly, favoring the left leg. Joanna studied his gait, noting that he was able to push off with his foot and flex his knee. She concluded that his problem was limited to the left hip and was probably traumatic in origin since he showed no evidence of generalized arthritis.

As they sat, Dimitri snapped his fingers and a waiter hurried over with a pitcher of retsina. Dimitri poured the cold wine, then toasted the couple with a long sentence spoken in Greek. Jake toasted him back with an equally long sentence in Greek. Both men raised their glasses to Joanna and said in unison, "Giassou."

Dimitri took out a pack of Greek cigarettes and offered them across the table to Joanna and Jake, who shook their heads. Dimitri lit up and inhaled deeply. "The world is going to hell. Nobody smokes or drinks anymore and the food tastes terrible." He sighed wearily. "And now they want everybody to eat oats. Goddamn oats! Horses eat oats."

Jake reached for a cigarette and lit it, inhaling, feeling the bite of strong Greek tobacco. It was the first one he'd had in two years. It tasted awful and great at the same time.

"Good," Dimitri approved. "You won't live as long, but you'll be a hell of a lot happier." He moved his chair in close and leaned across to Jake.

"Now, a little birdie told me you're working the 'Rooftop Strangler.' Right?"

"Right."

"This will be a tough one, Jake. Even for you. The cuckoos are always the worst because you can't predict them."

"Tell me about it."

"Not even close?"

Jake shrugged and poured more retsina.

"Well, if you find him, make sure you kill him. Don't take any chances. Just blow his goddamn head off."

The front door opened and a group of Greek sailors entered. Dimitri's face lit up. He knew that Greek-Americans held onto their culture and traditions tenaciously, more so than any other ethnic group in America. And the presence of boys from the old country would really liven things up. It would be like a homecoming. There would be great fun tonight. And great business.

"I must see to my new customers," Dimitri said, pushing himself up. "I'll send over the appetizers. After that, you're on your own."

Joanna watched him limp away, then turned to Jake. "He wasn't serious about you shooting the killer, was he?"

"Dead serious."

"I think it's best if you let the court decide his punishment."

"You tell that to Dimitri." Jake took a final drag from his cigarette and crushed it out in an ashtray. "Ten years ago, Dimitri was a homicide detective in the Metro Division. One night he's passing a mom-and-pop grocery store and sees a holdup in progress. He gets the drop on the guy and tells him to put the gun down. Some bleeding-heart customer at the back of the store yells out to Dimitri, 'Don't shoot him! He's dropping his gun.' In a flash, the stickup guy plugs the old lady behind the counter and makes his break out the back door. Dimitri runs him down, punches him out and puts on the cuffs. The guy is booked. Want to guess the end of the story?''

Joanna nodded quickly.

"They can't find the gun, the customer won't finger the stickup guy, the old lady dies, the stickup guy walks. And Dimitri is reprimanded for roughing up the suspect. Nice, huh?''

Joanna grimaced.

"That's not the end of the story. The punk wants revenge for being roughed up. Two months later, Dimitri is walking out of the station and the stickup guy is waiting for him with a semiautomatic. He puts two slugs into Dimitri's leg, then drops the weapon and surrenders, yelling that he's crazy. Dimitri's hip joint is shattered and he's retired on disability. And every step he takes for the rest of his life will cause him pain.''

"What happened to the stickup guy?''

"He's in some looney bin, trying to convince some simple-minded shrink to let him back into society.''

A waiter came to the table carrying a huge tray. He put down dish after dish of wonderful appetizers. Off to one side he placed a stack of large plates. He carefully refilled the glasses with retsina, then he smiled at Joanna and said something to her in Greek. Jake answered for her.

"What did he say?'' Joanna asked as the waiter disappeared from view.

"He said the eggplant was really good.''

"That's not what he said.''

"He said you looked like a goddess."

"And what did you reply?"

"I told him that he had good taste."

They hungrily went for the appetizers. The rice-stuffed grape leaves were the best, followed closely by the fried squid and souvlaki. Joanna bypassed the *gigantes*, huge kidney-shaped beans, and opted instead for the delicious cucumber salad. Then she went back for seconds on the grape leaves.

"Slow down," Jake warned. "There's a lot more to come."

"It's all so wonderful." She watched as he expertly took a piece of bread and swept it across the *taramasalata*. "How did you learn to speak Greek so well?"

"My ex-wife was Greek."

"Born in Greece?"

Jake nodded. "She was a stewardess for Olympic Airways."

"What happened?"

"To what?"

"The marriage," she said impatiently.

"It fell apart, like most things in life tend to do."

"There must have been a reason."

Jake stared out into space. "It was my fault, I guess. I was working twenty-hour days, coming home mostly to sleep and eat. I didn't try very hard." He picked up his glass and sipped the cold wine. "Yet she put up with me, hoping I'd change. Then she got pregnant and had a miscarriage. And while she was miscarrying, she was alone. I was out somewhere and couldn't be reached. That did it. She left and moved to Florida—married some developer in Tampa."

"Do you still think about her?"

"Not as much as I used to. I've got it down to once or twice a day now."

Joanna poked his chest with a finger. "You should have taken her here, to Dimitri's restaurant."

Jake smiled broadly. "She was the one who first took me to this damn place." Jake smiled broadly. "Eleni loved Dimitri. She could have come here every night." He sipped retsina and looked at Joanna mischievously. "I suspect once will be more than enough for you."

"Like hell," she said promptly, then laughed at herself.

"You know, when you stop using your brain, you have a hell of a good time."

"Do you think I'm inhibited?"

"No. It's just that you're too bright. People with big brains don't have much fun in life. They're always trying to think their way through things. They have trouble letting go."

"So I can have more fun if I become less intellectual?"

"Right. You've also got to be more physical."

Joanna made a face. "I'm not sure I believe that."

"Oh, sure you do. Like tonight when we were driving down here. You were a little uptight. But as soon as Dimitri kissed your hand, you began to melt, didn't you?"

"Yeah," she grinned.

"See? That was when your brain shut off and you got more physical."

Joanna nodded. "But I'm not sure that physical is the right word."

The musicians on stage picked up their instruments and music filled the room. The steel guitar began to blend in with the bouzoukis and tambourines. Two Greek sailors leaped onto the dance floor, feet shuffling, arms flailing gracefully. A third sailor joined in as they linked together, arms around each other's waists, and danced the dance of the Greeks.

The music grew louder and more intense. Joanna watched the lithe sailors as they moved effortlessly back and forth across the floor. She was mesmerized by the sensual sight and sound, her own body now moving rhythmically.

"Throw a plate," Jake whispered in her ear.

"What!"

"Throw a plate."

She picked up a large plate, not sure what to do next.

"Toss it like a Frisbee," Jake said.

She slipped it out and it shattered against the floor with a bang. The crashing sound sent electricity through her body.

"Do it again," Jake urged.

Joanna threw another plate, as did people at the adjoining tables. The sailors danced on, the music blared, plates smashed. The sounds were deafening, intoxicating.

The sailors came into the audience and looked over the women, searching for partners. One of them approached the table and held out his hand to Joanna.

"He wants you to dance," Jake said.

"I can't," Joanna said quickly.

"Sure you can."

"I don't know how."

"He'll show you." Jake gave the sailor instructions in Greek.

"Oh, Jesus!" Joanna moaned, getting to her feet.

"And don't forget to shut off your brain."

The music suddenly slowed and Joanna found herself in a row of young sailors, everyone linked together by arms around waists. The sailor showed her in slow motion how to do the dance step. And then again and again. He was very patient and waited until she had the basic step down pat. Then the music picked up and the dancers moved faster.

Joanna seemed to fly, her feet barely touching the floor. She felt strong arms around her and heard wonderful music filling her ears. She whirled back and forth, the audience now a blurred collage of colors. For a brief moment, Joanna's world disappeared.

Then there was applause. The sailor was kissing her hands and thanking her for the wonderful dance.

Joanna came back to the table and sat on Jake's lap, putting her arms around his neck. "You were right."

"About what?"

"About shutting off the brain."

"Want to make a dash for it?" Jake asked.

Joanna looked up at the sky. "We're going to get soaked."

They were standing near the mailboxes in the apartment complex where Joanna lived. A heavy rain was pouring down, causing large puddles to form along the cement pathway.

"I say we make a dash for it," Jake said.

"I think we should wait."

Jake reached for a Greek cigarette and lit it. The

taste was wonderful, but Jake cursed himself, vowing to throw the pack away in the morning. He didn't want to get hooked on nicotine and then have to go through the hell of quitting all over again.

"I didn't know you smoked."

"Only when I can get my hands on Greek cigarettes."

"And how often is that?"

"Whenever I see Dimitri."

The cigarette's aroma made Joanna think of the wonderful Greek music and dancing sailors.

"Do you really think of your ex-wife every day?"

"Naw. I was just making conversation," he lied.

The rain suddenly slackened. Jake flipped his cigarette away and grabbed Joanna's hand. They ran through the puddles, laughing, water splashing up into their shoes. They were at the door when a hard, driving downpour started again. Joanna fumbled endlessly through her purse until she found her keys. They finally stepped inside, soaked through to the skin.

Jake pulled off his clothes in the bathroom, then put on an old terrycloth robe that was four sizes too small. He walked into the living room and sat on some throw pillows in front of a blazing fireplace. He ran a hand through his hair and flicked droplets of water at the fire. The logs hissed and cracked loudly.

"Brandy or Scotch?" Joanna called out from the wet bar.

"Brandy."

She came over and handed Jake a large snifter. She was wearing a pale-blue silk robe that buttoned down the front. Her feet were bare, her hair combed straight back, accentuating her fine features. She sat on a pillow next to him, legs extended, ankles crossed.

"I loved tonight," she said, sipping brandy. "I haven't had this much fun in a very long time."

"It was the best."

They sipped their drinks in silence as the fire roared. A log split in two from the heat. Outside, a loud clap of thunder rattled the walls.

Joanna rested her head on his shoulder. "We're so different, Jake."

"I know."

"Like night and day."

He put a finger under her chin, lifting her head, and softly kissed her lips. "Like night and day."

She kissed him back, running her tongue along his lips. "This is never going to work."

"It'll never work." Jake began unbuttoning the front of her silk robe. Her skin was flawless, not even a freckle.

"You haven't heard a word I said, have you?"

"Joanna, do me a favor," Jake said quietly.

"What?"

"Shut your brain off."

Joanna smiled as he pulled her down on top of him.

13

"Where the hell is Dr. Blalock?" Simon Murdock barked into the intercom.

"She hasn't gotten to her office yet, sir."

"It's 10:20 A.M., goddamn it!"

"Yes, sir."

"Did you try her home?"

"I got her answering machine."

"Does her office know I wish to see her?"

"I told them that she's to report here as soon as she arrives in the hospital."

Murdock switched off the intercom and began pacing back and forth, his fists clenched so tightly that his knuckles were white. He spotted a recently arrived journal on his desk and hurried over. Murdock angrily picked up *The New England Journal of Medicine* and threw it across the room, its pages fluttering like a wounded duck. Then he kicked an empty wastebasket and sent it flying into the wall.

Murdock began to pace again, trying to gain control of his temper. I should have stepped down two years ago when I had the chance, he thought miserably. The board of directors at Memorial had suggested he give up the deanship and become chairman of the board. A distinguished professor of medicine at Stanford had been secretly contacted and had agreed to become the new dean if the position were offered. It would have been a perfect move for Murdock. More power, more money. But no, I wanted to stay on here as dean and complete my task. I wasn't satisfied that Memorial was considered on a par with Harvard and Johns Hopkins. I wanted Memorial to be better, to be the best.

And now everything had turned sour. Because some maniac was running around killing nurses, Memorial had a stigma that would be very difficult to remove. Recruitment of staff and faculty would become more difficult, patient referrals would dry up, benefactors would silently fade away. Nobody wanted to be associated with murder.

The best I can do for now is damage control, Murdock told himself. And I can't even begin to do that without first talking to Joanna Blalock. He glanced at the calendar on his desk. In two hours, he was scheduled to meet with the press. He needed to know all the particulars in the murder of Marissa Shaw. Otherwise the news media would eat him alive.

The phone on his desk rang. It was his private line, the number known to only a select few.

''Yes?''

''Blalock is on her way to your office,'' Arnold Weideman said.

''Good.''

''You might be interested to know why we couldn't reach her yesterday afternoon. According to my chief resident, she accompanied that police detective to look through Marissa Shaw's belongings.''

''Thank you, Arnold.'' Murdock placed the

phone down. He took several deep breaths, willing himself to remain calm. He looked out the window and studied the blue sky, the air still clean from last night's rain. "Congratulations, young lady. You've just become more of a liability than an asset. Much more."

Murdock picked up the magazine he'd thrown across the room and smoothed it out before placing it on a small table. He retrieved the wastebasket and put it beside his desk, turning it so that only he could see the big dent his kick had caused. He quickly straightened his tie. A sharp pain stabbed at his temple, then disappeared. Murdock reached in his desk drawer and took out two propanolol tablets. He swallowed them without water.

Moments later, Joanna Blalock entered his office.

"Have a seat, Joanna." Murdock watched her sit and briefly studied her. Her face seemed a bit puffy around the eyes, her hair not as carefully groomed as usual. "I hope this is not the time you customarily arrive at your office."

"I'm afraid I overslept."

"It happens." Murdock gestured with a hand, now watching the blinking buttons on his phone. "I know you're quite busy, so I'll try not to take up too much of your time."

Joanna nodded carefully. Her head was aching, her throat raw, her mind dulled. Too many brandies, she thought miserably.

"I need information, Joanna. In particular, I need to know everything about Marissa Shaw's death. And don't give me the same crap you gave Weideman about secrecy and confidentiality."

Joanna rubbed at her eyes, trying to clear her

brain. Murdock had caught her completely off guard. "It's not crap. There are some things that only the police should be aware of—and you know it."

"Give me an example," Murdock snapped.

Joanna tried to buy time. She felt as if her brain and tongue were not connected. She pointed to a small table that held a coffee maker and Styrofoam cups. "May I?"

Murdock was on his feet. "Black?"

"Yes, thank you."

Murdock poured the coffee and handed the steaming cup to her.

Joanna sipped the hot coffee and felt the caffeine speeding into her system. "I'm not going to give you anything specific about Marissa's murder."

"Well, let me see if I can help you. Why don't we talk about the rope?"

Joanna stiffened in her chair, all senses now alerted. "How did you learn about the rope?"

"Through a very devious mechanism. My secretary told me," Murdock said humorlessly. "When she left work yesterday, she spotted some policemen crawling into the sewers, complaining about the fact that they had to find a piece of rope several feet long. Of course, the press eventually heard about it, too. I learned about it from my secretary this morning. But only after I received a number of phone calls regarding the rope—which I knew absolutely nothing about."

"Jesus," Joanna groaned.

"And I've got to attend a press conference in two hours and I'll be goddamned if I'm going to allow myself to be embarrassed again. The press will not know things I don't. I can assure you that will not happen.''

"Simon, it's unfortunate that occurred, but you have to understand my position.''

The veins in Murdock's neck bulged. "I'm not the least bit interested in your position. I'm interested in the findings at autopsy. And I'll have them before I stand up in front of those hyenas. Is that clear?''

"You won't get them from me.''

"Oh, yes, I will.''

The two locked eyes, neither blinking, neither backing down. Outside a siren sounded in the distance, then disappeared, replaced by the put-put noise of a landing helicopter.

Murdock decided to ease off. He'd pushed her too hard. He knew that Joanna could be as stubborn and strong willed as any man, and he didn't want to waste time in a test of wills. And besides, some information was better than none. "Let's try for the middle ground, shall we?''

Joanna remained silent.

"Everyone knows about the rope. There's no secret to that.''

Joanna moved her head ambiguously.

"Was there anything unusual about the rope?''

"Simon, I'm not going to discuss the murder weapon with you. So drop the subject.''

Murdock nodded. *Good,* he thought, *now I know for certain that the rope was used to strangle the nurse. Before I was just guessing, like everyone else.* "Did she put up a fight?''

Joanna hesitated, weighing the pros and cons of giving out that piece of information. "Probably. But I won't tell you why I think that.''

"There's a rumor circulating that she was sexually mutilated."

"Not true."

"Then I can assume that she wasn't sexually assaulted either?"

"I didn't say that."

Murdock nodded again. But she didn't deny it either. So, he concluded, the nurse was strangled by a rope and was sexually molested. "Are we any closer to finding the man who killed our nurses?"

"You'll have to ask the police."

"Of course." Murdock now had the answer to his final question. The evidence must have shown that the same man killed both nurses. "Would you care for more coffee?"

"Yes, thanks."

Murdock refilled her cup, then sat back in his swivel chair and rocked gently. "There's one other thing we must talk about. I have learned that you've again involved yourself in the police investigation of these murders."

"That's not true. I have not returned to the Psychiatric Institute, nor have I spoken with any of the staff."

"No, no. I was referring to yesterday afternoon, when you accompanied the detective in charge on some kind of search."

"Lieutenant Sinclair asked me to go with him to Marissa's house and help him sort through her belongings. I saw nothing wrong with that."

"Did I instruct you not to involve yourself in police matters without first going through this office?"

"But I thought—"

"Yes or no, Joanna?"

"Simon, you're pushing me right to the edge and I don't like it. You're not my lord and master and I don't have to account to you for my every action." Joanna gave him a long stare, then sipped more coffee. "Now allow me to answer your question without interruption. I was asked by Sinclair to assist him. I didn't volunteer. I was asked. And if the police again request my assistance, I will give it. If you don't approve, that's too bad."

"I'm not the only one who doesn't approve."

"Who else? Weideman?" Joanna waited for Murdock to answer before she continued. She watched his face color, his neck veins beginning to bulge. *Screw you*, she thought, and locked eyes with him once again. "I know how we can get around this impasse. Call a meeting of the board of directors and make certain Mortimer Rhodes is present. Then ask them whether faculty members should assist the police if they are requested to do so. I'll abide by their decision."

Murdock felt his blood pressure rising. With effort he calmed himself. "I think they would answer in the affirmative."

"So do I."

"But they would also want these extracurricular activities of our staff to be centrally coordinated. That way we wouldn't have faculty members snooping into places they shouldn't or offending colleagues by their unwarranted suspicions. And, of course, we could also make certain that our staff was performing all of their duties at Memorial before prancing around doing police work."

"Simon, I'm not interested in protocol. I'm interested in catching the man who killed my friend.

I'm interested in stopping a vicious murderer who is going to kill more women if he isn't caught.''

Murdock nodded. "So am I. We should do everything possible to bring about the capture of this killer.''

"Exactly."

"So I know you'll have no objection to our bringing in another forensic pathologist to give a second opinion.''

Joanna's jaw dropped. "A second opinion?"

"Yes. We wish to leave no stone unturned, to cover everything in detail again. If necessary, we'll even exhume the body of Karen Rhodes for reexamination.''

"May I ask who will give the second opinion?"

"Peter Kranauer. Do you know him?"

"Yes." Kranauer was an outstanding forensic pathologist, second in command at the University of Michigan. Joanna wondered if Kranauer would be used only as a consultant or if he was going to be offered a full-time position at Memorial. Then she remembered Harry Crowe's comment about the *new* pathologist. Joanna felt a sudden hollowness in her stomach. She knew there was no need for two forensic specialists at Memorial.

"I know you'll extend him every courtesy."

"Of course."

"Well," Murdock said, rising up, "I won't keep you any longer.''

Murdock watched Joanna leave. Too bad, he thought, she should have played it smarter, then she wouldn't have to leave. He wondered what would be the best mechanism to push her out of Memorial. There were several options, none easy. But if Kranauer were to uncover something Joanna had missed, something important—well then, that would simplify matters. Too bad, he thought again. Blalock had promise.

Joanna returned to her office and found Peggy Collins waiting for her. The young nurse looked like a teenager in her outfit of Nike tennis shoes, jeans, and T-shirt. She sat on the edge of a chair, fidgeting, obviously upset.

"What's wrong, Peggy?" Joanna asked, sitting beside her.

"I want out of this damn city," Peggy said angrily. "I want to get away from the coldness and the craziness and the nuts. I want out."

Joanna noticed that the nurse was grasping an envelope so tightly she was crushing it.

"I can't believe it," Peggy went on. "I just cannot believe it."

"Believe what?"

"On the way to your office I ran into Bobby Hannah. I told him how terrible I felt about what happened to Marissa and how upset I was. And you know what he did? He put his arm around my waist and squeezed and asked if I had any plans for tonight. He actually tried to make a move on me. It was as if Marissa had never existed. Can you believe it?"

"Maybe you misinterpreted the hug. Maybe he was trying to console you."

"Not when his hand slides down and squeezes my butt. I'm telling you, he has the sensitivity of a shark. When I mentioned Marissa's name to him, it was as if I were talking about a block of wood."

"He showed no emotion whatever?"

"Not until I told him that I knew what he and

Karen had been doing on the roof of the Psychiatric Institute.''

Joanna's eyes narrowed as she leaned closer. ''Tell me everything in detail. Don't leave anything out.''

''When I told him that I knew about them on the roof, he wasn't really upset. He kind of smirked, as if to say, 'Prove it!' '' Peggy held up a white envelope. ''Then I waved *this* in front of his face. I told him it was a copy of Karen's diary and in it was everything about them and what went on on the roof. Well, suddenly Dr. Bobby Hannah wasn't so smug and cocky. I think he was dying to take the envelope from me, but we were standing in the hall and there were a lot of people around. Otherwise, I'm certain he would have tried.''

''What happened next?''

''He wanted to see the pages, but I wouldn't let him touch them.'' Peggy grinned malevolently. ''I told him I was going to give the diary pages to you, and if he wanted to see them he should give you a call.'' She handed over the envelope.

Joanna quickly opened it and unfolded the photocopied pages. There was a total of six. She thought back to the receipt for Xerox copies that was on Marissa's dresser. Marissa had paid for forty copies, not six. ''Where did you find these?''

''In one of Marissa's suitcases,'' Peggy said, her face blushing. ''The handle on my suitcase was broken, so I was going to use Marissa's. I hope that was all right.''

''Absolutely. Where in the suitcase did you find these pages?''

''In the lining.''

''And you found only six pages, huh?''

"That was it."

"Did you look for more?"

"No. What was contained in those six pages was plenty for me." Peggy got to her feet and tucked in her T-shirt. "Please tell that detective not to bother me in San Diego. When I leave here today, I want to leave all this behind me."

"I'll tell him that."

"I also left the key to the house in that envelope. I didn't know what else to do with it."

"I'll take care of it."

Joanna waited for the nurse to leave, then began reading the diary pages. The initial two pages contained talk about friends and family. The next two were about Bobby Hannah and how sweet and considerate he was and how much she loved him and wanted to be with him. Then came the part about her activities on the roof of the Institute—

We met just after 11 P.M. on the roof of the Psychiatric Institute. The stars were out, twinkling like a million diamonds. We were alone ten stories up, on top of the world. We took the ME 38 and waited for the magic. Funny how the pills worked. They were invented as mood elevators, but they also had a powerful effect on the sex drive. Within ten minutes, we were both so horny we couldn't stand it. I felt like I was going to explode. We tore our clothes off and got on the lounge chair. I had one orgasm after another, each bigger and better than the one before. Then he was nibbling on my neck and shoulders. And then he did something new. He told me to let him know just before I climaxed. As I felt it coming, I told him and he grabbed my throat and squeezed. For a moment I couldn't get any air. Then he let go at the exact time I climaxed. God! It was a spectacular orgasm. It went on and on and on. The best ever. It's so good it's almost addicting. But I know it's not. I can go for days without taking the drug and there are no withdrawal symptoms. I could stop taking it any time I want. But who wants to stop?

Joanna picked up the phone and dialed Jake Sinclair's number. He wasn't in, so she left a message for him to return her call as soon as possible.

Ten minutes later, Joanna walked into Hugh Jackson's office in the BRI.

"Is Dr. Jackson in?"

The secretary looked up from her typewriter. "I'm afraid not. At the moment he's in the auditorium conducting a symposium. He should be back in fifteen minutes or so. Would you like to wait?"

"What's the topic of the symposium?"

The secretary shrugged. "It's one of those 'Frontiers of Medicine' things."

"I think I'll go listen in."

Joanna hurried down the hall, wanting to hear as much of the lecture as possible. Frontiers of Medicine was a series of talks that delved into the most advanced, cutting edges of medical research. Last month she had listened to a group of physiologists describe a synthetic polymer gel that contracted in response to electrical stimuli. It behaved as if it were a muscle fiber. The scientists were currently arranging strands of gel into a bundle that could function like a human muscle.

In the future they planned to incorporate the synthetic muscles into artificial limbs.

Joanna quietly entered the auditorium and found a seat at the rear. The room was packed with full-time faculty, visiting physicians, and house staff. Jackson stood at the podium. Abels and Whitmore were seated off to one side.

"In conclusion," Jackson was saying, "let me tell you that I believe we are entering the golden age of medicine. It will be the time of miracles. We can already see them. Surgeons now transplant kidneys, lungs, hearts, livers, and bone marrows on a routine basis. We are rapidly breaking the genetic code, understanding the location and functions of thousands of genes. The day is not far off when we shall be able to manipulate those genes and eradicate a long list of diseases, including muscular dystrophy, cystic fibrosis, sickle-cell anemia, and diabetes, as well as many types of cancer, heart disease, and arthritis. It is now clear that we shall be able to extend the human life span to well over a hundred years. And, if we wished, we will be able to create a world in which all newborns are destined to be big, bright, strong, and handsome. We shall be able to accomplish in one generation what it would take nature thousands of years to do."

Jackson paused to take a sip of water. The audience was on the edge of their seats. There was a dead silence. "And now, let us turn our attention to the mind, that wonderful and elusive structure. Shall we be able to regulate it and dominate it as well? The answer is yes, a most definite yes. The mind is directed by chemicals or neurotransmitters that control its every function. By manipulating these neurotransmitters, we can govern the mind. We do it now, every day. We have mood elevators to lift depression, tranquilizers to suppress anxiety. These are chemicals acting on other chemicals to control emotions. And we are now unraveling the molecular mechanisms by which these chemicals work. An excellent example of this was provided today by my colleagues, Doctors Abels and Whitmore. They described for you a transport protein that's intimately involved in depression. This protein can be blocked by amphetamines or cocaine, and that probably explains why these drugs can function as mood elevators. So, depressive behavior may depend on a single transport protein and the treatment of depression may depend on blocking that single protein. This, I believe, will hold true for most human emotions, most mental illness. When we fully understand these molecular mechanisms, we will be able to control the mind completely. And when will all this occur? Soon. Much sooner than you think. Let me end by saying to you again, this is truly the golden age of medicine.''

The audience rose to its feet, applauding loudly. Joanna hurried down the aisle, wondering how best to approach Hugh Jackson. He was probably still upset about the way she had snooped around the BRI. And the last thing she wanted was to upset him more, to precipitate another phone call to Weideman or Murdock. Her position at Memorial was tenuous enough already.

Joanna waited for Jackson to finish talking with a group of house staff, then walked over. ''That was a fascinating talk, Hugh.''

''Thanks, Joanna. I'm glad you enjoyed it.''

''I need to talk with you.''

"I'm afraid you picked a bad time. I'm already late for an executive committee meeting."

"It's really important."

Jackson gave her a long look. "Is it regarding the police investigation?"

"I have something I want you to read." Joanna looked over her shoulder, making certain no one was within hearing range. "It will explain why Karen was on the roof of the Institute the night she was killed."

Jackson's eyes narrowed. "Why do you want me to look at it?"

Joanna moved in closer, lowering her voice. "I want you to tell me about the drug she was taking."

"What drug?" Jackson asked quietly.

"Let's talk in your office."

"I can give you ten minutes, Joanna. No more." Jackson took long strides up the aisle, with Joanna almost running to keep up. In the hall, a group of visiting Japanese scientists hurried over, cameras strapped around their necks, tape recorders in their hands, on and running.

"Very excellent talk, Dr. Jackson," said the leader of the group. "Please allow me to introduce myself. I am Professor Hashimoto from Tokyo University." He bowed respectfully.

"It's a pleasure to meet you." Jackson bowed his head slightly, still walking toward his office.

"May I ask a question?"

"Of course."

"This transport protein which is so important in depression—have you determined its chemical structure?"

"Not yet."

"Have you reported this work?"

"In last month's *Nature.*"

The Japanese scientist sucked air through his teeth and bowed again. "Thank you very much, thank you very much."

As they walked on, Joanna asked, "Do you think they'll try to synthesize your transport protein?"

"Of course," Jackson said matter-of-factly. "They know that's where the money is. If you can synthesize the protein, you can learn how to block it and then you can invent a whole new class of drugs to treat depression." He looked back at the visiting group as they all changed the tapes in their recorders. "Japanese scientists are a peculiar breed."

"How so?"

"They're not always imaginative or innovative. But pointed in the right direction, they can do the world's best research."

They hurried into Hugh Jackson's office, closing the door behind them, then sat opposite each other in wingback chairs.

Joanna took the photocopied pages out of the envelope and handed them to Jackson. "These pages were copied from Karen Rhodes's diary. I'd like you to tell me everything you can about the drug she was taking."

Hugh Jackson put on his reading glasses and quickly read through the first four pages. Then he slowed as he reached the part describing Karen's escapades on the roof of the Institute. He reread the final two pages.

Joanna watched as Jackson let the pages slip from his hands onto his lap. His whole body seemed to sag. He shook his head sadly. "You try to do something worthwhile. You spend your entire professional life making things better for people. You devote all of your time to building an institute where the very best research will be done. And then, this happens. Everything is destroyed by a foolish young woman who wanted to enhance her sexual drive."

"Nobody will blame you. It certainly is not your fault or the fault of the BRI."

Jackson sighed wearily. "Joanna, an institute runs on its reputation. Nothing is more important. It is the reputation that attracts brilliant faculty and large research grants. If the reputation is damaged, faculty will leave and research grants will dry up. Our name is about to be badly tarnished."

Joanna felt a twinge of sympathy, but the future of the BRI was not her major concern. Poor Karen, she thought, as a picture of her dead friend flashed into her mind. "I take it that ME 38 was an experimental mood elevator."

"That's correct."

"With side effects of enhancing the sex drive."

"Apparently."

"You don't seem to be very familiar with the drug."

"That project belonged to Abels and Whitmore."

"I think we'd better talk with them as well."

Jackson went behind his desk and punched the intercom button, instructing his secretary to have Abels and Whitmore report to his office immediately.

Jackson slumped down in his chair, a forlorn expression on his face. "Is there any possibility that this story is a fabrication?"

"I don't think so, Hugh."

"Young women sometimes have very vivid sexual fantasies."

"She wasn't that young. And besides, her descriptions were too graphic, too explicit."

Jackson nodded disgustedly.

"I have to make one quick call." Joanna dialed her office to see if Jake had returned her phone call. He hadn't. She made a mental note to have him check through all of Marissa's belongings again. Thirty-four pages of the diary were still missing. Joanna leaned back in her chair and wondered why Marissa hadn't turned the diary over to the police. Probably to protect Bobby Hannah, she guessed. No, no, that wouldn't fit. If Marissa wanted to protect Bobby she would have destroyed the entire diary. But instead she made copies of selected passages. Why? What type of information was so important to Marissa that she not only had to copy it, but hide it away as well?

There was a sharp knock on the door and Abels and Whitmore walked in. Julian Whitmore smiled and waved to Joanna. Abels gave her a long, suspicious stare.

Jackson waited for them to sit on the couch. "Tell me about ME 38."

"It's an experimental mood elevator," Abels said promptly. "It was quite effective, but we had to give it up. Too many side effects."

"Such as?"

"Irritability, increased sex drive, rash, occasional nausea. In some cases, we saw aggressive behavior."

Joanna asked, "How aggressive?"

Abels looked at her, then at Jackson. "What the hell is she doing here?"

"Just tell her what she wants to know," Jackson said curtly.

Abels didn't answer at once. He could tell from Jackson's tone of voice and expression that there was trouble. Real trouble. Probably stirred up by that nosy bitch, Joanna Blalock. "I deserve a better answer than that," he said.

Joanna thought that Richard Abels looked even more unattractive than usual. "It seems that Karen Rhodes was taking ME 38."

Abels asked quickly, "Why was she taking the drug?"

"We'll get to that in a moment," Joanna said. "Please answer my question. How aggressive did the patients on the ME 38 become?"

"Some of them became combative. Several of the males got into fights, a few of the women into screaming bouts." Abels's photographic memory easily retrieved the data. He could have given Joanna specific information on the number of patients involved and the degree of their aggressiveness, but decided not to. Screw her.

"Nothing really violent?"

"Not that we're aware of."

"How frequently did this occur?"

"In approximately twenty percent of the patients."

"And the incidence of irritability?"

"About the same."

"What about the increased sexual drive?"

"That was the most common side effect. Almost half the patients exhibited it to one degree or another." Abels scratched at an armpit. "Why are you asking all these questions about ME 38?"

"Because Karen Rhodes was taking the drug to increase her sexual drive," Joanna said evenly.

"That's impossible!" Julian Whitmore blurted out.

"Why?"

"Because we haven't used that drug for months. And our supply of ME 38 is safely locked away in our medicine room."

"Who has the keys to the medicine room?"

"Just the senior physicians."

Joanna thought back to the time she was a resident in Psychiatry and had worked on drug trials. "But the nurses dispense the pills for all the drug trials, right?"

"Correct."

"How do they get the pills?"

"They have access to the medicine room, so they . . ." Whitmore stopped in midsentence as his voice trailed off.

"So Karen was in the medicine room quite a bit without anyone else in attendance?"

"Yes," Whitmore admitted softly.

Abels asked, "How do you know she was taking ME 38? Did you find it in her blood?"

"In her diary."

Abels and Whitmore looked at each other. If a message passed between them, Joanna didn't see it.

"Are you telling us that she was taking the drug to increase her sex drive and then writing about it in her diary?" Julian asked incredulously.

"In detail."

Abels leaned forward, a worried look on his face. "Don't tell me she was screwing patients. Don't tell me that."

"No patients were involved. She was meeting her lover on the roof of the Institute."

"Oh, great!" Abels said sarcastically. "Was she giving him the pills as well?"

"Yes."

Abels slumped back on the couch, throwing his hands up in despair. His career would be badly damaged by this nightmare. News of the scandal would race like wildfire through the academic community. Anything associated with the BRI, including himself, would be looked at with a jaundiced eye. And what about the recent offer of a professorship he'd received from Harvard? They'd now say forget it. Who needs this kind of trouble? they'd think. And they'd be right. "We're ruined, Hugh. We may as well pack our bags and look for another place to do research. As soon as this becomes common knowledge, they're going to run us out of town."

"Things do not look good," Jackson said grimly.

"Jesus! I can see it now on the front page of the *Times*: 'Psychiatric Institute a sexual hot spot. Nurses taking drugs to make them horny. Murdered nurse involved.' And on and on and on."

"Perhaps we could find a way to keep this quiet," Julian Whitmore suggested.

Abels shook his head. "You're dreaming. And they're going to uncover a lot more, too. I'll bet Karen Rhodes was into other drugs as well."

Jackson looked over at Joanna. "Does the diary talk about other drugs as well?"

"We only have six pages of her diary."

"Where's the rest?"

Joanna shrugged. "I don't know. These Xeroxed pages were found by Peggy Collins, a nurse who lived with Marissa and Karen."

Jackson strummed his fingers on the desk,

thinking. "Perhaps we could find a way to keep it quiet."

"I'll have to give these pages to the police," Joanna said quietly.

"Obviously. But they could be persuaded to keep them under wraps. And besides, they may wish to keep the diary confidential—particularly if they believe it relates to the murder of Karen Rhodes."

Abels squinted an eye skeptically. "It's bound to leak."

"Maybe not. The first thing is to control the number of people who know about the diary pages. Thus far, there are the four of us and the nurse." Jackson glanced over at Joanna. "Do you think this nurse will talk about the diary?"

"I doubt it. She's now left Los Angeles and has no plans to return."

"So there's only the four of us who know. Correct?"

"There's one other. The surgical resident who is mentioned in the diary."

Hugh Jackson picked up the pages and quickly scanned through them. "Are you referring to this Bobby she writes about?"

"Yes."

"What's his last name?"

"Hannah."

Jackson's jaw dropped. "Are you certain?"

"Positive."

Jackson pushed himself up from his swivel chair and walked over to the window. Outside the sky was blue, the sun bright. "Bobby Hannah is a patient of mine."

"What's his diagnosis?" Joanna asked, quickly covering her surprise.

''I can't divulge that, Joanna. But my advice is for you to talk with your detective friend and have him obtain a court order that will allow him to examine the boy's chart.''

''Is Bobby Hannah dangerous?''

Jackson took a deep breath and exhaled loudly. ''I would obtain that court order as quickly as possible.''

14

Edward made his move at the moment a drifting cloud blocked out the moonlight. He pounced up from a crouched position and ran across a cement pathway, ducking into shrubbery planted next to the building. Slowly he rose and looked through the bedroom window. Everything was dark. With ease he pried the sliding glass window off its track and removed it. As he placed it on the ground, he heard footsteps approaching. Edward quickly lowered himself back behind the shrubbery.

The footsteps came closer and closer. A young couple, arm in arm, chatting and laughing. A big dog on a leash. A black Doberman. The dog barked at the bushes, smelling the human but not seeing him. Edward took out his knife and waited.

"Come on, boy!" the young man said, pulling hard on the leash. The dog resisted and barked even louder, but his owner jerked him away and down the pathway.

Edward remained motionless until everything turned quiet again. Then he climbed through the window and into Joanna's bedroom. He paused and allowed his eyes to adjust to the darkness before snapping on a pair of latex gloves. Off to the right was a night table and telephone with its answering machine. Edward had called Joanna several times that evening and had gotten only the answering machine. He left no message. He had also checked her parking space in the garage, making certain she was not yet home.

Edward glanced into the bathroom, illuminated by moonlight streaking in through the window. Hanging over the bathtub were lacy panties and bras. He took them down and rubbed the silk against his face and nose. So fresh, so sweet. That's how Joanna would taste. Just thinking about her made his penis throb. Reluctantly he replaced the delicate lingerie and hurried into the living room.

There were things he had to do before Joanna arrived.

Joanna watched the mechanic at the all-night service station push himself from underneath her car. His hands were covered with grease and he had a silly grin on his face. Joanna knew the news was going to be bad.

"You've got a cracked axle," he reported.

"What does that mean?"

"Well, the axle is—"

"I know what the axle is. What I want you to tell me is how much will it cost to repair and how quickly does it have to be fixed."

"It's going to run you three or four hundred dollars, depending on the time involved. And as far as when you got to fix it—well, it'll hold for a while. But I wouldn't take any long trips if I was you."

Joanna sighed wearily, wondering where she was going to find four hundred extra dollars. She was barely squeezing by as it was. "It'll have to wait. Please check under the hood and fill the tank while I use your phone.''

She walked over to the pay phone and dialed her home, then punched in the number code that signaled her answering machine to relay its messages to her. There were several calls with no messages, just hang-ups. Joanna shook her head, not understanding why people were so intimidated by a machine. Then she heard Jake's voice. He'd gotten her message and tried to reach her at the hospital, but she'd already left. He'd call her again later.

Joanna replaced the receiver, her mind now drifting back to the night before. It was the best ever. The wonderful wine, the Greek food and dancing, and Jake. He'd surprised her in so many ways. Joanna smiled to herself, remembering what he had said about everybody having three faces—the one they showed the public, the one they showed their family, and a third that they kept secret in their heart of hearts. She had seen two of Jake's faces. She wondered what the third was like.

Joanna went back to her car. The mechanic had another silly grin on his face.

''More bad news?'' she asked.

''Your hood is fine, but your right front tire has got a slow leak.''

''What does that mean?''

''It'll cost you ten bucks to patch it. But it'll hold as is for a while.''

Joanna checked her watch. It was late and she was tired. ''Another time. I've got to run.''

Edward waited in the darkened living room. He had positioned himself against the far wall, away from the faint light that penetrated the closed drapes. Everything was quiet, so quiet that he could hear himself breathe. Edward wiggled his fingers in the latex gloves, making certain of a snug fit. In his mind, he again rehearsed the upcoming Event. Joanna would enter the apartment and leave the door open for light. He'd seen her do this a number of times while watching from the shrubbery outside. She would then walk to the lamp beside the sofa and lean over to switch it on. At that moment he would move quickly and apply a sharp karate chop to the back of her neck. Perhaps even a second blow to make certain she was well out. Then he would close the door and begin.

Edward took out his knife and tested its sharpness against a throw pillow. Its point easily penetrated the woven fabric, its blade slicing through the thick material with minimal resistance. The knife would be perfect for what he had in mind. This Event was going to be special, he promised himself, very special.

Outside, Edward heard the clicking sound of high heels approaching. Then he saw a feminine shadow pass in front of the drapes. He silently closed the switchblade and placed it in his pocket. Now she was fumbling with the keys, cursing under her breath. Then the door opened and he saw her profile. She walked over to the lamp and leaned over.

Edward catapulted out of the darkness.

Kate Blalock switched the lamp on and at the same instant saw the approaching shadow. She turned just as Edward's hand came down. The karate chop caught her high on the shoulder, knocking her to the floor, the lamp and small table falling with her. Instinctively, she kicked out with both feet and landed a glancing blow to his stomach. Kate was up on one knee when he swung again, hitting the top of her head and sending her flying toward the fireplace. Quickly he was on top of her, grabbing for her throat.

"Help!" Kate screamed at the top of her lungs.

Edward smashed her in the face, but Kate still managed to let out another loud shriek.

"Bitch!" he hissed, now gripping her by the hair and slamming her head against the slab floor. Kate felt warm fluid flowing down her face. Then a terrible pain. Then blackness.

Joanna was at the mailbox when she heard the screams. She ran toward her apartment and saw the opened door, the overturned lamp and table, the man on top of her sister slamming her head against the floor.

"Oh, God!" Joanna mumbled, paralyzed with fear.

She frantically looked around for a weapon, for anything to use. Her gaze went back to the overturned small table. She picked it up by its legs and swung with all of her might, catching the man on the upper arm and knocking him off Kate.

Joanna screamed loudly, then drew the table back for another swing. But the man was on his feet, charging at her, fists flailing. She felt a sharp pain high on her right temple and dropped to the floor, badly stunned.

Edward stared at Joanna, then at her sister, now realizing his mistake. He picked up a heavy stoker from the nearby fireplace. "Do it!" a voice inside his head commanded. "Do it! There's still time. Crush their heads!"

But outside Edward heard voices and footsteps

approaching, doors opening and closing, yells of "Call the police!"

He dropped the stoker and ran into the bedroom, locking the door behind him. Then he dove through the opened window and disappeared into the night.

Jake Sinclair hurried through the emergency room, dodging gurneys and wheelchairs, looking for the house staff office. He spotted the sign on a partially opened door and walked in.

Joanna was seated in a folding chair, her hands tightly clasped together, her hair disheveled. There was dried blood all over the front of her blouse.

"Are you all right?" Jake asked.

"I'm fine."

Jake got down on one knee and looked up at her face. "Are you sure?"

"Positive." Joanna managed a small smile, touched by Jake's concern.

He pulled up a chair next to her, then lit up an awful-smelling Greek cigarette.

"I thought you were going to quit today."

"Tomorrow."

"Liar."

"Yeah." He took a deep drag and exhaled slowly. "Do you feel up to talking about it?"

She nodded slowly, then took the cigarette from his hand and puffed without inhaling. "I was at the mailbox when I heard Kate screaming. I ran into the apartment and saw this man on top of her, slamming her head against the floor. I picked up a little table and hit him, then he hit back. The next thing I remember was a lot of people in the living room and blood pouring from Kate's head. Then the paramedics came . . .''

"The blood on you is from Kate?"

"Yes."

"Is she badly hurt?"

Joanna puffed on the cigarette and handed it back to Jake. "She still hasn't regained consciousness. There's a question of a skull fracture and maybe a subdural hematoma."

"A what?"

"A subdural hematoma. It's when blood collects between the skull and the brain."

"Is it serious?"

Joanna's lower lip began to quiver and she bit down, trying to stop it. Then tears filled her eyes and overflowed. She covered her face. "I'm so scared, Jake. She's all the family I've got left."

Jake put his arm around her shoulder and gently squeezed.

Joanna got to her feet and walked over to a table and grabbed a handful of Kleenex. She dabbed at her eyes, then blew her nose. "Enough of that!" she said, sounding much braver than she felt. "You're dying to know what I remember about the attacker, aren't you?"

"It can wait."

"No, it can't. Unfortunately, the light was poor, so I can't tell you very much. He was average size, and he was wearing a black leather jacket and a baseball cap."

Joanna paused for a moment, thinking back. "And his left upper arm probably has a hell of a bruise on it. That's where I hit him with the little table."

"That's it?"

"That's it."

"Didn't you see his face?"

"Not really. The bill of the baseball cap was pulled way down."

"Over his nose, huh?"

"I—I think so," Joanna said hesitantly. "I'm not being very helpful, am I?"

"You're doing fine." Jake walked over to a large sink and doused his cigarette. He decided not to push Joanna for the physical makeup of her attacker. He knew that victims frequently blocked out the faces of their assailants, sometimes temporarily, sometimes forever. It was the mind's way of coping, of trying to forget, a police shrink had told him once. "Did he have latex gloves on?"

Joanna shrugged. "It all happened so quickly, Jake."

"A baseball cap and a black leather jacket, huh?"

"Right."

"Well, at least he's a creature of habit. That's the outfit he wore the night he killed the hooker in Hollywood. The night clerk at the hotel said the guy was wearing a Los Angeles Dodgers cap. Did you see an emblem on the attacker's cap?"

Joanna tried to concentrate. She remembered the cap, but not its color, and couldn't recall whether there was an emblem on it. For a brief moment she saw the attacker's chin, but the image quickly faded. She forced her mind back to the baseball cap. "I'm not sure about the emblem."

"Well, I figure it's the same guy, don't you?"

"I think so. I also think he mistook Kate for me in the dim light. It was me he was trying to kill, not her."

"Why you?"

"Why the others?"

Jake got up and started pacing the room. "A baseball cap and a black leather jacket. That's not much to go on. We're not any closer to this guy than we were before."

"I'm not so sure about that."

Jake stopped in his tracks. "Oh?"

"Do you remember you once told me that a central question in this case was, 'What was Karen Rhodes doing on the roof of the Institute the night she was killed'?"

"I remember."

Joanna reached in her purse and took out the diary pages. "This will tell you why."

Jake quickly read the papers, then read them again. He kept his expression even, but inside he was boiling. The son of a bitching little surgeon was lying his ass off. Hannah was on that rooftop plenty of times, screwing Miss Goody Two-Shoes, and squeezing her windpipe for a little extra kick. Did he squeeze once too hard, too long? Did he try to cover the murder by throwing her body off the roof? Sinclair could barely wait to question the young surgeon again. "So she was banging Bobby Hannah on that roof?"

"So it seems."

"What's this ME 38?"

"It's a mood elevator that's used to treat depression. One of its side effects is increased sex drive."

"How'd she get the drug?"

"It was used in a drug trial that Karen was involved in. The drug had so many adverse reactions that it was eventually discarded." Joanna's eyes narrowed as she wondered if Marissa was also involved in the ME 38 drug trial. Maybe Marissa was also taking ME 38, and maybe, just maybe, she was involved in a twisted love triangle with Bobby and Karen. Joanna looked over at Jake, but decided not to say anything. First, she'd check with Julian Whitmore and see if Marissa was part of the ME 38 study.

Jake started pacing again. "Bobby Hannah keeps moving up on my list. Pretty soon, he's going to be at the top."

"There's more. Bobby Hannah is a psychiatric patient under the care of Hugh Jackson."

"Is he a real wacko?"

Joanna shrugged. "Jackson wouldn't divulge Hannah's diagnosis. But you can bet he has a big-time mental illness."

"Violent?" Jake was now thinking about Karen Rhodes's crushed throat and the distance her body was thrown in order to clear the fence around the rooftop. And he was also thinking about Bobby Hannah's well-muscled arms and shoulders.

"Maybe. Hugh advised me to tell you to get a court order so he can let us examine Bobby Hannah's chart. And he said for you not to waste any time getting that court order."

Jake took out his writing pad and began scribbling notes furiously. "How did you find the diary pages?"

"Peggy Collins discovered them in one of Marissa's suitcases. She brought them over to my office this morning. That's why I tried to reach you all day."

"How much of the diary did she find?"

"Just six pages. But I'm almost certain there's more."

''Why?''

''Remember that receipt for Xeroxing we found on Marissa's dresser? It was for forty pages, not six. And I'll give you odds that the reason Marissa used a private shop rather than making the copies in the Institute was because she was copying Karen's diary.''

''Clever bastard,'' Jake grumbled.

''Who? Bobby?''

''Maybe. Our killer. On my way over here, I was notified that Marissa Shaw's house had caught on fire earlier this evening. It burned to the ground. And they found kerosene everywhere. It's arson, sure as hell. Somebody torched that house and now we know why.''

''Just in case there were more hidden copies of the diary.''

''Exactly.'' Jake reminded himself to have all the banks checked and see if the Shaw girl had a safe-deposit box. There was also a small safe in the burned wreckage of her house yet to be opened. ''Now tell me, who else knew about the copies?''

''Hugh Jackson, Julian Whitmore, Richard Abels, and Bobby Hannah.''

Sinclair slapped his forehead with an opened hand. ''Christ! Why so many?''

''I had to tell Hugh, Abels, and Whitmore. It was their drug study and only they could give me all the details about ME 38. Peggy told Bobby Hannah when she ran into him at Memorial.''

Suddenly Joanna's face lost color. ''Oh, shit.''

''What?''

''Peggy told Bobby Hannah that she was going to give the diary pages to me and if he wanted them he could give me a call.''

"Cute. Real cute."

Joanna nervously patted her hair in place. "But it does narrow down the number of suspects, doesn't it? I mean, only five people knew about the Xeroxed diary pages."

"But those five could have told half the hospital before sundown. And then there's the possibility that Marissa talked to other people, too."

"Shit!"

"Yeah."

The door opened and a tall, thin man with sharp features and swept-back gray hair entered. He was wearing a long white coat with his name and department—Paul Schroeder, M.D., Neurosurgery—embroidered in script above the left breast pocket.

"Paul, this is Jake Sinclair. He's the detective assigned to this case," Joanna said.

Schroeder nodded. The beeper on his belt sounded and he pushed a button, silencing it. "I've got good news and bad news, Joanna. The good part is that there's no skull fracture and no evidence for intracranial bleeding. The MRI was absolutely negative. The bad news is that your sister remains poorly responsive. She may be even deeper than when she first arrived."

"But there's no permanent damage, right?"

"I can't be sure."

Joanna felt a streak of fear shoot through her body. "Maybe it's just a severe concussion that's going to last for a while."

"Maybe. But there's another possibility. She may have severe cortical contusions, and sometimes that results in permanent damage."

"Such as?"

"Speech impairment. Memory loss. Things of that sort."

"Or a coma from which she never awakens."

"That's very rare, Joanna. Very rare, indeed." Schroeder's beeper sounded again and he silenced it. "Now, let's not discuss some nightmare that will probably not occur."

Joanna felt a painful lump lodge in her throat, but she held back the tears. "So we just wait and watch."

"There's one other thing we can do. We can include your sister in an experimental study that may well help her. Of course, I'll need your consent."

"Tell me about it."

"We give large doses of corticosteroids intravenously to patients who have had severe trauma to the central nervous system. To be precise, we administer 250 mgm methyl prednisolone I.V. daily for three days. There's some evidence that the drug reduces the swelling and inflammation associated with the trauma. I'm certain you're aware that steroids have possible adverse side effects. But in your sister, I believe the benefits far outweigh the risks."

"Give it," Joanna said without hesitation.

"Good." Now, I'm having your sister admitted to the ICU, where we can monitor her carefully. I'd like you to go home and get some rest." Schroeder leaned over and touched the bruise on Joanna's temple. "And put some ice on that."

"I want to stay with Kate."

"You'll just be in the way. I'll be here all night and if there's any change, good or bad, I'll call you immediately."

Before Joanna could protest, Jake said, "I'll see that she gets home."

Schroeder reached for a phone and spoke with the operator, then hung up. "I've got to run."

"Are you headed for the ICU?" Jake asked.

"Yes."

"I'm going to send two uniformed officers with you. I want Kate protected around the clock."

"Why?" Joanna asked.

"Because she might be able to identify the guy who attacked her. And the attacker might know it."

"In her present condition, she can't describe anything," Schroeder said.

"But our killer doesn't know that, does he?"

The Crime Scene Unit was packing up their equipment when Joanna and Jake returned to her apartment. Jake saw his partner, Lou Farelli, standing by the wet bar and waved him over.

"What you got?"

Farelli chewed vigorously on a toothpick. "Well, let's start at the beginning. Our boy comes in through the bedroom window. It's one of those sliding types, easy as hell to pry off their tracks. They ought to have those things outlawed. Anyhow, he's in with no sweat. Then he looks through the drawers and closets. The guy is neat, not messy. Like he's searching, but he doesn't want us to know he's searching." Farelli glanced at Joanna's bruised temple, deciding she'd have a real lump there by morning. "Doc, when you feel up to it, you should do an inventory and let us know if anything is missing. Anyhow, he attacks the girl and does most of the damage over there by the fireplace, where you see the blood. Then he's surprised by the doc, gives her a punch, and makes his break through the bedroom window. On his way out, he steps in blood and leaves us some nice footprints on the carpet. And outside the window the ground was wet and soft, so he left us some more prints. The boys will do some measurements on the depth of his footprint and the length of his stride, then come up with the guy's approximate weight and height."

"Any witnesses?"

"Nada. Not a one." Farelli rubbed the stubble on his chin, thinking. "Oh yeah. Doc, was one of your throw pillows cut up?"

"No. They're almost new."

"Well then, our boy had a knife, a real sharp one. He was planning on doing more than a little punching tonight. And he used the pillow for practice."

Joanna shivered, thanking God that she hadn't let the mechanic fix her tire. If she'd been delayed just a few minutes, Kate would now be dead.

Farelli saw the head of the Crime Scene Unit leaving and called out to him. "Got a minute, Howie?"

Howie Moskowitz strode over, carrying a small suitcase. He was a thin, middle-aged man with hawklike features and penetrating dark eyes. "What?"

"Let the doc take a look at the pen."

Moskowitz opened his suitcase and took out a small plastic bag containing a gold pen. He held it up to Joanna. "This yours?"

"No. It doesn't belong to me or my sister."

"Good," Moskowitz said. "It's got a wonderful set of prints on it."

Farelli and the Crime Scene Unit hurried out of

the apartment en masse. It was after midnight and they still had a lot of work in front of them.

Jake closed the door behind them. "Want me to help straighten things up?"

"I'll do it." Joanna returned the small table to its original position, then placed the lamp on it. She spent a long time smoothing out the shade and making it stand upright. There was a small clot of blood attached to the bottom of the shade. Joanna went into the kitchen and returned with a cloth and a bottle of club soda. "Are you going to stay?"

"Yes."

Joanna leaned over and carefully cleaned the spot off the shade. It required all of her effort to keep her hands steady. "I'm frightened, Jake."

"I know."

"Suppose he comes back here?"

"He won't. He's not stupid."

"But suppose he does?"

"Then he'll have to get by the two cops outside and by me in the living room."

"Am I going to be protected twenty-four hours a day?"

"Yes."

"So you think he'll try again, don't you?"

"Not as long as there're cops around."

Joanna got down on her knees and poured club soda into the bloodstain on the carpet. She waited for it to fizzle and begin breaking down the hemoglobin, then gently wiped at the stain with a cloth. She found herself applying more and more pressure, trying to make Kate's blood disappear. She scrubbed harder and harder, as if removing the stain would make Kate better, would lift her out of the coma.

Joanna didn't hear herself crying or mumbling Kate's name.

Jake hurried over and helped her to her feet. "We'll take care of the stain in the morning."

"It'll be a lot more difficult to—"

Jake put his index finger on her lips. "I'll take care of it. Now I want you to get some sleep."

He watched her walk into the bedroom and close the door behind her. Then he heard her sobbing.

Jake took out a Greek cigarette and lit it, inhaling deeply. Well now, Mr. Killer, it's no longer professional between you and me, is it? Now it's personal, real personal.

Jake decided to take Dimitri's advice. When you find him, don't take any chances. Just blow his goddamn head off.

Good advice.

15

Joanna looked down at Kate and her heart sank. Kate appeared more dead than alive. Her skin had a peculiar greenish tint from the overhead fluorescent lighting in the ICU. And she wasn't moving. Not even a muscle twitched. The only sign of life was the sound of air flowing in and out the endotracheal tube.

Joanna wanted to touch Kate's hand, but she waited while Paul Schroeder completed his neurologic examination. "Why was she intubated?"

"Because she wasn't handling her secretions very well. The last thing we need is an aspiration pneumonia."

"She looks so awful."

"If anything, she's better. When we were putting the tube in, she resisted and moved all of her extremities. Then, about an hour ago, the nurse heard your sister mumbling. It sounded like she was saying, 'Kay-Girl.' "

Joanna touched Kate's forehead and moved a few strands of hair back in place. "That's what our father used to call her."

"Have you notified your parents?"

"I'm the only family she has left."

"Oh. Sorry." Schroeder was now testing Kate's reflexes. He ran the metal end of a reflex hammer over the sole of Kate's foot. Her big toe flexed. "Babinski's negative," he reported.

Joanna nodded. There was still no evidence of any structural damage to Kate's brain. Except for her unresponsiveness. "Are you planning any further tests?"

"I may repeat the MRI study if she doesn't improve."

"But you said she was getting better."

Schroeder looked down at Kate, his expression impassive. She should have shown more improvement by now. Much more, if all she had was cerebral contusions. "She is better, but she still has a long way to go."

"Maybe the methyl prednisolone will bring her out of it."

"Let's hope so."

Joanna left the ICU, saying a silent prayer. *Oh, God! Help her. Please let her recover.* And then Joanna felt guilty. The only time she spoke to God was when she needed Him.

She saw Jake leaning against the wall outside the visitors' lounge and waved to him.

He hurried over. "How's Kate?"

"A little better."

"Good. Is she awake?"

"Not yet."

"Well, hell, give her a little time."

Joanna shook her head sadly. "It's so tough when it's your own family, Jake. So tough."

"I know." He reached out and touched her shoulder with a finger. "Look, I can meet with Hugh Jackson by myself. You don't have to come along if you don't feel up to it."

"This is one of the few times you're really going

to need me. Psychiatric terminology can be very difficult, even for a physician.''

''You sure you feel up to it?''

''Let's go.''

They took the elevator down to the third floor and entered the glass-enclosed bridge that connected Memorial Hospital with the Psychiatric Institute. Outside, a helicopter was landing on the roof of a small adjacent building. It seemed so close that Jake felt as if he could reach out and almost touch the rotor blade. The noise of the engine caused the glass walls of the bridge to vibrate vigorously.

They walked into the Institute, the door automatically closing behind them. The deafening sound quickly faded away.

''Why did they build the landing pad so close to the bridge?'' Jake asked.

''They didn't mean to. First, they expanded the emergency room facilities by adding on a small building. That's the two-story structure next to the bridge. Later on, someone decided they needed a heliport, so they stuck it on the roof of the new building.''

''Good planning, huh?''

''Your tax dollars at work.''

The corridor of the BRI was deserted and very quiet. Jake noted that all the doors were closed. Everybody guarding their precious secrets, protecting them from the outside world. The doors were shut most of the time, he figured, and that's why Karen Rhodes and her boyfriend were never seen by anyone when they went to the roof for fun and games.

Hugh Jackson was waiting for them in his office. He offered them coffee, which they declined.

Then Jake handed him the court order granting permission to open Bobby Hannah's chart.

Jackson quickly reviewed the order and handed it back. "Where would you like to start?"

"How long have you been seeing Bobby Hannah as a patient?" Joanna asked.

"He came to see me about two years ago, shortly after he began his surgery residency."

"What was his diagnosis?"

"Bobby was referred to me by the chief of surgery because of difficulty controlling his temper. There had been a number of shouting and shoving episodes with some of his colleagues and coworkers. Bobby actually struck an intern during an argument, and that precipitated his referral to me. Obviously, he was displaying very aggressive behavior, even for a surgeon. In any event, when I first evaluated Bobby, I wasn't certain of the diagnosis. But as the past revealed itself, it became clear he was a borderline personality."

Jake leaned forward, his ears pricked. He had heard the term 'borderline personality' used before by police shrinks. But it was a long time ago, way back. He tried to remember the case, but couldn't. "I think I'd better get your definition of a borderline personality."

Joanna touched Jake's arm. "There is no simple definition. It's a personality disorder with a long list of characteristics. Let me explore it with Hugh for a moment and I think it will become clear to you."

"Right," Jake said, but he wrote down the words 'borderline personality' in his notepad.

Joanna turned back to Hugh Jackson. "You were saying that at first you weren't certain of the diagnosis."

"That's correct. When I first saw Bobby he was a very bright, talkative, persuasive young man. I would describe him as being charming, almost ingratiating, someone who you tended to like immediately. When asked about his temper tantrums, he had some very plausible reasons to explain them away. He told me about the great stress of being a surgery resident and how he had become upset with others because they had performed in a substandard fashion. And on and on. To be frank, he seemed quite normal at the time. But then that's how borderline personalities appear initially because they are notoriously good liars. They are very smooth and adept at lying because they've been doing it most of their lives. They lie, of course, to cover up their behavioral problems, and by doing so they obscure the true diagnosis."

Jackson took out his pipe and lit it, puffing softly. "His diagnosis became clear several months later when he had a transient psychotic episode while on holiday in his hometown. It was triggered by his estranged wife demanding a divorce. The psychiatrist caring for him called me and then everything came to light. You see, that psychiatrist had been looking after Bobby Hannah for years. When I found out the truth about Bobby's past, the diagnosis jumped up at me."

Jackson glanced at Jake Sinclair. "These patients are incredibly talented liars. They can fool everyone. Often it is only when the story of the patient is checked against that of a family member that it becomes clear that his present behavior has caused endless problems over the years."

Jake scribbled down another note. "So these temper tantrums were nothing new?"

"Exactly. There was no question in my mind that Bobby Hannah was a borderline personality. He met virtually every criterion needed to make that diagnosis."

"Could you list some of the other features of his illness?" Joanna asked.

"Surely. He'd been through one relationship after another, never able to sustain one beyond a period of weeks or a few months. There had been fights and brawls, always the fault of someone else, according to Bobby. At one time, there was a drug habit, mainly marijuana. And he'd been married twice before the age of twenty-five."

"Could you describe the psychotic break he had?" Joanna asked.

"Mainly paranoid delusions. It was transient, lasting only a few days."

"And the cause of his divorces?"

"The temper tantrums, the lying, the abusiveness. In brief, the obnoxious behavior."

Jake jotted down a note, reminding himself to see if Bobby Hannah had an arrest sheet. "How the hell do women marry these guys?"

"As I told you, Lieutenant, initially they're very charming people who seem to be full of action and fun. Those features entice women to marry them. But then, the other side appears."

"And the divorce proceedings start."

"Not always. Most women will run as if their lives depend on it. But there are a few who stay, who believe the lies, who tolerate the abuse, who make excuses for their husband's behavior."

"Why would they stay in something like that?" Jake asked incredulously.

Jackson gestured with his hands. "There are some things that even psychiatry can't answer."

Jake looked up at the ceiling, thinking aloud. "So, most of the time these borderline personalities act fairly normal. Right?"

"For the most part."

"When they're having their crazy spells, can they control it?"

"Only at times and only with great effort. For the most part, they act on impulse without really giving thought to the consequences."

"And when they're caught screwing up?"

"Then they start lying and making excuses to cover up their impulsive behavior."

"You'd think they'd learn how to control it?"

"In a capsule, that's the problem, Lieutenant. These people never learn from their past experiences. They have no insight into what they did or why they did it. And so they concoct wonderful lies in an effort to explain their behavior."

"Can they kill?"

"Anyone can kill."

"I'm talking about Bobby Hannah."

"It's possible."

"Possible or probable?"

Jackson slowly relit his pipe. "Do you recall that I told you Bobby Hannah was referred to me for aggressive behavior, for hitting an intern?"

"Yes."

"The blow knocked the intern backwards, causing him to trip and strike his head on the corner of a table. It required twenty-five stitches to close the wound." Jackson puffed gently, sending spirals of smoke upward. "Does that answer your question?"

"Yes, it does."

Joanna and Jake left Hugh Jackson's office with a copy of Bobby Hannah's psychiatric file. They rode the elevator down with a group of research technicians, so they remained silent until they were walking across the enclosed bridge back to Memorial.

Jake flipped through the pages of Hannah's chart, making certain the copies were legible. "I'll give this to the police shrinks so they can go over it and give us their opinion. Is there anything in particular they should focus in on?"

Joanna nodded. "Bobby's hometown psychiatrist. He's the one who will know the most about Bobby's past behavioral problems."

"Behavioral problems?" Jake forced a laugh. "That's kind of understating it, don't you think?"

"It's just a psychiatric term."

They came to the automatic door and waited for it to open, then walked on.

"Let me ask you something, Joanna. How the hell do they let a nut like this guy become a doctor?"

"Medical schools don't require a psychiatric evaluation before they accept a student."

"But wouldn't they want to know something about his health?"

"Oh, sure. So the student goes to his family doctor, who happily fills out the form. The doctor probably doesn't even know the student is seeing a psychiatrist."

"But wouldn't the family doc know about his crazy behavior?"

"Not necessarily. And even if he did, the doctor may simply think that the student is a little wild or immature."

"So, they always manage to get by with their craziness."

"At first they do. But eventually it catches up

with them. Just like what's happening to Bobby Hannah. They're found out."

Jake slowly shook his head. "Can you imagine being on a rooftop ten stories up at night with a bastard like that?"

Joanna shuddered to herself. "Do you really think he killed Karen?"

"It's like Jackson said, anyone who can split an intern's head open can push a girl off a roof." Jake patted his inside coat pocket. "And I just happen to have a search warrant for Bobby Hannah's apartment. I'm going over there now and I'd like you to come with me."

"I can't, Jake. I'm so far behind in my work."

"You might really help."

"How?"

"In two ways. First, sometimes the wackos like to take little mementos from their victims. Kind of like souvenirs. Don't ask me why. It's just part of their sickness. So he might have taken something from your apartment last night that we would never recognize, but you would. He might also have something that belonged to Karen Rhodes, which you'd also spot."

"And the second reason?"

"You're under police protection around the clock. If you stay here, I've got to assign a cop to stand outside your door. And we're shorthanded as is."

"Do you think the killer would try something at Memorial?"

"He already has. Twice."

They turned into a wide corridor and entered the Department of Pathology. Up ahead, Joanna saw Arnold Weideman hurrying towards them, signaling with his hand.

"Damn," she said. "Just what I don't need now."

"Who's he?" Jake asked.

"The chairman of Pathology."

Weideman walked up to Joanna, ignoring Jake. He glanced at his wristwatch. "You're making a habit of arriving at work late."

"I was visiting my sister."

"Well, I suggest you visit her on your time, not the department's."

Joanna glared at him, fists clenched, trying to control her anger.

"Now, our consultant pathologist has arrived and is just beginning his reexamination of the Shaw girl. I want you to report immediately to the autopsy room, where you will observe and, if asked, assist."

"Piss off!" Joanna snapped.

"What!"

"You heard me. Piss off!" Joanna took a step forward and was eye to eye with Weideman. "Now listen carefully, because I don't plan on repeating myself. You wanted to get a second opinion. Good! Great! Get it. But don't expect me to stand around and watch some son of a bitch do something I've already done and done well. I won't do it."

"Now you listen to me, young lady," Weideman seethed. "It's customary for the staff pathologist to be in attendance while the consultant—"

"That's crap and you know it." Joanna cut him off. "You want me in that room so you can embarrass me, so you can make me feel like an underling."

"That's absurd."

"Really? Then tell me, will Simon Murdock be there as well?"

"He will. The dean requested—"

"I can envision it now. You and Simon standing off to one side, arms folded across your chests, looking at me as if to say, 'See? This is what happens when you don't obey commands.' "

"I would strongly advise you to report to the autopsy room."

"I've already told you to piss off. Would you like me to say it again?"

Weideman's face reddened. "This may very well be your last day in the Department of Pathology."

"Good! Then we can walk out together."

"Together?" Weideman asked, now puzzled.

"That's right. Because in addition to being full of crap, you're also incompetent and everybody knows it. Even Mortimer Rhodes. He's not very happy with you." Joanna looked over at Jake. "Didn't you get that impression when you spoke with Mortimer?"

Jake nodded quickly. "Yeah. He didn't seem too happy."

"They're going to push you out of here so fast you won't know what hit you." Joanna smiled mischievously at Weideman, enjoying the stupid look on his face. "Now get the hell out of my way!"

Jake watched Joanna nudge Weideman aside with a forearm and walk into her office. He was astounded by the way she had attacked Weideman, cutting him to ribbons with her tongue. There was real anger there mixed in with a healthy dose of indignation. Maybe she was so upset because of what was happening with Kate, Jake thought. Yeah, that was probably the reason.

Lou Farelli was waiting for them outside the door to Bobby Hannah's apartment. Standing next to him was a small, wiry man in his mid-sixties with reddish-gray hair and heavily freckled skin. He was grumbling about missing the Dodgers game that was being televised on cable from Atlanta.

"This is the apartment manager, Mr. Sanders," Farelli said.

Jake nodded and handed over the search warrant. "How long has Dr. Hannah lived here?"

"About two years." The manager held the warrant at arms length and struggled with the small print.

"He cause any problems?" Jake asked.

The manager passed the warrant back. "Nope. I hardly see the doctor, with him being at the hospital so much. What's he done?"

Jake ignored the question. "Open the apartment up."

Sanders fumbled with a ring of keys before inserting a master key into the door and opening it.

Joanna noted the roughened appearance of the manager's hands. There were calluses over the fingers and palms and a few recent cuts and abrasions. Several nails were split and all had dirt deeply encrusted beneath them. "Are you a carpenter?"

"Part-time. Why?"

"Do you use any rope?"

Sanders stared at Joanna suspiciously. She didn't look like a cop. He glanced up at Jake. "Who is she?"

"A consultant," Jake said.

"What does that mean?" Sanders asked.

"That means it's none of your business," Joanna snapped. "Now, do you use rope or not?"

Sanders glared at Joanna. A real bitch, he decided. "No, I don't use any rope."

Jake motioned with his head and Farelli took the manager's arm and guided him to the stairs, thanking him for his assistance.

"This isn't one of your better days, is it?" Jake said to Joanna.

"How do you mean?"

"Well, first you chewed that doctor at the hospital into little pieces. Then I got the feeling you were about to do a number on the manager."

Joanna shrugged. She didn't know why she was so irritable and on edge. But she knew when it started. When Weideman told her to visit Kate on her time and not the department's. The insensitive bastard!

Farelli came back, jotting down numbers in his writing pad. "Jake, I'm going to check out some of the people who live here. They're nurses and stewardesses with funny schedules. So I'd better get to them now and find out what they know about Dr. Hannah."

"Good. Zero in on last night and on the night the Shaw girl was iced."

"Right." Farelli turned, then stopped and turned back. "There's one other thing. When you told me about this Hannah guy, I did a real fast run on him. And guess what? He's got a sheet. Mainly misdemeanor stuff—brawls, disorderly conduct. Last year he was arrested for felony assault, but he walked."

"Was that the fight with an intern?"

Farelli shook his head. "A hooker. He beat the hell out of her, broke her jaw and nose. And there were witnesses. But after careful consideration, the hooker decided not to press charges."

Jake saw the perplexed look on Joanna's face and explained, "That means she was bought off."

"This guy's a real sweetheart," Farelli said and headed for the stairs.

Joanna and Jake walked into the apartment. He closed the door, locking it, then opened the drapes and let the morning light flood in.

"How'd you know he was a carpenter?" Jake asked.

"His hands were covered with calluses and his nails were split and dirty."

"He could have been a mechanic."

"I don't think so. The calluses were too well developed, and I didn't see any grease. Also, his heavily freckled skin told me that he spent a lot of time outdoors." Joanna shuddered to herself as she again thought about the mechanic in the service station who wanted to fix her tire. If she had let him, if she'd have been delayed another few minutes, Kate would be dead.

Jake stood motionless, letting his eyes scan the living room, then the small kitchen off to one side. Then he scanned the area again, now looking for more detail. "Before I search a place, I always try to get a feel for the person who lives or works there. In particular, I like to know whether he's messy or not. That'll tell me where he tends to hide his stuff."

"I'm not sure I follow you."

"If the guy is neat, he'll hide his things neatly. Like, he'll unroll a pair of socks, deposit his good- ies, then reroll the socks back into a ball. And then he'll return the socks to his drawer. If he's messy, he'll just put the thing underneath a pile of dirty clothes and then throw more crap on top of the pile.'' Jake looked over the room once again. ''Kind of messy, isn't it?''

''More like a pigsty.'' Joanna waved a hand in front of her face, trying to remove the aroma of stale garbage coming from the kitchen. There was dust on everything, and the coffee table was covered with unopened mail, several empty bottles of Bud Lite, and an aluminum tray containing a partially eaten TV dinner. Dirty clothes were piled up on a chair, and newspapers and magazines were strewn about the floor.

''If you see anything important, don't touch it. Even if it belongs to you, don't touch it.'' Jake led the way across the living room. ''Let's start in the bedroom.''

The bedroom had a strong smell of body odor that emanated from sheets that looked as if they hadn't been washed in months. The pillows had no pillowcases on them. Dirty clothes were piled up in a corner next to an overflowing hamper.

Jake got down on all fours and searched under the bed, then turned the pillows and mattress. Nothing. Next, he walked over to the corner and rummaged through the hamper. Smelly socks, soiled underwear, used handkerchiefs. Then he came to the top of a scrub suit with dried blood on its front. He picked it up with a pen, holding it up to the light. ''Well, well.''

Joanna moved in for a closer look. ''That blood-stain is days old. It didn't come from Kate.''

''But it could have come from Marissa Shaw's neck.''

Joanna shrugged. ''Surgeons frequently get

bloodstains on their scrub suits. It probably won't lead anywhere, but we'll type it and match it against the blood of the victims."

Jake put the scrub top on the bed and walked over to the closet. On the floor were shoes, hangers, a dusty baseball glove, and an umbrella. There was no baseball cap. But there was a black leather jacket hanging between two sportscoats. Jake picked the jacket up by its hanger and patted the pockets and lining, then placed it on the bed. "Can you match this coat up against the black material you got from underneath the hooker's brass knuckles?"

"I can't, but the FBI can. They have a special lab for this sort of thing."

Jake quickly went through the dresser, finding a stale marijuana cigarette and a packet of condoms. Such a nice fellow, Jake thought sarcastically. All of Hannah's girlfriends probably considered him to be socially responsible. Until he beat the shit out of them.

Reluctantly, Jake walked into the bathroom, with Joanna a step behind. As expected, it was filthy. The basin and tub had heavy rings of dirt around them. Hanging towels smelled damp and moldy. The toilet seat was cracked and peeling. The tile shelf next to the sink held a half-used cake of soap with hairs embedded in it. The medicine cabinet contained toothpaste and brush, deodorant, shaving utensils, and aspirin. There were no prescription drugs.

They hurried out and into the living room, where Jake cracked the window and let fresh air in.

"What a goddamn pig," Jake growled.

"Do you think he's ever had this apartment cleaned?"

"Probably not. Let's get finished and get the hell out of here. You want to take the kitchen?"

"Not particularly, but I will." She took a deep breath of fresh air and walked into the small kitchen. The odor of stale garbage was intense and Joanna hoped it wouldn't permeate her clothes. She glanced at the sink that was heavily spotted with rust stains. Pots and pans were piled up and half-filled with water. The gas burners on the stove were thickly coated with grease. Joanna opened the refrigerator door and stepped back, expecting a blast of foul air. But there was none. The refrigerator was empty except for a six-pack of beer and a wedge of cheese wrapped in cellophane.

Joanna went to the small corner closet and glanced into a soiled, plastic garbage can. It contained empty milk cartons, empty beer bottles, and decaying food. Behind it was a stack of dirty rags. She pushed the garbage can to one side, then reached for her pen and rummaged through the rags. Her eyes suddenly widened as she bent over for a closer look. "Jake!"

"What?"

"Get in here, Jake!"

Sinclair hurried in to her side and with his gaze followed her pointing finger. "The garbage can?"

"Next to it."

Jake leaned over and saw it, mixed in with the rags.

A piece of rope.

Three feet long.

Encrusted with blood.

* * *

"You can't come in here." The head nurse jumped up from her seat at the nurses' station that was located adjacent to the operating rooms.

Jake flashed his shield. "I'm Lieutenant Sinclair from Homicide. Are you the head nurse?"

"I am."

"Good. I need to talk with Dr. Robert Hannah. Right now."

"That's not possible," the nurse said curtly. "Dr. Hannah is currently in surgery."

Joanna stepped forward. She was wearing her long white coat with her name embroidered over the upper left pocket. "Is he the surgeon in charge?"

"Oh no," the nurse replied, her voice now softer. "He's the second assistant on a cholecystectomy."

"Would it be possible for you to get him for the lieutenant? It's very, very important."

"I'll try." The nurse gave Sinclair an unpleasant look. "And don't you take a step beyond this point. I will not have you contaminating my operating room."

Jake glanced around the area, then over at a young nurse standing behind the desk. She seemed so young. Like a teenager. *Christ! I must be getting old.* "Miss, is there another door out of here?"

The young nurse pointed to a nearby corridor. "That leads to the fire exit."

Jake motioned with his head and Lou Farelli quickly moved into the corridor, where he planted his feet firmly.

"You don't think he'd try anything that stupid, do you?" Joanna asked in a whisper.

"You never know."

The head nurse returned. Bobby Hannah was a few steps behind her, still fully gowned, capped, and masked.

"Dr. Robert Hannah?" Jake asked formally.

"That's right."

"You're under arrest for the murder of Marissa Shaw."

"What!" Hannah was suddenly aware of the onlookers now gathering around him. Nurses, surgeons, aides. "You can't be serious."

Jake signaled with a hand to Farelli, but his eyes never left Bobby Hannah. "Cuff him and read him his rights."

Bobby Hannah looked remarkably calm for a man accused of murder.

Joanna watched Hannah through a specially designed one-way mirror that allowed her to see into the interrogation room. Bobby sat upright at a table, hands folded in front of him. Only his eyes moved, periodically glancing at a running tape recorder. Jake was seated across from him. Farelli stood near the door.

Jake was carefully going over the ground rules with Bobby Hannah. "Now, Dr. Hannah, we have arrested but not booked you yet because you claim to be innocent and you say you can prove your innocence. Is that correct?"

Bobby nodded.

"Don't answer by moving your head, Dr. Hannah. The machine can't record a nod. Answer yes or no."

"Yes. I'm innocent," Hannah said in a clear voice.

"You've agreed to answer all of our questions

without the benefit of an attorney being present?''

''Yes.''

''And you understand that anything you say can and will be held against you?''

''I understand.''

Joanna watched Jake stand and begin to pace. Then her gaze drifted back to Hannah. He was so calm, so confident he could wiggle out of his predicament. He'd pleaded with Jake not to arrest him, to let him prove his innocence. He would answer any and all questions. So sincere. But Bobby Hannah was already as good as convicted. The blood on the rope found in Bobby's apartment belonged to Marissa Shaw. Joanna had spent the last two hours typing the blood for twenty-three different antigens. A perfect match.

''Can you tell us where you were last Monday night?'' Jake asked.

Hannah hesitated. ''I'm going to have to think for a moment, sir. I'm on call at the hospital so much that . . .'' His brow wrinkled in thought. ''No. I was on duty all weekend, so I was off Monday night. And I went to a movie.''

''What time did you arrive at the theater?''

''About 7:25 P.M. A few minutes before it started.''

''You're sure about that?''

''Yes, sir. I remember because I thought I was going to be late, but my watch was running fast. The clock in the movie read 7:25.''

''Did you take a date?''

''No, sir. I was really tired and I just wanted to see the flick and then go back to my apartment.''

''Did you see anybody at the movie you knew?''

''No, sir.''

"Anyone who could vouch for your being there?"

"No, sir."

"What was the movie?"

"It was a Japanese film with subtitles. The name of the movie was *Sensei*. That means 'teacher' in Japanese."

"What time did the movie let out?"

"Around nine-fifteen."

Jake continued to pace, now circling the table, slowing briefly to study Bobby Hannah. The doctor's blond hair was neatly groomed, his face clean shaven, his nails manicured and clipped short. So fastidious in his personal appearance, yet he lived in a filthy pigsty. Sinclair wondered if that was part of Bobby Hannah's illness.

Jake thought for a moment about Hannah's alibi. The doc lied well, smooth and unhurried. And he picked a good place to be the night of the murder. A movie theater, probably not far from Memorial. "Where was this show?"

"On Santa Monica Boulevard, near Sepulveda."

Jake nodded to himself. An easy ten-minute drive from Memorial.

"I may even have the ticket stub," Hannah volunteered. "Sometimes I just throw them on my dresser and they stay there for a while."

"That could be helpful," Jake said.

"It would prove I was there."

Jake gestured with his head ambiguously. That would prove nothing. He could have bought a ticket and left after five minutes. And he still would have had plenty of time to get back to Memorial and strangle Marissa Shaw.

Jake paused to light a Greek cigarette; his eyes

looked over the flame at Bobby Hannah. The boy was a good liar, but he was an amateur when it came to constructing an alibi. A pro would have gone to the movie the night of the murder and caused a little scene. He would have spilled his soda on the girl at the counter. He would have apologized, offered to pay for cleaning her uniform, called the manager over and explained what happened, given the girl five dollars to cover the cost of the cleaning. Maybe even left his name and phone number in case five dollars didn't cover the cost. Then they would have remembered him and he would have had a decent alibi. "Where were you last night?"

"On call at the hospital," Hannah said promptly.

"All night?"

"Of course. When you're on surgery call, you must stay at the hospital. Even if you have a beeper." Hannah's lips began to curl into a grin. "And I've got plenty of witnesses, too."

"I'm sure you do."

Joanna quickly reached for the phone and pushed the intercom button. She heard the buzzer sound in the interrogation room and waited for Jake to pick up the receiver. "Jake, residents sneak away from the hospital a great deal when they're on call. Find out where he was between ten and eleven last night. See if he was in the OR, if the operator called, or if somebody beeped him. Make him account for every minute of his time."

Jake put the phone down and looked over at Farelli. "The test was positive, Lou. You were right. Good thinking."

Lou Farelli didn't know what the hell Jake was referring to, but he nodded back solemnly.

Jake turned to Bobby Hannah, now seeing a glint of concern on the doctor's face. "Where were you last night between ten and eleven?"

"At the hospital."

"Where? In the OR? In the ER?"

Hannah's narrowed eyes started to dart back and forth. He shifted around in his chair, trying to buy time. "I was probably in the on-call room."

"Did anyone see you there?"

"I don't know. I was resting."

"Resting or sleeping?"

"Mostly dozing."

"And no one saw you."

"I don't know."

Jake smiled to himself, enjoying the cat-and-mouse interrogation. Suspects, particularly the bright ones, always thought themselves so superior to the police, so sure they could think their way out of trouble. "Were you beeped? Did the operator call?"

"I don't think so."

"So you really don't have any witnesses, do you?"

"I was there," Hannah insisted.

"Right." Jake took a final drag on his cigarette and crushed it out. "Were you sleeping with both Marissa Shaw and Karen Rhodes?"

"That's none of your business," Hannah said sharply.

"I just made it my business. Yes or no?"

"There was a time I went with Marissa and a time I went with Karen."

"Recently? During the past few months?"

"No."

"Are you telling me that you weren't screwing

Karen Rhodes on the roof of the Psychiatric Institute?''

"How did you—?'' Hannah caught himself in mid-sentence, suddenly remembering the pages of the diary that Peggy Collins had waved in his face. The nosy little bitch!

"Yes or no?''

"Yes, but—''

"And when was the last time?''

Hannah hesitated. His lips moved for a second before the words came. "A few days before she was killed.''

Jake's instincts told him that Hannah was lying. He decided to push harder. "You're lying.''

"It's the truth.''

"Don't forget. We've got the diary.''

The color drained from Hannah's face. Shit! She probably wrote that we were going to meet that night. "I was supposed to meet her on the roof the night she was killed. But she asked me to come fifteen minutes later than usual.''

"Why?''

"She didn't say. Anyway, I was just leaving the emergency room for the parking lot when they wheeled Karen in.''

"Did anybody see you in the ER?''

"No. I don't think so.''

"You seem to do a lot of things without anybody seeing you, don't you?''

Hannah's eyes widened. "You don't think I pushed Karen off that roof?''

"What happened up there? Did she get you angry? Did you lose your temper?''

"I wasn't up there, I'm telling you.''

"Or did things get a little rough when you were banging her? Did you squeeze her throat too hard?

Did you throw her off the roof to make her death look like a suicide?''

"You're crazy!"

"No, Dr. Hannah. You're the one seeing a psychiatrist because of a real mean temper you can't control.''

"I've never done anything like that, and you know it.''

"I know otherwise. I know about the intern whose head you split open and about the hooker who you kicked the hell out of and then paid not to press charges. Shall I go on?''

Hannah was on his feet, staring coldly at Jake. "You're just blowing hot air. You can't prove a damned thing.''

"Oh yes, I can," Jake said evenly. "We just finished searching that shithole you call an apartment and we found something very interesting. It was a piece of rope.''

"What rope?"

"The one you used to strangle Marissa Shaw. It had some dried blood on it, too. Want to guess whose blood it was?''

Bobby Hannah was stunned speechless.

"Well, I'll tell you," Jake went on. "We had the lab type out the blood twenty-three different ways. They told us it definitely belonged to Marissa Shaw. It could have also belonged to Marissa's identical twin, if she had one, but she didn't.''

"You set me up," Hannah hissed.

"We'll let a judge and jury decide that."

"I want a lawyer."

"I don't blame you. I'd get a damn good one, if I were you." Jake motioned to Farelli with his head. "Book him. Murder one."

16

"God damn it!" Simon Murdock slammed his fist on the desk. He glared down at the front page of the *Los Angeles Times* and a picture of Bobby Hannah smiled back at him. Not really a smile. More like an inappropriate grin. The press were now calling him the Memorial Murderer. And somehow they'd found out about his psychiatric problems.

The intercom buzzed loudly. Murdock reached over to it. "What?"

"Mortimer Rhodes is on line two."

"Tell him I'm talking with the police. I'll have to call him back."

"Yes, sir."

"Shit!" Murdock hissed under his breath. He looked over at Hugh Jackson and Arnold Weideman, the two men at Memorial he'd known the longest and trusted the most. "How should we handle this mess?"

Weideman said, "The first thing we should do is disassociate ourselves from the crazy bastard."

"We can hardly do that," Murdock said. "After all, Hannah was a member of our house staff for three years. You can't simply ignore that fact."

"Sure you can. It's done all the time. Issue a statement saying that it's terrible and dreadful and that we're relieved the murderer has been apprehended. Tell the media that the matter is now in the hands of the legal system. Then we just walk away and refuse to answer further questions."

Murdock weighed the suggestion carefully. "It won't work. Not in this instance. Not with Bobby Hannah's psychiatric history now public knowledge. We had a maniac on our staff and the press will never let us forget it."

"How the hell did the media find out about Hannah's mental problems?" Weideman asked irritably.

Hugh Jackson shrugged. "The police probably leaked it. They're very good at this sort of thing. It makes their case sound stronger."

"I still say we should disassociate ourselves and let the bastard hang and twist in the breeze. That's how I'd handle it." But deep down Weideman knew there was no way out of this mess. Memorial's reputation was about to drop like a deadweight and all the staff would go down with it. Weideman thanked his stars that next year he would be retiring and moving to Santa Barbara, well away from Memorial and its headaches.

"Maybe he's innocent," Jackson said softly.

"What!" Murdock looked at him oddly.

"He's been charged, but he hasn't been proven guilty. Has he?"

"No. But I've been told that the evidence is overwhelming. He's as good as convicted right now. The only question is what his sentence will be."

"You missed my point," Jackson said.

"Which is?"

"We don't have to accept any blame until he's convicted. For now we should issue a statement saying that Robert Hannah, a member of our house staff, has been charged with a very serious crime. He has been suspended from Memorial until his innocence or guilt is clearly established. Say no more than that.''

''But the media will bombard us with questions about his psychiatric problems. They're going to have a field day. They're already implying that we don't adequately screen our house staff, that we could have other lunatics running around Memorial.''

Jackson felt a twinge of pain over his left eye and ignored it. ''Let them imply all they want. When the media bring up the matter, refer them to the police. If they persist, tell them that we will not participate in a trial conducted by the media. Tell them that in this country we have a court system to establish guilt or innocence.''

''The press are like sharks. They stop at nothing once they've smelled blood.''

Jackson sighed deeply. ''There's really no good way to handle this matter, is there?''

''Not that I can see.'' Murdock disgustedly swept the newspaper off his desk and into the wastebasket.

Hugh Jackson's face suddenly went pale as a knifelike pain shot through his temples. His vision began to blur, images becoming wavy. He rubbed at his eyes.

''Are you all right, Hugh?'' Murdock asked, concerned.

''I'm afraid my migraine headaches are coming back.''

Murdock opened his desk drawer. ''I've some propanolol if you'd like.''

"It won't help. I have some very effective medicine in my office." Jackson got to his feet shakily.

"Perhaps I should accompany you."

"Please don't bother. I'll be fine."

Weideman watched Hugh Jackson hurriedly leave the room. "I didn't know his migraines had returned. I thought they were under control."

"They were. But I suspect his involvement in this Bobby Hannah fiasco has brought them back."

"What involvement?"

"Didn't you know that Hugh was Bobby Hannah's psychiatrist?"

Weideman sucked air through his teeth. "My God! When the press finds out . . ."

"Exactly."

Joanna and Jake hurried past the nurses' station and into the ICU. Kate was sitting up in bed, sucking orange juice through a straw. She still appeared pale and weak. Her hair was brushed back, exposing a shaved area where a laceration had been sutured.

Kate smiled at Joanna. "I must look like hell."

"You look beautiful." Joanna kissed her sister's forehead and gave her a gentle hug. So close, she thought, so close to death and all because of me. Joanna tightened her hug.

"Careful," Kate grimaced. "I'm sore from head to toe."

"You had us pretty scared there for a while."

"Exactly what happened to me?" Kate slurped the last of the orange juice.

Joanna hesitated, wondering how much to tell her still fragile sister. "A man had broken into the apartment and you surprised him."

''That's it?''

''That's it.''

''You're such a bad liar, Joanna.'' Kate lay back and carefully positioned her head on the pillow. ''One of the nurses told me that there was a policeman standing guard outside the ICU. I wouldn't need protection from a common burglar, now would I?''

Jake said, ''You'd make a pretty good detective.''

''Archaeologists *are* detectives.'' Kate grinned weakly, then looked at Joanna. ''What really happened?''

''The man in the apartment was the killer from Memorial Hospital. He had mistaken you for me.''

''Jesus,'' Kate groaned, swallowing hard. ''Why was he after you?''

''We're trying to find that out now.''

Kate shook her head slowly. ''God! He must be a crazy old man.''

''Why did you say old man?'' Joanna asked quickly.

''Because he was.''

Jake moved closer to the bed. ''Did you see his face?''

''No. His neck. He had one of those wrinkly necks where the skin hangs loose. You only see that in old people.''

''You're sure?''

''Positive.''

''Do you remember anything else?''

Kate stared at the ceiling, thinking back. She remembered opening the door and walking in. There was very little light and everything was quiet. Then a sound, a movement behind her.

Then the pain. "I was reaching for the lamp when he hit me from behind."

"Did you actually turn the lamp on?" Jake asked.

"The lamp was on," Joanna said. "It had been knocked to the floor, but it was on."

A small lamp on the floor makes a very dim light, Jake thought. "What happened next, Kate?"

"I went down and I think he hit me again. And then he was on top of me, with his hands on my throat. It was the last thing I—" Kate stopped in mid-sentence and squinted an eye suspiciously at Jake. "If this guy was after Joanna, why did you station a cop to guard me?"

Smart, Jake thought. Almost as smart as your sister. "Because there was a chance you could identify him and, if he believed that, he might come back for you."

"Do you think he still might come back?"

"No. We got the guy."

"For sure?"

"About as sure as you can get."

"Who is he?"

"Some guy who works at Memorial."

Kate's eyelids started to grow heavy, and she let them slowly fall. "I feel so tired."

Joanna kissed her forehead. "You get some sleep. We'll see you in the morning."

They left the ICU and walked down a long corridor, deserted except for a nurse pushing a medicine cart in the distance. They passed a patient's room with its door opened and glanced in. A young couple held onto each other, tears streaming down their cheeks. A doctor was speaking to them in a low, soft voice. The news was not good. Joanna thought again about how lucky she was and closed her eyes and thanked God for answering her prayers. They turned onto another corridor and headed for the elevators.

"What do you think about Kate's story?" Joanna asked.

"Seeing a wrinkled neck in dim light is kind of slim evidence."

"You do believe her, don't you?"

Jake shrugged. "There wasn't much light in that room, Joanna. Remember, it was a small lamp and it was on its side on the floor."

"But Kate has very good eyes and she's been trained to be observant."

"I've got two problems with her story. First, during the assault we know where Kate's head was from the bloodstain on the carpet, and we can tell where the attacker was from his bloody footprints."

"So?"

"When the guy was on top of her, he was between her head and the lamp. His body was blocking out most of the light."

"That's weak, Jake. If Kate were positioned at the slightest of angles to the lamp, the light would have come through."

"Maybe," Jake conceded. "But now I'm going to give you a stronger point. I don't think she really saw his neck."

"Why not?"

As they approached the visitors' lounge, Jake took her arm and guided her into the empty room. "Lie down on the couch."

"What?"

"Just lie down on the couch." Jake waited for her to assume a supine position, then turned off the overhead light, leaving a small lamp on in the corner. He came back to the couch and placed a knee between Joanna's legs and leaned over her, his hands lightly grasping her throat. Their noses were a foot and a half apart. "What do you see?"

"Your face."

"What about my neck?"

"No. Mainly your face and chest."

"That's my point. And you had plenty of time to look and you weren't scared out of your wits."

Jake helped her up and they walked back into the corridor. "A long time ago," he said, "I had a similar case in which a witness claimed to see a scar on a guy's neck. I watched an attorney do in court what I just did in the visitors' lounge. He destroyed the witness's credibility."

"It still bothers me."

"I wouldn't worry about it. We've got too many other things. Hannah is as good as nailed."

Joanna nodded. "It's hard to get around that bloodied piece of rope we found in his apartment."

"But his lawyer will try. Believe me, he'll try."

Joanna suddenly remembered the bite marks. If Bobby had a chipped central incisor, he'd be convicted, regardless of how clever his attorney was. "Did you do a dental mold on Bobby Hannah?"

"We got one in the works."

Joanna thought again about the wrinkled neck Kate had seen. If her sister's observations were accurate, the killer had to be at least in his fifties. A wrinkled neck. Not much to go on. She turned suddenly to Jake. "Have a doctor check Bobby Hannah's neck for wrinkles."

"But you only see that in old people, don't you?"

"Check him anyway. And make certain a doctor does the examination. Sometimes people have congenital abnormalities of the subcutaneous tissue and their skin is quite loose, even when they're young."

Jake took out his writing pad and scribbled down a note.

"Also have a doctor check him for bruises over his left shoulder and upper arm. That's where I hit him with the table and knocked him off of Kate."

"Did you hit him that hard?"

"You want a demonstration?"

"Left side, huh?"

"Left side."

17

The next morning Joanna arrived at the police station late. She hurried into the small room and sat beside Lou Farelli, who was intently watching the ongoing interrogation through the specially designed window.

"Hi, Lou," she whispered.

"Hi, Doc. You can talk louder. They can't hear us."

Joanna briefly studied Bobby Hannah. The young doctor sat at the table relaxed, his posture upright, his expression impassive. Cool as a cucumber. Just like a borderline personality, Joanna thought. Her gaze drifted to a fashionably dressed, middle-aged man sitting next to Hannah. He wore a dark-blue Armani suit with a striped shirt and a brightly colored tie. His face was nicely tanned with sharp features, and his thinning hair was black.

Joanna motioned with her head. "Is that Hannah's attorney?"

"Yeah. That's the famous John Weitz."

"He looks expensive."

"Fifty thousand for starters. But if you're in big trouble, he's the one you want." Farelli took out a toothpick and began to nibble on it. "Oh, yeah. Jake said to tell you that Hannah's neck ain't wrinkled and he doesn't have any bruises on his body."

"Damn," Joanna said.

"Don't sweat it. We still got him good. He's not going to walk."

Joanna watched Bobby Hannah and his attorney huddle, speaking in barely audible whispers. Jake leaned against the far wall and waited patiently. "Did Hannah's teeth match the bite marks?"

"Don't know. Something went wrong with the first mold, so we had to go back and do it again. By then, the great John Weitz was on duty, screaming illegal search and seizure, invasion of privacy, all sorts of crap. He claimed you can't mold a guy's teeth without his permission. You know, like you can't do a blood test until you get the okay."

"What happens next?"

"We've got a friendly judge reviewing the matter right now."

Bobby Hannah and his attorney broke from their huddle. "I think my client has already answered that question," Weitz said, his voice strong and articulate.

"I just want to make double certain of the times," Jake said. "Dr. Hannah stated he arrived at the movie around seven-fifteen and left when the show ended at approximately nine-fifteen. Correct?"

Hannah looked at Weitz, who nodded his consent to answer. "That's correct," Hannah said.

"But you have no way of proving you were there. Right?"

Weitz said quickly, "He doesn't have to prove he was there. My client states he was at that movie and that's all he has to say on the matter. If you have evidence to the contrary, let's hear it."

"You're right," Jake said agreeably. "He doesn't have to prove it now. But before this is over, I can damn well assure you that your client will have to prove where he was the night Marissa Shaw was murdered."

"If and when that time arrives, we will be prepared to do so."

Jake smiled thinly at the attorney, respecting his ability, yet disliking the man. Weitz was very clever and over the years had gotten off too many guilty people through technicalities and legal loopholes. "So you found the ticket stub for the movie that night, huh?"

"Among other things."

"And of course Dr. Hannah remembers everything about the movie."

"He enjoyed it immensely. He can even recall lines from some of the scenes."

Jake shrugged. "He could have seen the movie the week before."

"Not really, Lieutenant. You see, my client went to the very first showing of the movie in Los Angeles. It would have been impossible for him to have seen it the week before or even the night before."

Bobby Hannah smiled at Weitz, obviously pleased with his attorney's performance.

Jake's expression remained impassive. "Maybe he did see it that night."

"Exactly."

Jake looked down at Hannah. "What did you do after the movie let out at nine-fifteen?"

Hannah hesitated, thinking, remembering his attorney's advice—keep your answers short and to the point, don't volunteer information, and when in doubt say nothing. "I went back to my apartment and crashed."

"That means you went to sleep?"

"Yes."

"Did anyone see you come back to your apartment?"

"No."

"What time was the second showing of the movie that night?"

"I don't know. Maybe nine-thirty or nine-forty-five."

Jake nodded at Weitz. "Like I said, maybe your client did see the movie the night Marissa Shaw was murdered. Maybe he saw the second showing."

Weitz brushed a piece of lint from the sleeve of his dark suit. "He went to the first showing and we are now searching for a witness who we believe will testify she saw Dr. Hannah at that movie."

"Well, when you find the witness, make certain she sat next to Dr. Hannah through the whole movie. Otherwise, your client is still in deep trouble. Any prosecutor worth his salt could punch a hundred holes in Hannah's alibi."

Jake began to pace the floor slowly, glancing occasionally over at Bobby Hannah, making him squirm and wait. Earlier that morning Jake had spoken at length with a police shrink about borderline personalities. The shrink had told him how to deal with Hannah, how to unravel the little shit-ass. "Tell me what you think about this sequence of events. Dr. Hannah goes to the seven-thirty movie and, as he takes his seat, he waves to a girl way across the room. Five minutes into the film, he leaves unnoticed, goes to Memorial, where he murders Marissa Shaw. He scoots back to his apartment, hides the murder weapon, then returns to the theater and waits outside. As the movie lets out, he sees the girl who he had waved to earlier and he waves again. A few minutes later he buys another ticket and goes in to watch the movie. How does that sound, Counselor? Plausible?"

Weitz shook his head wearily and wondered why Jake Sinclair was going through all the theatrics. Nothing he'd said would hold up for two seconds in a court of law. "The only thing you're lacking is proof. My client was at that seven-thirty movie and you cannot refute that fact. And you don't have one shred of evidence to show that he was in the parking lot at Memorial Hospital when Marissa Shaw was murdered."

"Oh, yes, I do," Jake said, holding his hands several feet apart. "I have a piece of rope this long that's covered with Marissa Shaw's blood. And we found it in your client's kitchen."

"It could have been planted there."

"By whom?"

"That's for the police to determine."

"No, no. That's for *you* to determine, Counselor." Jake put his knuckles on the table and leaned toward Weitz. "The jury is going to be told that we found the bloody rope in your boy's kitchen closet. If you want those jurors to believe it was put there by somebody other than Bobby Hannah, you're going to have to prove it."

Jake walked toward the mirrored window. He couldn't see in, but he now felt Joanna's presence in the adjacent room. He wondered if he was developing a sixth sense for her. His father had had a sixth sense for Jake's mother, somehow always knowing when she was about to arrive home.

Joanna turned to Farelli. "Actually, it wasn't the police who discovered the rope. I found it."

"Yeah. I know."

"Does that matter?"

"Not really. It was the murder weapon and it was found in his apartment. That's all that counts."

"So, he's as good as convicted."

"For sure."

"Then why is Jake continuing to question him?"

"Because he wants to pin all the other murders on young Dr. Hannah."

"I hope he doesn't forget the attack on my sister."

"That's at the top of his list."

Jake started pacing again. "Now, Dr. Hannah, when I first interrogated you, you gave me some information on your whereabouts the night Karen Rhodes was murdered. I'd like to go over that with you again."

Weitz held up his hands, palms out. "Whoa! Has my client been charged with the murder of the Rhodes girl?"

"Not yet."

"Then I don't see any reason why he should answer your questions regarding her."

Jake sighed loudly. "We can do this the easy way or the hard way."

Weitz arched an eyebrow. "Is that a threat?"

"Absolutely not. Let me explain it a little better. The hard way is I walk over to the phone, call the DA's office, and ask them to add Karen Rhodes's murder to the charges. The easy way is we just continue the questioning."

"You have proof that—?"

"I have evidence connecting your client to other crimes committed by the serial killer."

"May I have that evidence?"

"Shall I make the phone call or not?"

Weitz thought at length, wondering if Jake were bluffing and, more importantly, if Hannah were as innocent as he claimed to be. "Ask your questions."

Sinclair looked over at Bobby Hannah. "You were meeting Karen Rhodes on the roof of the Institute regularly?"

"A couple of times a week," Hannah said evenly.

"Always at night?"

"Yes. I was usually on call and couldn't get away from the hospital."

"But why the roof? Why not in the backseat of a car?"

"She liked the roof. And besides, it was private and we knew we weren't going to be interrupted."

"Tell me what you usually did on the roof."

Hannah hesitated, smiling thinly for a moment. "You want all the details?"

"What did you do on that rooftop?" Jake demanded.

Hannah looked over at his attorney, who gave him no sign or signal. He scratched at the back of his neck nervously and decided to be very careful here, very careful. "We screwed. Okay? We screwed."

"Did you do anything else?"

"Like what?"

"Smoke cigarettes?"

"She did. I don't smoke."

"Have a little wine?"

"I was on call. I never drink when I'm on call. Not even a sip of wine."

You're so upstanding, Jake thought. No drinking while on duty. But murder, well now, that's permissible. "Any marijuana? Drugs?"

"I don't do drugs. And even if I did, I wouldn't while I was on call."

"That's understandable," Jake said smoothly. *You lying bastard*, he thought, remembering the ME 38 Karen had described in her diary. "Was Karen taking any drugs?"

Hannah shrugged. "She smoked an occasional joint. That was about all."

"Now, let's go back to the night she was murdered. You claim you never made it to the roof."

"That's right. I was walking out of the emergency room when they wheeled her in."

"And nobody saw you in the ER?"

"Not that I can remember."

"Why did you go through the ER? Were you seeing a patient or what?"

"No. I just wanted to check out the suites on the surgical side and make certain I wasn't going to be needed. It's also a shortcut to the Institute."

Joanna quickly reached for the phone and punched the intercom button. The phone sounded in the interrogation room and Jake picked it up.

"He's lying, Jake."

"Are you certain of that, sir?" Jake asked.

"Positive."

"Why are you so sure, Chief?"

"A whole lot of reasons," Joanna said, envisioning an aerial photograph of Memorial. "First of all, no house officer would ever go from the hospital to the Institute via the ER. It's so far out of the way. It would be like going from Los Angeles to San Francisco via Dallas."

Jake wrinkled his forehead, confused. Hell, it was a straight line from the ER to the Institute.

He'd walked it himself. "Let me get to a more secure phone, Chief."

Jake excused himself, then hurried out to the corridor and into the adjacent room. He lit a Greek cigarette and inhaled deeply, vowing to quit tomorrow. "I don't follow you, Joanna. The Institute is right across the parking lot from the ER."

"Only if you're planning to go through the front door of the Institute, which Hannah would never do. There's a guard on duty. He'd have to sign in."

Jake nodded slowly. "So he'd have to walk all the way around the hospital to get to the main lobby, then he'd have to walk over the bridge to the third floor of the Institute."

"Right."

"Doesn't make sense."

"Furthermore, he'd never go through the ER to see what's happening. There's always somebody who wants something. A student, an intern with a problem patient. No, he'd stay away from the emergency room. And if Hannah were really interested in making sure the coast was clear, he would have done it with a phone call."

"So he wanted to go through the ER?"

"Exactly. But I don't know why."

Jake crushed his cigarette, then hurried out and back into the interrogation room. He studied Bobby Hannah briefly. The doc was lying his ass off and sticking to his story. And with Weitz present, Jake couldn't push too hard. But he decided to continue to push, firmly and persistently, just like the police shrink had told him to do. Hannah would eventually make a mistake—his type always did. "Sorry about the interruption," he said. "Let's see, Dr. Hannah, we were talking about you walking through the ER to make certain you weren't going to be needed. Correct?"

"Yes."

"Everything was calm?"

"Yes." Hannah glanced over at Weitz, who nodded back his approval. Keep your answers short, monosyllabic if possible, Weitz had advised while Jake was out of the room.

"Did you make any stops in the ER?"

"No."

"Do you have a locker in the ER?"

"No. I have one in the surgery lounge adjacent to the operating rooms. That's on the other side of the hospital."

"So you left the ER. What happened next?"

"I saw them wheeling Karen in."

"All right." Jake began pacing slowly. He wondered if Hannah knew another way into the Institute, a shortcut from the ER. "You said you were meeting Karen Rhodes twice a week on the roof."

"About that."

"Did you always go through the ER?"

"Almost always."

"Tell me the route you took from the ER to the Institute."

"I walked across the parking lot, then turned right and went into the underground garage, and then—"

"An underground garage?" Jake interrupted.

"There's a big parking area located beneath the surface lot."

"Who parks there?"

"Mainly house staff and students."

"Do you park there?"

Hannah's eyes narrowed. Then his eyelids twitched ever so briefly. "Yes."

Jake smiled to himself. Bingo! "Do you usually stop at your car?"

"No," Hannah said quickly.

"Where do you go next?"

"To the other side of the garage, then up the stairs that lead to the front of the hospital. Then I go into the main lobby, hang a left, and walk over the bridge to the Institute."

Jake nodded. "Let's go back to your car."

"What about it?"

"Why did you have to stop at your car on the way to the roof?"

"I didn't," Hannah said firmly, but his eyelids twitched again, a little more this time.

"Oh yes, you did."

"I swear to you, I didn't."

Joanna quickly reached for the phone and pressed the intercom button.

Jake picked it up. "Yes?"

"I think I know why he stopped at his car," Joanna said.

"Go ahead."

"I'll bet you that's where he kept the supply of drugs he and Karen were taking before they climbed into the sack."

"Why there?"

"Because Karen wouldn't carry a bottle of pills around in her purse, and she wouldn't leave them at home, where her roommates might see them."

"Maybe."

"And the reason Bobby is being so secretive is that he doesn't want you to know he was taking those pills while he was on call. If that became known to his superiors, they'd throw him off staff. Remember, those drugs were mood elevators—happy pills—as well as aphrodisiacs."

"Thanks, Chief." Jake put the phone down, then turned to Bobby Hannah. *Well now, Dr. Hannah, we're going to squeeze your balls a little and see what happens.* "Do you want to tell me what's in your car or should we go ahead and search it?"

Weitz said, "Not without a search warrant."

"I'll have one in half an hour," Jake said, his eyes still on Hannah. "And if I have to obtain a search warrant, I'll ask the chief of Surgery at Memorial to accompany me while I go through your car."

Hannah's face lost color. His lips moved, but no sound came. Then he swallowed hard. "And what if I just tell you?"

"That's where you kept the drugs, wasn't it?"

"Yes," Hannah said, his voice almost inaudible.

Weitz looked back and forth between Hannah and Sinclair. "What drugs?"

"Some experimental pills that make you horny," Jake said.

"Shit," Weitz groaned, looking disgustedly at Bobby Hannah and wondering what other important information the stupid little prick had withheld.

"She took them," Hannah said, now squirming in his chair. "But I never would. She pestered the hell out of me, but I would never take those damn drugs."

"That's not what she said in her diary," Jake said evenly.

"She was *lying*," Hannah yelled, losing his composure.

"No, I don't think so." Jake took out a cigarette and lit it. *This is the last pack I'll ever buy,* he promised himself. "Let me tell you what happened that night. You went to the roof and met Karen and you both swallowed those experimental drugs. Then you banged her and started playing rough games, like squeezing her throat until she almost passed out. It made for great orgasms, didn't it?"

"That *never* happened."

"But things went a little too far," Jake went on. "You squeezed too hard, too long. And then you had a dead girl on your hands, didn't you?"

Hannah jumped to his feet, fists clenched, glaring at Jake. "Lies! All lies! You're trying to frame me."

Jake stared back, hoping Hannah would make a stupid move.

In the adjacent room, Joanna grabbed Lou Farelli's arm. "I think he's going to attack Jake."

"I'd pay money to see it," Farelli said earnestly.

"You don't understand. When someone with a borderline personality snaps, he can be very strong and very dangerous."

"Well, if Jake can't handle him, I will."

Joanna looked at him quizzically.

Farelli read her mind. "I know what you're thinking. I'm just a roly-poly guy. What could I do? Well, let me tell you. I wouldn't use a choke hold or some restraining maneuver. Uh-uh. I'd whack him right in the balls. Works every time. It'll calm down just about anybody, even the fruitcakes."

Jake continued to stare at Bobby Hannah. "Yeah, you killed her. That's for damn sure."

"You can't prove it."

"And all caused by drugs. Jesus! Look what it's going to cost you. Your freedom, your profession, maybe even your life."

Now Weitz was on his feet, standing next to

Hannah. "This has gone far enough. Either produce your evidence or stop this line of questioning."

Jake ignored the attorney, his eyes still fixed on Hannah. He could see that Hannah was becoming unglued, his confidence rapidly draining away. Now was the time to crack him. "First thing I'll do is get the chief of surgery to help me search through your car."

"You can't do that!" Hannah yelled. "You promised—"

"I lied. I do it all the time," Jake said. "You killed that young girl. Anybody who reads her diary will know that."

"I didn't kill her. I loved her."

"Oh, sure! Like you loved the prostitute you almost beat to death."

Weitz looked at his client strangely, no longer convinced he was defending an innocent man. "What prostitute?"

Jake moved in closer. "You beat the shit out of her, didn't you? You broke her jaw and her nose. Did you enjoy yourself?"

"I was never charged."

"That's because you bought her off. But you ain't going to buy your way out of this one." Jake took another step closer. "Terrible things seem to happen to the people you love. Have you ever noticed that?"

"What are you talking about?"

"I'm talking about Karen Rhodes and Marissa Shaw. Both now dead with crushed throats because you couldn't control yourself."

"You're framing me! You're setting me up!" Hannah backed away from the detective, his eyes frantically darting back and forth.

"And two nights ago you beat the hell out of another young woman. But you made another mistake, Bobby boy. You left something behind." Jake reached into his coat pocket and took out a plastic envelope containing a Cross pen. "Is this yours?"

Hannah stared at the pen, eyes bulging.

"It must be yours," Jake went on. "It's got your fingerprints all over it."

"No! No!"

"Have you ever seen the inside of a gas chamber?"

Hannah suddenly backed up against the wall, eyes dancing everywhere. "Get away from me! Get away from me!"

John Weitz extended his hand. "Just take it easy, Bobby."

"Don't touch me! I know you've got electricity in your fingers. I know they're lethal weapons."

"What!"

"I know those electrical weapons. They cause a lot of pain, but I won't talk. Torture can't make me reveal those secrets."

"What secrets?" Weitz asked, now aware that something was very wrong.

"You know. You're one of them, aren't you? I can see right through your disguise." Hannah backed his way along the wall, wild eyed. "Don't touch me. If you do, we'll both burn up. I have my defenses. You'd better be careful."

Joanna quickly reached for the phone and pushed the intercom button.

Hannah jumped, startled by the buzzing sound. "It's probably the special forces. They'll come to my rescue."

Jake picked up the phone very slowly and listened. "Jake, watch yourself! He's had a complete psychotic break."

Weitz pointed to a folding chair. "Why don't you have a seat, Bobby? We'll get you some help."

"I don't feel very good," Bobby said in a monotone.

"I know." Weitz pushed the chair toward Hannah. "Just sit down for a little while."

Bobby Hannah nodded meekly and walked past Weitz. He placed a hand on the back of the chair, pausing to take a deep breath. "Could I have a drink of water?"

"Of course," Weitz said and turned toward the door.

Bobby Hannah suddenly spun around and grabbed Weitz, picking him up as if he were almost weightless, then throwing him across the room at the onrushing Jake. Weitz slammed into Jake with a thud, both men going down hard.

Hannah dashed through the door and into the crowded corridor, yelling, "Fire! Fire!"

Jake untangled himself and got up on one knee. He waited for his head to clear, then stumbled out into the corridor. People were packed shoulder to shoulder, pushing against one another as they tried to reach the fire exits. A loud, piercing alarm filled the air.

Jake stood on his tiptoes and looked over a sea of heads.

Lou Farelli shoved through the crowd and made his way over to Jake. "Which way did the bastard go?"

"I'm not sure. Call upstairs and have them seal off the exits."

"Okay. But it's going to be a real bitch to nab

him. Hundreds of people are flooding out of here as fast as they can."

"Yeah, but only one of them is wearing a prisoner's uniform." Jake bounced up on his toes again and looked down the corridor. For an instant, he thought he saw a blond head bobbing in the crowd, but then it disappeared.

Bobby Hannah kept his shoulders hunched and his head down as he moved with the tide of people. He felt safer now, away from the two men who tried to harm him. And the people around him didn't even notice his green uniform. They were all too concerned with saving their own asses. But once they were outside that would quickly change. Then they too would become the enemy. They would recognize his prisoner's outfit and scream, and he would be captured and brought back to the small room where the two men would torture him.

Off to the right, Hannah saw an open office door. Head down, he quickly peeled off from the crowd and entered the deserted room. There were no windows, no other exits. The ventilation shaft was too small to accommodate him. Hannah looked behind the door and saw a raincoat hanging on a hook. He hurriedly tried it on. It was a size too big, but it would do. He placed his hands in the pockets and felt a pair of glasses. They had tinted lenses with a wire frame.

Bobby Hannah stepped back into the corridor and moved with the people streaming to the exit. He smiled at the woman next to him. She was thin and in her mid-thirties with frizzy blond hair and designer glasses.

She smiled back at him. "Well, at least we get an early lunch break."

"Too bad we don't have fires every day."

"Yeah," she giggled.

"Do you have lunch nearby?"

"Naw. The restaurants around here are so boring. I usually drive into Westwood. I know a great Thai take-out place."

"I've never eaten Thai food," Hannah lied. "By the way, my name is Bobby Steward."

"I'm Sandy Collins. Are you a cop?"

"Nope. I work with the computers."

They walked up a short flight of stairs and entered another crowded corridor. Up ahead Hannah saw the main exit. Two cops were stationed at the door, carefully eyeing everyone who passed through.

Hannah moved closer to the blonde, their shoulders now touching. She didn't seem to mind. "Is this Thai restaurant close to Memorial?"

"Sure. It's only a couple of blocks away. Why?"

"I've got to stop over there for a blood test and my car is in the garage being fixed."

"Are you sick?"

"No. They're going to check and see if I can donate blood to a good friend who needs a transfusion."

"I'll be glad to give you a lift."

"Thanks." Hannah put on the tinted glasses as they approached the door. He leaned closer to the blond. "Maybe we can have lunch together tomorrow."

"I'd like that."

They passed by the cops and walked into bright sunshine.

18

Joanna and Jake hurried across the enclosed bridge leading to the Psychiatric Institute. Off to the left and beneath them, a helicopter had just landed on the adjacent rooftop. Its blade was still spinning, its engine whining down.

"At this moment, John Weitz is the happiest man in Los Angeles," Jake said glumly.

"Why?"

"Because his client is now a bona fide wacko. He'll plead Bobby-boy innocent by virtue of insanity."

"Maybe," Joanna said slowly, "but then again, maybe not. Bobby Hannah is quite psychotic now, but that doesn't mean he was mad when he was killing those women. As a matter of fact, these types of psychotic breaks are usually transient. In a few days or weeks, he'll be entirely sane."

"Ha!" Jake forced a laugh. "You've got to be kidding!"

"I'm being very serious."

Jake looked over at the adjacent rooftop and watched medical personnel run over to the helicopter and unload a patient strapped onto a stretcher. "Well, let me tell you how things are going to go. Every time Bobby Hannah looks as if he's back to normal, somebody in the DA's office will set a court date. At that very moment, John Weitz will snap his fingers and suddenly Bobby Hannah will start seeing spaceships from Mars circling around his head. Do you get the picture?''

''There are experts who can determine whether someone is faking insanity.''

''Forget it. Believe me when I tell you, Bobby Hannah will never come to trial.''

''But at least he'll be confined and no longer able to terrorize the women of Los Angeles.''

''Tell that to Karen Rhodes's family. I'm certain they'll find it comforting.''

The walkie-talkie Jake was holding suddenly clicked on and Lou Farelli's voice came through the static. ''Jake, Hannah's locker is clean and so is his car. No pills. Nothing.''

''Where are you now?''

''In the underground garage.''

''Stay put. I'm on my way.''

Joanna asked, ''Do you think Bobby Hannah came back to Memorial just to get those pills?''

''Who the hell knows?'' Jake said irritably. ''We're dealing with a first-class fruitcake.''

''That fruitcake was smart enough to escape from a building surrounded by police.''

''Tell me about it!'' Jake stopped on the bridge and reached for a Greek cigarette, ignoring the ''No Smoking'' sign. He still couldn't understand how Hannah had escaped. Goddamn it! All the exits were covered and he was wearing a prisoner's uniform. Maybe he jumped from a window.

''I thought you were going to quit.''

''Tomorrow.'' Jake lit a cigarette and inhaled deeply. ''And the answer to your question is yes. I think he came back to Memorial to get his pills.

That's why he was spotted at his locker and in the garage less than an hour after he escaped. Those are the places where he would keep his cache.''

Joanna squinted an eye, not at all certain that Jake was correct. More likely, Hannah returned to Memorial because it was huge, with a thousand hiding places. And he knew his way around it. ''But why risk capture just to get the experimental drugs?''

Jake shrugged. ''Maybe he thinks that if he removes that part of the evidence we won't be able to convict him.''

''That's crazy.''

''Not to him.'' Jake took a final drag and crushed it out on the floor. ''Now I want you to tell Jackson that I got tied up and that you're acting on my behalf. Okay?''

''No problem.''

''I need two pieces of information from him. First, describe Bobby Hannah's breakdown to Jackson and see if he can give us a precise diagnosis. Find out if Jackson thinks Hannah was really wacked out and if so, how long he will remain that way.''

''He's going to tell you the same thing I just did.''

''I know, but I need the opinion of a psychiatric expert for my report. Then ask Dr. Jackson if he has any idea where Bobby Hannah might be hiding.''

''Why would Jackson know?''

''Maybe Hannah mentioned some secret place—you know, like when he was lying on the couch in Jackson's office.''

''You're really grabbing at straws.''

"I do it all the time." Jake's eyes narrowed as he began to think about hiding places. The best spots were away from people, secluded, quiet. And near a means of escape. Like a car. "How many routes are there in and out of the underground garage?"

Joanna thought for a moment. "Three. Two are stairs. The third is a roundabout way."

"Tell me about the third route."

"Not many people use it. It circles around to the back of the hospital, where the laundry facility and utility rooms are located."

Jake reached under his coat and adjusted his weapon. "Show me where it is."

Joanna rode the elevator up, still thinking about the cold looks on the faces of Jake and Lou Farelli as they checked their weapons and began to search the roundabout way out of the garage. They would take no chances with Bobby Hannah this time. If he turned violent, they would kill him. Joanna was certain of that. She looked over at a group of student nurses who were describing a handsome intern they were all attracted to and wanted to go out with. Gorgeous. Funny. Brilliant. Joanna looked up at the overhead floor panel, wondering about the features that had attracted Karen Rhodes to Bobby Hannah. Bobby was good looking, charming, lively, fun to be with. Qualities that all women loved. How was Karen to know that those features represented the surface of a borderline personality? How could she have possibly known she was falling in love with a murderer? How could any woman have known? Faces, she thought. Everyone has so many faces.

Joanna was ushered into Hugh Jackson's office by his secretary, who closed the door behind her.

As Joanna took her seat, she briefly studied Jackson. The distinguished psychiatrist looked tired and old, the lines in his face more obvious than usual.

"Hugh, I appreciate your seeing me so promptly."

"I hope I can be of some help."

"Detective Sinclair is busy conducting the search for Bobby Hannah, so he can't be here with us. But he would like your opinion on a few matters regarding Bobby Hannah." Joanna reached into her purse and took out several handwritten pages. "As you know, Bobby escaped from the police while he was being interrogated. I was in an adjacent room, watching through a one-way mirror, when all this occurred. I think Bobby had a psychotic break just prior to his escape. I've written down exactly what happened. I'd like you to review my notes and tell me what the most likely diagnosis is."

Jackson quickly read the pages. "He's blatantly psychotic. He has all the characteristics of paranoid schizophrenia."

"Is there any way to predict how long the psychotic episode will last?"

Jackson gestured with his hands. "I'm afraid not. Most of the time the psychosis lasts days or perhaps a week. However, in some cases the episodes keep recurring until the patient becomes chronically psychotic."

"Was he psychotic when he was killing people?"

Jackson shrugged. "There's no way to know."

"Then take a guess!" Joanna snapped angrily.

"I—I would guess not." Jackson winced as a knifelike pain shot through his temples and into his eyes. For a moment his vision dimmed, then returned. The pain eased. He looked down into an opened desk drawer and saw two plastic vials of medicine. He reached down for the one containing the pills for his migraine headaches, then decided against it. He was already feeling sedated from a dose he'd taken a few hours earlier, his mind not nearly as sharp as usual. He didn't want to make any mistakes. Not here. Not now.

Jackson was suddenly aware that Joanna was staring at him. He began tapping a finger against his chin, feigning deep thought. "But then again, I do recall a case in which the psychotic episodes lasted for only hours."

Joanna sighed wearily. "So what you're saying is that if Bobby Hannah remains psychotic, we'll never know if he was sane when he committed the murders."

"That's correct."

Jackson felt the migraine returning, now jabbing at his temples and eyes. The pain suddenly intensified, blinding him with brilliant flashes of light. He squeezed his eyes shut, but the pain worsened, becoming excruciating. He groped around in the desk drawer and found the medicine vial. He opened it and hurriedly swallowed two pills.

"Are you ill, Hugh?"

"I'll be fine," Jackson said. He rested his head on the back of his chair, waiting for the flush that always came after he took his migraine medication.

"I just have a few more questions. I'll need another five minutes or so of your time. Lieutenant

Sinclair and I would like to bring this matter to a close as quickly as possible.''

"I understand," Jackson said agreeably. The headache pain was less now, but he still hadn't experienced the flushing sensation.

"We're going to need some additional information on ME 38, the drug Karen was taking."

Hugh Jackson now felt energy surging through his body, his muscles tensing. He looked over at Joanna, studying the softness of her neck, the outline of her breasts protruding under a silk blouse. He wetted his lips, knowing she'd be delicious.

"What the hell are you staring at?" Joanna demanded.

"I—I'm sorry. I'm feeling a little bit under the weather." Jackson looked down at the vials in the drawer. The medication for his migraines still had the cap on it. The other vial was opened and empty. *Oh, my God! I've taken the wrong pills! I've taken the experimental drug!* He quickly got to his feet. "Would you excuse me for a moment?"

"Of course," Joanna said.

Hugh Jackson hurried into a small adjacent bathroom and locked the door. He leaned over the toilet and stuck a finger down his throat. He heaved and retched, bringing up a small quantity of greenish fluid that splashed into the water. He got on his knees and examined the bowl, looking for fragments of the pills he'd swallowed. The water was clear and free of any particles.

Jackson jumped to his feet and looked into the mirror. His reflection looked normal, but energy was pulsating through his body and his genitals felt on fire. He reached quickly into a drawer beneath the basin and took out an ampule containing a new tranquilizer the Institute was developing. It had a superior calming effect without causing sedation. He took a small syringe from the medicine cabinet, filled it halfway with the tranquilizer, and injected it into his thigh muscle.

The drug entered Jackson's bloodstream, and within minutes he felt calm and tranquil. His muscles relaxed. The sensation of energy flowing through his body subsided. He turned on the faucet and splashed cold water on his face, then looked into the mirror. Again he saw only his reflection. *Good. Hold on a little longer. Just a few minutes more and it will all be over.* He splashed cold water on his forehead, then reached for a hand towel and dried his face. He glanced in the mirror again. His facial expression looked meaner now; his eyes narrowed and his lips partially retracted. And he could feel his muscles again bulging and rippling beneath his white coat. His mouth made a chewing motion as he thought about Joanna's neck and breasts. So soft. So sweet.

Jackson stepped back from the mirror and performed a vicious karate chop, lightning fast, the edge of one hand smashing into the palm of the other. That's all it would take, he thought confidently, and Joanna Blalock would be down and out. Then he could take his time, particularly with her breasts. Sink his teeth into them and chew until they bled. Jackson's penis began to throb and he grabbed at it, thinking back to the nurses. Oh, so nice! Particularly Karen Rhodes—so young and so sweet—like a little bird. And that's how she died, too. Her throat crushed, she flew off the roof and floated down to earth. A gentle dove on her last flight.

Don't be stupid! Jackson berated himself. *If you*

kill Joanna Blalock in your office, there will be no escape. You'll be trapped and cornered. And don't forget, there are police all over Memorial at this moment, searching for Bobby Hannah. And if the police catch you, you'll be finished.

Hugh Jackson's mind was racing now, thinking about self-survival. The goddamn drug was still in his system, maybe a little yet remaining in his stomach. *Get it out! Get it out!* He turned on the faucet and gulped water, then got on his knees in front of the toilet. He stuck a finger deep down his throat and retched and heaved, bringing up a small amount of green-yellow vomitus. In the toilet water he thought he saw a few white particles. Probably fragments of the pills. Yes! Yes! He felt better now.

But his mind went back to Joanna Blalock with her tender neck and beautiful breasts. So nice, so irresistible. Of course, he could do her and get away with it. He had outsmarted the police every step of the way thus far. Yes, he could do her and put the blame on Bobby Hannah—the nasty little shit!

Perfect! Perfect!

Jackson decided to practice the karate chop maneuver once again. In a flash, he smashed the edge of one hand into the palm of the other. The blow made a loud, cracking sound. *Perfect! Perfect! Okay, now she's down on the floor. Rip all her clothes off, everything. Then do her. Nice and slow. Savoring each bite. Maybe even fuck her before crushing her throat.*

There was a sharp knock at the door. "Hugh, are you all right?" Joanna called out.

"I—ah—I'm fine. I'll be out in a moment," Jackson replied. He quickly splashed cold water on his face, then took several long, deep breaths. His muscles began to relax and he felt the aggression within him subsiding. He wondered whether he should take more tranquilizer just to be sure. No. He wanted his mind sharp and clear. No mistakes now. Jackson smiled at himself in the mirror as he straightened his tie. *I've got plenty of the tranquilizer left in me*, he thought, *more than enough to get me through the interview.*

He opened the bathroom door and returned to his swivel chair. "I've been having these headaches," he explained. "Migraine, I think." He sat down heavily. "Now let's finish up. You had a few final questions."

"I need more information on the drug Karen was taking, the ME 38. Did you find out how she was able to get the pills? And how many of them are missing?"

Jackson shrugged. "I haven't really looked into it."

"Why the hell not?" Joanna asked irritably.

"Now, look here—"

"No! You look here! A very good friend of mine died because of your goddamn pills. And you don't seem very interested in that fact."

"I'll have Julian check into it immediately."

"Fine. But don't strain yourself, Hugh."

"Why are the ME 38 pills so important?"

"Because the police say they are."

"I understand." Jackson rocked back in his chair, feeling wonderfully at ease. Almost done, he thought, almost home free.

Joanna shifted around in her chair, trying to control her increasing anger and irritability. She felt like hitting him, like scratching his eyes out. "Maybe you'll get a better idea of how long his psychosis will last when you've had a chance to reexamine him."

"Perhaps. But I wouldn't count on it."

Joanna glared at him, hating his ambiguity and his noncommittal answers. "I'll try not to count on it."

Jackson picked up his pipe, but it slipped through his fingers and fell to the floor. He reached for it, but stopped abruptly as pain shot into his left shoulder. "Oww!" he complained, now rubbing the shoulder.

"Is something wrong?"

"It's my shoulder. I fell the other day and bruised it rather badly."

Joanna's eyes suddenly widened, her gaze now focused on the wrinkled skin of his neck. *It's him! It's him!* She pushed her chair back a little and glanced over at the door. *I've got to get the hell out of here!*

"It was stupid of me," Jackson went on, now studying Joanna's face and seeing the change in her expression. Something was wrong. "I tripped and fell here in my office." He stood and walked over to a small table by the door, then reached into a drawer for a fresh supply of tobacco.

Joanna shifted around in her chair, eyes fixed on Jackson as he packed his pipe. He continued to stand next to the small table, directly in front of the door.

Joanna watched Jackson light his pipe, her mind racing to fit all the pieces into place. Now she began to understand the reason for her uncharacteristic anger. The same thing had happened after her meeting with Jackson the day before. He was a violent psychotic and she was picking up his disturbed psyche.

Jackson suddenly felt his muscles tensing beneath his long white coat. Energy was pushing through his body again, his genitals burning up. He went back behind his desk, his eyes never leaving Joanna. He now saw the fright in her face and watched as she slowly tried to inch her way out of her seat. So she'd put all the pieces together.

In a split second he flew over the desk and picked Joanna up and spun her around, her back to him. He had a forearm locked under her chin, a hand grasping the crown of her head as if it were a coconut.

Joanna sucked for air. Jackson's arms felt like the two halves of an iron vise.

"Don't move. Not even an inch," Jackson hissed.

Joanna tried to swallow. Jackson tightened his grip.

"I know what you're thinking, Joanna. You're wondering if you can scream before I harm you. Right? Well, the answer is no. You make the slightest sound and I'll snap your neck. Then you will become a quad. You remember what a quad is, don't you, Joanna? Sure you do. A quadriplegic is someone who has complete paralysis of the arms and legs. The person can't urinate, so a catheter has to be in place permanently. They can't even have a bowel movement, so someone has to come in every day and stick a finger in their rectum to help fecal evacuation. Isn't that nice? And all it would take is one quick jerk of my hands and your spinal cord would be severed. So my advice to you is not to move."

Jackson wetted his lips, pleased with the situation. "Then again, perhaps I should do it anyway. What do you think?"

Joanna trembled with fear. The purse clutched in her hands shook like a leaf.

"Do exactly what I say and I might allow you to live. I want you to take one hand and slowly lift your dress up to your waist, front and back. Do it!"

Joanna used her left hand to lift her skirt up.

"Good. You've got on nice silk panties. I like that." Jackson pushed his erection against her buttocks and gently humped, now breathing harder. "You wanted a motive, Joanna. Well, you're feeling it now."

Joanna tried to concentrate, to think of a way to escape. Keep him talking, she told herself, buy more time. Maybe Jake will come up.

Jackson pushed up harder against her, and she gritted her teeth, repulsed by him.

"Yes," he was saying, "my cock is my motive."

"What?"

Jackson laughed, now sounding like a madman. "Let me briefly tell you the story. A year ago we developed a very powerful mood elevator. Unfortunately, it had serious side effects, so we changed its chemical structure. When we tested it again, it had very little mood-elevating activity, but some of the patients reported increased sexual drive. We shelved the drug, but I still had great interest in it. At the time I was having a problem with impotency. So I decided to try the drug and it worked wonderfully. But after a month it began to lose its effectiveness. So I doubled the dose."

Jackson nibbled on her ear. Delicious. He felt like biting it off.

"What do you think happened when I doubled the dose?" he asked. "You'd better answer quickly."

"Its—its activity was increased," Joanna stuttered.

"Yes. Exactly. But then I began to notice other effects. I became very powerful and aggressive, and I developed an irresistible urge to *kill*. I enjoyed the killing more than the sex. It was ecstasy. And I had no remorse. None. Not even when I killed Karen Rhodes. You feel a lot like her."

Jackson started humping Joanna's buttocks forcefully. Joanna felt a wetness seeping through her panties and she reflexively pulled away from him, but he jerked her back, pushing down on her head and stretching ligaments in her neck.

"Oww!" Joanna cried out.

"Stand still! I'll tell you when to move," Jackson snarled in her ear.

Slowly he began humping her again.

"Let's see. Where was I? Oh yes. Karen Rhodes. She was a simple little twit. She came to see me because she thought she had become addicted to ME 38. She tried to have sex without the drug and it didn't work. She became furious, believing she couldn't respond without the drug. She demanded that I cure her or she would go to her grandfather. I agreed to do so, but of course no cure existed." Jackson chuckled hoarsely. "Then again, perhaps there *was* a cure. I threw her off the roof. *That* cured her."

He's going to kill me! Joanna screamed to herself. *I'm going to die. Here. Now. He's told me everything and now he'll kill me.*

"Hugh," she gasped, "the police know everything. There's no way for you to escape."

"Bullshit! If they knew everything they'd be up here with you, wouldn't they?"

"But they know I'm up here with you. If anything happens to me, they'll blame you."

"No, they won't. I'll tell them that Bobby Hannah was hiding in my bathroom. He surprised both of us, knocking me unconscious, then killing you. I'll tell the police he escaped through the side door. They'll buy that. Just like they bought the bloody rope I left in Hannah's apartment and his pen that I planted in yours. They're so fucking stupid."

He squeezed her neck tighter.

"Don't—don't kill me! Please!" Joanna begged.

Jackson pushed her farther forward. "I want you to lean over and reach out, placing both hands on top of the desk. You make one wrong move and I'll snap your neck."

The pressure on Joanna's throat increased and she heard herself wheeze. "I can't breathe," she choked.

Jackson shoved her onto the desk. "After you've bent over, I want you to pull your panties down."

As Joanna leaned over, Jackson loosened his grip slightly. Her right hand was still grasping her purse. She glanced back, now seeing Jackson's groin, his erection bulging. In a flash she remembered Lou Farelli's advice on handling psychotics.

She suddenly twisted around and slammed her purse into his groin. The heavy purse only grazed his testicles, but it caused enough pain to make Jackson lose his grip on Joanna.

She ran for the door, but Jackson dove for her and caught her by the feet, tripping her. She rolled on the carpet to the far wall.

Jackson was up on one knee, glaring at her. "You're dead, bitch. Dead."

Joanna pushed herself to her feet with her back to the wall. She tried to scream, but no sound came. She reached for a framed diploma and threw it at Jackson. It crashed against the desk, the glass shattered loudly. She hurled another framed certificate at him, then a bronze plaque.

Jackson ducked. The objects flew past his head and slammed into the wall. He jumped to his feet.

The door opened and Jackson's secretary looked into the room. *"What in the world—?"*

Jackson swept her out of the way and raced out of the office and down the corridor. He ran into a female technician head-on, knocking her senseless to the floor. At the elevator he glanced at the overhead panel. Both cars were in the lobby. Quickly he went through the fire door and down the stairs, taking them two at a time.

Up above he heard footsteps coming after him. He speeded up, bounding down the stairs, using the railings to keep his balance.

Don't go to the lobby, Jackson told himself. *And don't go to the parking lot, either.* Cops would be everywhere. That's what Joanna had said. She talked too much. The next chance he got he'd kill her.

He decided to go to the main hospital. He knew a hundred places to hide there.

He exited on the third floor and entered the glass-enclosed bridge that led to Memorial Hospital. He glanced over at the roof beneath the bridge. A helicopter was on the pad, its blades beginning to whirl in preparation for takeoff. The engine noise grew louder and louder.

Perfect!

Jackson grabbed a heavy fire extinguisher and smashed it into the glass again and again. At first the glass would not give, but then it cracked and finally shattered completely.

Hugh Jackson jumped from the bridge onto the roof and ran for the helicopter as it was just lifting off.

At the last possible moment he leaped up and grabbed the landing strut. The helicopter began its ascent.

Joanna hurried onto the enclosed bridge and saw Jake running toward her at full speed.

"What the hell is happening?" Jake asked.

"Hugh Jackson is the killer."

"What!"

"He confessed to everything."

Joanna pointed up at the sky through the gaping hole in the glass enclosure. Jackson was holding on with both hands and was now straddling the landing strut with one leg. The helicopter continued to gain altitude but tilted noticeably because of the added uneven weight.

"He's not going to get away, is he, Jake?"

"No. The pilot knows Jackson is there. He'll set the craft back down. How in the hell did you get a confession out of him?"

Joanna ignored the question. "But what if Jackson manages to crawl into the cabin?"

"That only happens in the movies."

Joanna shielded her eyes from the glare, watching Jackson hanging on in the distance. He looked more like a marionette than a human. "He's totally psychotic."

"Did he attack you?"

"He tried."

The helicopter began its slow descent, still noticeably tilted. A sudden downdraft caught the aircraft and it veered crazily, now heading directly for the enclosed bridge.

Jake pulled Joanna through the door and back into the Institute just as the helicopter slammed into the bridge. It hung there for a brief moment, then crashed to the roof below.

Hugh Jackson was pinned under the helicopter's landing strut. He smelled gasoline, then saw smoke, then felt the heat.

The pilot leaped out of the helicopter's door. He glanced over at the man pinned beneath the wreckage. An old man with a kind, soft face. The smoke thickened and the pilot ran for his life.

Hugh Edward Jackson stared up at the burning metal. He saw his own image, now framed by curls of fire.

With his life rapidly ebbing away, Hugh Jackson uttered his last word. "Murderer."

And then the flames consumed him.

Epilogue

"Congratulations to you, Lieutenant Sinclair, for a job well done," Mortimer Rhodes said.

"Thank you, sir. But most of the credit belongs to Dr. Blalock. We would have never cracked this one without her."

"I'm aware of her contribution. And I'm also aware that some people went out of their way to make it difficult for her to assist you." Rhodes glanced over at Simon Murdock, who busied himself studying a figurine on his desk. "I also know there were others who went out of their way to help her." Mortimer Rhodes nodded to Julian Whitmore, who nodded back. "Now, Lieutenant, I've gotten this story in bits and pieces from a variety of sources, but I want you to tell me everything, particularly about Hugh Jackson. I still can't understand his vicious behavior."

"It'd probably be better for Joanna to tell you. The part on drugs is way over my head."

"Fine. Tell me everything, Dr. Blalock. Leave out no detail."

Joanna sipped coffee from a Styrofoam cup. Her throat still hurt, and she was still finding it difficult to swallow. "Hugh Jackson was experimenting on himself with various drugs. I think he started out with the best of intentions, believing he could control the drugs. But the reverse happened. He wanted to feel young and virile and powerful, and the drugs accomplished this. It was ecstasy to him. And when the dreadful side effects occurred, he was willing to accept them as long as the drug made him feel incredibly young and potent."

"What were the side effects?"

"He became psychotic and very aggressive. Then came an almost irresistible urge to kill. And the act of killing gave him great pleasure—pleasure so intense that it was addicting."

Rhodes shook his head in disbelief. "Hugh Edward Jackson—a name that should have been associated with greatness. Instead, he turns out to be a murderer. And you're telling us that he took lives just for the joy of it?"

"I'm afraid so. At least the first two victims, a prostitute and a young mother, were murdered purely for pleasure."

"What about my—my granddaughter, and the other nurse?"

Joanna slowly sipped her coffee. Some things were better left unsaid, she thought to herself. "Karen was killed because she found out that Hugh Jackson was experimenting on himself with drugs," Joanna lied convincingly. "We're not certain why Marissa Shaw was killed, although I think I can give you an accurate guess. I think Marissa found Karen's diary, which probably described Hugh Jackson's experiments on himself. She went to him with the diary and he murdered her."

"Why would she take the diary to him?"

Joanna shrugged. "No one will ever know the answer to that."

"A distinguished physician turned murderer." Rhodes shook his head again. "Do you think the drug simply uncovered a dormant madness that was always there?"

"I doubt it. Hugh Jackson was considered a very stable, outstanding scientist who contributed greatly to our understanding of the mind. But I think he became too ambitious, too arrogant. He firmly believed that the drugs in his laboratory could control every aspect of the human mind."

"But the drugs ended up controlling him."

"Yes."

"And he was more than willing to accept the awful side effects as long as the drug made him feel young and virile?"

"Exactly."

"It sounds like Doctor Faustus selling his soul to the devil."

"In a way it was." Joanna looked over at Jake, who held up three fingers and pointed to his face. He was referring to Jackson's third face, the one he kept hidden away in his heart of hearts.

"Why did he kill only women?" Rhodes asked.

"He got pleasure from loving them and pleasure from killing them."

"Are you referring to sexual love?"

"Yes."

Rhodes's expression hardened. "Are you saying he was having a relationship with my granddaughter?"

"Absolutely not," Joanna said firmly. "As I told you a moment ago, Karen was killed because she found out about Jackson's experiments."

"Why didn't she come to me?"

"I think she planned to, but she—she ran out of time."

Mortimer Rhodes sighed sadly. "Why did she go to the roof with him?"

"She didn't. Karen went to the roof to meet a resident she was in love with. On that particular night, Karen arrived before her boyfriend."

"And Hugh Jackson simply followed her to the roof and killed her?"

"Yes, sir. I'm afraid she was in the wrong place at the wrong time."

Mortimer Rhodes looked out the window at the clear blue sky, thinking about his dead granddaughter, the apple of his eye, the love of his life, never to be seen again. For a moment, a deep sadness darkened his face. "I was told that the young resident who was initially arrested was Karen's boyfriend. Is that correct?"

"Yes."

"What happened to him?"

"He had a nervous breakdown and is currently under therapy."

"Was that caused by his arrest?"

"It's difficult to say. He has a long history of psychiatric problems."

Rhodes wanted to know more about the relationship between the young resident and Karen, but decided not to pry. Besides, what difference would it make now?

He took out a handkerchief and blew his nose loudly. "Well, let us now go on to other matters. I met with the board of directors yesterday and we decided on a number of changes. First, the Department of Pathology is to be reorganized. We have decided to establish a new Division of Forensic Pathology. It will be part of the department, but it will be independently funded by an endowment from the Rhodes family. The new division will have a forensic laboratory second to none. And that laboratory will be named in memory of my granddaughter."

"Karen would like that," Joanna said softly.

"I think she would also approve of the fact that you will be named the director of the new division."

Joanna's jaw dropped.

"Close your mouth, Dr. Blalock, or you'll catch flies." Mortimer Rhodes shifted uncomfortably in his chair. He was wearing a topcoat and shawl despite a pleasant room temperature of seventy-five degrees.

The old man turned to Julian Whitmore. "Now, let's talk about the Institute. Hugh Jackson managed to disgrace the BRI as well as everything else associated with Memorial Hospital. We may never recover from this, but we have no choice other than to go on. With changes, of course. The tenth floor will no longer be referred to as the BRI. Instead, it will be called the Institute for Clinical Investigation, or ICI. And you, Dr. Whitmore, will be acting director. Do you accept?"

"Yes," Julian said without hesitation.

"Good. Now let me tell you the conditions that you will work under. Everything is to be tightly controlled and there are to be no exceptions. We will not tolerate even the slightest hint of misconduct or scandal. And we have ways to make certain this is accomplished, don't we, Simon?"

Simon Murdock nodded firmly. "Indeed we do. Every bit of research that goes on in the Institute will be carefully monitored. An oversight committee will review all research protocols. No research will be allowed without the committee's approval. All drugs being studied will be registered and catalogued and dispensed only through the pharmacy. Furthermore, all drugs used by Hugh Jackson in his experiments are to be destroyed, as are all the lab books that refer to those drugs. We have drawn up a rather extensive list of rules and regulations that are to be closely adhered to. If any violations occur, those staff involved will be immediately dismissed. Is that clear, Dr. Whitmore?''

"Quite clear.''

Mortimer Rhodes pushed himself up from the chair, using his cane for support. ''I believe that concludes our business.''

The old man shuffled slowly toward the door. The others followed very slowly and well behind.

In the hall, Julian Whitmore shook Joanna's hand. ''Congratulations on your appointment.''

''And the same to you,'' Joanna replied with a broad smile.

''I'm afraid mine is only acting chief. I suspect they'll be looking for a permanent director very soon.''

''I don't think so, Julian. Acting chairmen have a great tendency to become permanent chairmen.''

Whitmore smiled. ''Yes, I know.''

Julian Whitmore hurried down the corridor, heading for the glass-enclosed bridge. His appointment as director was a real feather in his cap, and he knew it. It was the second most important and powerful position in the entire Psychiatric Institute. Some thought it the most important. And now, he was in total control.

Whitmore waved to a colleague as he turned into another corridor. And of course Joanna was correct. He would soon be permanent director. Mortimer Rhodes had suggested that in a phone call earlier that morning. *I promised to follow his instructions to the letter*, he thought to himself. *And I will. There will be no violations, no irregularities. I will run a tight ship, free of any misconduct.*

Whitmore thought about the conditions he would be saddled with. The oversight committee could be handled with ease. Its members would all be from Memorial, people he knew, people who trusted him. Cataloguing and dispensing drugs through the pharmacy was a cinch. Any administrative assistant could set that up. And finally, there was Hugh Jackson's drugs and lab books. He had already destroyed the drugs as well as the lab books. But he still knew the chemical formula of the drug Jackson had used. After all, Julian was the one who helped him develop it, who worked side by side with him on the drug. He couldn't erase the formula from his mind even if he wanted to.

Why throw away a wonder drug? Whitmore asked himself. Because a foolish man abused it? Nonsense. There was something magical about that mood elevator. It made an old man feel young and powerful. It restored his virility and potency. So it had side effects. Didn't every drug?

Whitmore was now crossing over the glass-enclosed bridge, where a big sheet of plywood covered the hole made by Hugh Jackson in his futile attempt to escape. Whitmore looked up through the glass ceiling at the tenth floor. *Mine. All mine. I'll wait until I've cemented myself in place as chairman and then I'll begin to study the drug again.*

Carefully this time. Very carefully.

I'll alter its chemical structure, removing its evil side effects, maintaining its beneficial actions. I know I can do it and, unlike Hugh Jackson, I can control it.

Just think! A chemical that makes old men feel young, restoring their strength and virility. It would be the wonder drug of the century. An elixir of youth.

There's a Nobel Prize in that, he thought. There most certainly is.

Dimitri rushed over to greet the newcomers with his arms extended out wide. He studied Joanna, undressing her with his eyes, then looked at Kate. "How is it, Jake, that a man so ugly ends up with the two most beautiful women in the world?"

"Charm," Jake said gruffly.

Joanna grinned. "Dimitri, this is my sister Kate."

Dimitri bowed gracefully and kissed her hand. "You have the same face as your sister, the same eyes, the same genes. But I hope your taste in men is better. Your sister has chosen badly and ended up with this lout."

"He's a hunk," Kate said happily.

"He's also a pain in the ass."

Dimitri led the way through the crowded restaurant. He snapped his fingers loudly and yelled over to two waiters. Instantly a space was made ringside at the dance floor and an empty table appeared.

Dimitri poured a round of retsina and sat down with his guests. "Giassou," he said, toasting the women, then turning to Jake. "So you got him, huh?"

"Yeah."

"The newspaper said he died in the helicopter crash."

"Not right away."

"Oh?" Dimitri brightened up.

"When the pilot jumped out, he glanced down at Jackson. The old guy was still alive."

"So he felt the flames?"

"For a while."

"Good. The bastard should have suffered. With any luck at all, he's in hell at this moment, still feeling the flames."

Dimitri glanced over to the entrance. New customers were arriving. He stood up quickly and barked orders to a nearby waiter. "Your table will soon be filled with appetizers. Enjoy."

Joanna watched Dimitri limp away, then turned to Kate. "How's your retsina?"

"It's great," Kate beamed. "What type of appetizers was he referring to?"

"They're super. You'll see." Joanna studied her sister's face. So young, so pretty. *And almost so dead because of me.* She shuddered, thinking back to the night of the assault. If she had allowed that mechanic to change her tire—that was the difference between Kate's life and death.

"Throw a plate," Jake said.

"What?" Joanna said, snapping out of her thoughts.

"Throw a plate."

"I'm really not in the mood."

Jake handed her a platter. "You keep looking at Kate like she's made out of fragile china."

Joanna glanced over at Kate. "Is he telling the truth?"

"I'm afraid so."

"That's because you're so important to me." Joanna leaned over and kissed her sister's cheek. "You're the only family I have left in the world."

"Well," Jake said, "she's not fragile. She's tough as hell, and the fact that she's here with us now proves it. Now throw the damn dish."

Joanna let the dish fly and it crashed in the middle of the dance floor. A dozen other plates followed, and suddenly the mood in the restaurant changed, becoming loud and electric. The musicians quickly picked up their instruments and music soon filled the air, the steel guitars blending with the bouzoukis and tambourines. Handsome couples dashed to the floor, feet shuffling, arms flailing to the raucous sounds.

A young Greek approached the table. He was tall and good looking with dark eyes that had probably broken a hundred hearts. His jeans were tight, his shirt unbuttoned halfway down his chest. He extended his hand to Kate. "Dance with me," he said.

"I don't know how," Kate said quickly.

"I will show you."

"Go ahead," Jake urged her. "If your sister can do the dance, so can you."

Kate got to her feet. "Can you really do this?"

Joanna nodded.

"Is there any particular trick to it?"

"Yeah," Joanna grinned. "You've got to shut your brain off."

"Here goes," Kate giggled.

Joanna watched her sister on the floor, tentative at first, then learning the steps, then dancing the dance as if she had been born to do it. She whirled and laughed, her feet moving in perfect rhythm to the music. So young. So beautiful. And so alive.

Joanna leaned her head against Jake's shoulder. "Do you know what, Jake?"

"What?"

"Life is pretty damn good."

"Particularly when you shut your brain off."

"Yeah."